Praise for

THE MAGIC OF MELWICK ORCHARD

"Readers will fall in love with strong-willed, spunky Isa in this magical story about hope, resilience, and what it means to be family."
—Abby Cooper, author of *Bubbles* and *Sticks and Stones*

"Caprara beautifully captures the unbreakable bond between sisters when life throws a curveball. A tender and imaginative debut."
—Jenn Bishop, author of *14 Hollow Road* and *The Distance to Home*

"A beautiful bloom of a book, rooted in friendship, hope, and love. This stunning debut will make you believe in magic—on the page, and in your heart!"
—Bridget Hodder, author of *The Rat Prince*

"Rebecca Caprara has beautifully walked the line between magic and real life in *The Magic of Melwick Orchard*. For families with children who have illnesses, they will see the truth of what it is like when one member of the family is sick. This story will hold your heart, break it, and then mend it back together."
—Kati Gardner, author of *Brave Enough*

THE MAGIC OF MELWICK ORCHARD

REBECCA CAPRARA

CAROLRHODA BOOKS
MINNEAPOLIS

Carolrhoda Books
A division of Lerner Publishing Group, Inc.
241 First Avenue North
Minneapolis, MN 55401 USA

For reading levels and more information, look up this title at www.lernerbooks.com.

Apple illustration by Rina Oshi/Shutterstock.com.

Main body text set in Bembo Std regular 12/16.5.
Typeface provided by Monotype Typography.

Library of Congress Cataloging-in-Publication Data

Names: Caprara, Rebecca, author.
Title: The magic of Melwick Orchard / by, Rebecca Caprara.
Description: Minneapolis, MN : Carolrhoda Books, [2018] | Summary: While her
    sister Junie, six, is in the hospital fighting cancer, Isa, a twelve-year-old loner, feels
    forgotten until a magic tree helps her whole family to heal.
Identifiers: LCCN 2017040104 (print) | LCCN 2017053233 (ebook) |
    ISBN 9781541523739 (eb pdf) | ISBN 9781512466874 (th : alk. paper)
Subjects: | CYAC: Cancer—Fiction. | Family problems—Fiction. | Magic—Fiction. |
    Trees—Fiction. | Friendship—Fiction. | Schools—Fiction.
Classification: LCC PZ7.1.C385 (ebook) | LCC PZ7.1.C385 Mag 2018 (print) | DDC
    [Fic]—dc23

LC record available at https://lccn.loc.gov/2017040104

Manufactured in the United States of America
1-43078-32452-4/11/2018

For my grandparents

The world is a great library, and fruit trees are some of the books.

They have a voice, and speak plainly to us, and teach us many good lessons.

—Ralph Austen, 1653

CHAPTER 1

Mom forgot to pick me up from school. Again.

So I walked the two miles home, which usually felt more like ten. But that first afternoon in April, it felt like one hundred miles. Endless and annoying. The least funny April Fools' prank ever. Probably because it wasn't a prank at all. And also because my shoes stunk. I don't mean they smelled bad. They just stunk. Crummy, broken down, too small. No one heard me when I said I'd grown out of this pair weeks ago. By the end of that walk, my big toes stuck out and a blister was erupting on my right heel like a miniature volcano. I'm just glad the other kids from school weren't nearby to see. Between my shoes and my patched jeans, I looked a real mess. Almost worse than Mom, and she barely got out of her bathrobe or brushed her hair anymore. At least she still had hair, though. Junie's hair was all gone.

And it was a crying shame, because she looked awful cute in pigtails.

I shuffled up our driveway, my cranky toes leading the way, kicking at pebbles and thinking about pigtails. My feet veered left, away from the house. I crossed the backyard, past the old shed that doubled as Dad's workshop. I paused to peer in the window. The glass was cracked from a ball I'd accidentally thrown too hard during a game of catch last September. I'd expected Dad to say something like, "Isabel! We just moved here, and you're already smashing the place to smithereens." To my surprise, he wasn't mad. He sucked in his breath, inspected the damage. Instead of scolding me, he let out a long whistle. "I knew you had the Fitzwilken arm," he said beaming with pride, which made my heart expand to at least three times its normal size. We called that pitch the *window breaker* from then on. Even though I hadn't practiced it with him in a while, I still considered it my secret softball weapon.

I lifted a finger and very carefully touched the glass. If someone came along and tapped it in just the right place, the whole thing might shatter to pieces. Lately, I felt the same.

Dad promised he'd fix the cracked pane months ago, but other things came up. Now, looking in, I could see a curtain of cobwebs draping the window frame. Dust coated the tools. No one had been inside for a long time, except for an army of spiders apparently, and probably a few mice. A half-finished dollhouse sat on a table in the far corner. I wondered if we'd ever finish building it for Junie, but those thoughts made me feel too scratchy, so I continued on my way.

I climbed the grassy hill that sloped up behind the shed. With one swift leap, I cleared the gate at the top and kept on going straight into our orchard. I zigzagged between the rows of ancient apple trees until I arrived in an open meadow as big as a softball diamond. Traces of an old barn foundation were visible near the center of the clearing. Junie and I used to walk along the exposed foundation stones, testing our balance with our arms stretched to the side, pretending we were crossing the parapets of our own personal castle, while the scraggly looking apple trees marched beside us like loyal sentries.

The trees right along the edge of the clearing were bigger than the others in the orchard, probably because they were less crowded and could soak up more rain, catch more sunlight. When our parents first told us about our new home in Bridgebury, they tried to soften the blow of yet another dreaded move by promising my sister and me that we'd have the same as those trees: room to grow, fresh air to breathe, sunshine to bask in. There would be fields of grass to run through, mud puddles to stomp in, trees to swing beneath. We'd only ever lived in tiny city apartments, so it was hard to imagine having a real backyard, let alone acres of land to explore. It all sounded so perfect at first.

I walked over to our swing, the one Junie used to love. The one Dad built from barn wood and braided ropes, before he got too busy. The one Mom helped us hang from the strongest, safest branch she could find, before she got too sad. I used to lift Junie up, tell her to hold on tight, then give her a push. Let her fly. She'd hoot and holler and scream for me to stop, which I knew was actually sister code for *go higher!* Junie-to-the-moonie high.

That was last fall, which wasn't really so long ago, if you looked at a calendar. But to me, those five months, three days, twenty-two hours, and nine minutes felt like a million years. Like a different life.

The wind shifted. The orchard seemed to sigh. I had this strange sensation that the trees were listening to me, which was just plain silly, because I wasn't actually saying anything out loud. And also, trees don't have ears.

Just then, my own ears pricked. Something high-pitched trilled through the branches. My heart leapt in my chest, until I realized it was only birdsong. For a few fleeting seconds, I could've sworn it was Junie, laughing. Which made me want to cry. I looked at our swing, then down at my poor feet, and just about every part of me started to ache.

So I sat on that swing, even though I'd vowed to never touch it again. Not after what happened to Junie. Or me. Heck. I might as well have changed my name to Isabel-Invisible. For all I could tell, I was disappearing. Except this wasn't superpower invisibility, or something cool like that. Nope. It was the opposite of cool. Junie would say it was the *worstible*, a word reserved for the worst-most-horrible things, like brussels sprouts and salamanders and shots at the doctor's office.

Back and forth, the ropes and wood creaked as I kicked my legs, swinging higher. Up, up, then down with a whoosh that made my stomach drop. The higher I went, the more I could see. Not quite a bird's-eye view. More like a squirrel's-eye view. Little green leaves sprouted on crooked branches. Robins flitted here and there, building nests. Crocuses peeked up purple, and yellow forsythia blossoms scattered like confetti at a birthday party.

I hoped we'd have a party for Junie this summer. She'd never met a cupcake she didn't like—any flavor would do. Chocolate, vanilla, strawberry, even carrot cake, which she refused to believe was actually made from a vegetable. Dad used to joke that somewhere in Junie's pint-sized body was the stomach of an elephant. She could probably eat an entire dozen cupcakes if you let her, though Mom never would. I bet she'd make an exception this year though.

If there was a birthday.

I'd save up my lunch money and buy seven of the biggest, brightest balloons I could find. Instead of making wishes by blowing out candles (which leave holes in the tops of precious cupcakes), Junie preferred popping balloons, one for each year. Last year, Mom even gave her a wishing pin—a sparkly red brooch in the shape of a butterfly that she found for a dollar at a rummage sale. The latch was broken and it was missing some rhinestones, but Junie thought it was *perfecterrific* and proceeded to make her birthday wishes using it on the balloons. *Pop. Pop. Pop. Pop. Pop. Pop!* Six very loud wishes. And I'm pretty sure none of them involved getting sick.

There was a rustling in one of the trees. My eyes followed the sound. A squirrel skittered down a nearby trunk and ran across the clearing, his tail bouncing behind him, all jolly and fluffy. Junie and I watched that same squirrel collecting acorns last fall. I recognized him right away by the notch in his left ear and the patch of missing fur on his rump—souvenirs from a scuffle with a hawk, or a cat, or maybe our neighbor's notoriously feisty chickens.

I remembered that squirrel digging holes all over our lawn and dropping nuts into the ground for safe-keeping. I learned in Ms. Perdilla's science class that squirrels are awfully forgetful and easily distracted, and often forget where they buried their nuts.

Which I could totally relate to. Take that wishing pin, for example. I told Junie I'd put it in one of my special hiding spots, for safekeeping. Trouble was, after a few weeks, I forgot where that spot was. It wasn't the first time this type of thing had happened either. Mom said I turned the entire house upside down searching for my lost treasures. That was ridiculous, of course. Look, I was pretty strong: I could do eight chin-ups, and I could run the bases faster than any other girl on my softball team. But I was nowhere near strong enough to lift up an entire house and flip it over.

Although I wished I could. I'd shake it until my mother tumbled out of her room and all the change came clinking out from between the couch cushions. Then, maybe, Mom and Dad might've noticed that even though I was healthy and strong enough to lift up a house, I still needed them too.

The squirrel was bounding through the grass, looking hungry. *Swish, swish.* His tail curved behind him like a question mark. *Where are those nuts?* he seemed to ask. I dragged my feet along the ground, slowing the swing to a halt. Dirt filled my holey, too-small shoes. I took them off and tossed them aside. Good riddance.

The squirrel stopped. He turned and stared right at me. *Well?* He cocked his head. *Care to help?*

I stood up and scanned the trees. For generations, Melwick Orchard had been famous for growing the most delicious fruit for miles and miles. People would travel hours just to buy a bushel of those apples. The farmers could barely keep up with the demand, so they started experimenting with ways to increase harvests. Unfortunately, something went wrong and the trees sort of rebelled, sprouting wild limbs in any direction they pleased, and refusing to produce so much as a single bud.

There was no fruit that fall, or the next, or any year since. People in town whispered all sorts of strange stories, but no one really understood what had happened. Maybe the pruning had been too aggressive? Maybe the pesticides and fertilizers had been too harsh? Maybe there weren't enough bees to pollinate all those trees? Maybe the owners had gotten too greedy? Maybe it was something else entirely?

Of course, Junie was convinced it was magic. As much as I loved my little sister, I knew she was wrong. I'd stopped believing in *that* a long time ago.

Whatever the reason for the trees' sudden change of heart, the family who owned the orchard eventually gave up and moved away. By the time we arrived, the property had been abandoned for years. The pale blue farmhouse was about as run-down as my lousy shoes, and the apple trees were peculiar, but I didn't mind. As long as we stayed put.

I was tired of moving, moving, always moving.

In the past, just as soon as I'd start making friends someplace, Dad's company would offer him a transfer. This bugged me for a bunch of reasons. First of all, the transfer was never really an offer; it was basically a demand dressed up real nice, like when my parents said things like, "Isabel, could you clean your room?" or "Junie, don't you want to finish those lovely brussels sprouts on your plate?" Secondly, *transfer* was a deceptively smooth-sounding word for something that was actually a total pain in the butt, involving cardboard boxes, packing, and long, bumpy rides to some unfamiliar place. Thirdly, and perhaps most importantly, it meant I'd have to say good-bye all over again. And on my list of worstibles, good-byes ranked pretty high, alongside walking home from school and being invisible.

That's why, after transfer number five or so, I decided Junie would be the only friend I needed. Even if we moved again, we'd move together. I'd never have to say good-bye to my sister. At least that was the plan.

The squirrel's tail swished impatiently. *Well?*

"Sorry," I said. "I'm a little distracted these days. And apparently a little nuts too. Talking to a squirrel. This is a new low."

Nuts? Did you say nuts? The squirrel blinked eagerly.

I couldn't help but laugh. Just a little. I looked at the trees around us. Overgrown, in need of attention. I felt like I was looking in a mirror, except beneath the ground they had deep roots, tying them to one spot forever. It was a feeling I'd never known, but one I desperately wanted.

"There," I said to the squirrel. I pointed to a sapling, fresh and new, pushing its way up through the grass in the center of the clearing. I walked closer to it, feeling the cool ground beneath my bare feet. "That's one of your nuts. At least it was, before it started growing into an oak tree."

The squirrel scampered over, looking puzzled.

"It's true," I said with a shrug. "You probably buried your acorn right there in the fall. You forgot all about it. Nature did its thing, and now it's growing! Ta-da!"

The squirrel scratched his notched ear, then bobbed his head up and down. I felt so wise, imparting my wisdom to that confused creature. I knelt down next to the sapling, which was nothing more than a skinny gray-brown stick. It stood about knee high with several fragile green shoots poking out. Crinkly paper-thin leaves were beginning to open. Oddly, the whole thing glistened with dew, even though the afternoon sun should have dried it out.

I squinted at the leaves. Upon closer inspection, they *didn't* look like the oak leaves Ms. Perdilla had shown us during our fall foliage unit. They didn't look like maple, elm, beech, birch, or apple leaves either. Then I remembered Ms. Perdilla telling us about a special type of plant that turns out differently than expected. She said it happened when science met serendipity— something Junie probably would've called *sciendipity*: a rare combination of seed, flower, pollen, and pure luck that produced something brand new.

She called those plants *chance seedlings*.

When the kids in my class asked how that was even possible, Ms. Perdilla told us to think about ourselves. "Are you exactly one hundred percent the same as your parents?" she asked. Of course, the answer was no. "We all share certain similarities with our family members, but we are each entirely original." She picked up an apple from her desk. Ripe red streaked with gold. She took a bite, chewed, smiled. "Not as good as a Melwick," she said, "but it'll do." She took another bite. "Can anyone tell me what sort of apple this is?"

After a few guesses, we learned it was a Cortland. Ms. Perdilla told us that if a Cortland tree was pollinated by a Red Delicious tree, you'd get an apple like the one in her hand, but the seeds inside that fruit would be a cross of the two parent varieties. Things might get interesting if you planted one of those seeds, because it could grow into a new, totally unique variety of apple.

"Take the Granny Smith apple, for example," I said to the squirrel, who was listening to me intently. After months of feeling forgotten, it was nice to have such an appreciative audience. "Some old lady named Mary Ann Smith supposedly dumped kitchen scraps with a bunch of bitter Tasmanian crab apples near a creek in Australia. Bet she was surprised to discover a tree full of deliciously crisp green apples growing out of that garbage heap a few years later!"

I didn't think squirrels could actually smile; at least Ms. Perdilla never mentioned it in science class. But I could've sworn that funny little squirrel smiled at me. Then he turned and looked the sapling up and down, sniffing the air.

An unusual scent swirled in the breeze. I inhaled. A bizarre combination filled my nostrils: sawdust from Dad's workshop, cinnamon from Mom's sticky bun recipe, the leather of my softball glove, Junie's strawberry chewing gum. All mixed together, the result should've been gross. But somehow it wasn't. It was like the perfume of a happy memory, if such a thing existed. And it seemed to be coming from the sapling.

I gently touched one of the wrinkled leaves. It unfolded in my palm. The smell grew stronger. When I closed my eyes and breathed deeply, memories flickered behind my eyelids, like a movie reel of the Fitzwilken family's greatest hits. For a split second, I forgot about my sore feet, my invisibility dilemma, my sick sister. My whole body fizzed with delight. We were building the dollhouse in the workshop. Eating cotton candy and riding the Ferris wheel at a fair. Baking with Mom in the kitchen. Feeding swans in the park. Blowing pink gum bubbles as big as our faces. Playing catch in the backyard.

I opened my eyes and shook my head. As soon as the happiness wore off, pain set in. It left me wondering if we'd ever do those things again, together as a family. I quickly pushed the memories away.

The squirrel studied my face. His nose twitched.

"What?" I said, letting go of the leaf.

He lifted his tiny, furry shoulders, as if to say, *How should I know?* Then he looked at my hand. I followed his eyes.

My palm shimmered with a silvery, sticky sheen. Apparently the dew coating the tree wasn't dew at all. It was some sort of sap. I tried to wipe it off on my pants, but it wouldn't budge. I crouched and rubbed my palm vigorously on the grass, the way Junie did whenever we ran out of napkins at a picnic. When my hand accidentally brushed the sapling's thin trunk, a tiny shock traveled through me, similar to the harmless jolts of static electricity I felt when I shuffled around our living room carpet in my fleecy socks. Except this feeling lasted longer. By the time I raised my hand, the glittery sap had disappeared.

"Weird," I muttered, more to myself than to the squirrel.

But the sapling seemed to think I was speaking to *it*. It bent and swayed, then dropped a single leaf by my bare feet. Before I could pick it up, the leaf disintegrated into the grass. I blinked and it was gone.

"Did you see that?" I asked the squirrel. Now I felt like the confused creature. "That's definitely not something a normal tree or leaf would do."

The squirrel inspected the patch of grass, equally perplexed. We walked in a slow circle around the sapling, looking at it from all angles. The trunk straightened up. The leaves fluttered proudly, almost like that tree was showing off and enjoying the attention.

"There's got to be a scientific explanation for whatever's going on here, right? Do you think . . ." I chewed my lip. "Maybe *this* could be a chance seedling?"

The squirrel's tail shot up, from a curling question mark to an excited exclamation point.

"You really think so?" So much for my great wisdom. Who was I kidding? I was just a barefoot fool, talking to a bushy-tailed rodent.

Swish, swish, went the squirrel's tail. His glassy black eyes twinkled. Then he sprang toward the base of the sapling. He started to dig right below the spot where the leaf had landed.

"The leaf is gone," I said. "And I told you, you won't find an acorn under there either. It's already sprouted."

He kept digging. His paws worked quickly, flinging dirt in my direction.

"Cut that out. You're making a mess."

But the squirrel was determined. He dug and dug. The sapling trembled.

"Be careful not to hurt its roots!" I said, feeling strangely protective of that weird tree, even though it was basically a glorified stick.

After a few minutes, the squirrel stood up on his haunches and inspected his work. The hole was half a foot deep and wide enough to store an entire lunch box full of acorns. A few disoriented earthworms wriggled around at the bottom, wondering who turned on the lights. Some of the sapling's roots were exposed, but thankfully they didn't appear to be injured. Oddly, the roots weren't brown or green, or any of the colors I expected them to be. Even caked with dirt, the roots were a very faint shade of blue.

"Look!" I pointed to the roots. The squirrel wasn't interested. He just kept looking past me, his tail twitching. He eyed the sneakers I'd tossed aside earlier. Then me. Then the hole. *Ahem.*

"What exactly do you want me to do? Put my sneakers in there?"

He nodded.

"Why?" It was a question I asked a lot lately, but it rarely came with an answer. So I changed my question. "Why not?" The sneakers were pretty useless at this point. Maybe they did deserve a proper burial. I picked them up and placed them in the hole. As soon as I did, the roots brightened ever so slightly. It was very strange, but then again, so was hanging out with a squirrel.

"I feel like I should say something." I cleared my

throat. The squirrel held his tail in his hands, out of respect. "May your souls . . . and soles . . . rest in peace."

As I tossed a handful of dirt into the hole, I spotted the tiny blue root tendrils snaking down toward the sneakers. One wove through the laces, another curled around the heel. Before I could investigate further, the squirrel jumped in front of me. His hind legs kicked the rest of the dirt back into the hole, completely covering the sneakers and twisting roots.

When he was finished, he moved aside and flashed another squirrely smile. With one last tail swish, he scurried away, disappearing through the orchard. I patted the ground with my palm, being careful not to disturb the sapling. Our work was done. And now my parents would have no choice but to buy me a new pair of sneakers.

CHAPTER 2

Dusk was pouring through the windows by the time I got home. I rubbed my grubby feet on the mat and started switching on lights, room by room. The gloom retreated, hovering in inky pools at the windowsills.

"Mom?"

No answer. I was disappointed, but not surprised. Recently she'd become MIA—Mother Increasingly Absent. At least when it came to mothering me.

I went to the kitchen. No supper simmered on the stove. No music played on the radio. No one hummed to a tune. A smashed teacup lay on the floor like a clue from a crime scene.

"Mom!" I shouted, breaking the quiet into a million pieces. Still no answer. I mopped up the cold tea and swept the shards of china into the dustpan. I climbed the stairs, flicking on more lights as I went.

I stood in the open doorway of my parents' bedroom, feeling like a cardboard cutout of a girl. Like one of Junie's paper dolls come to life.

"It's dinnertime," I said flatly.

The heap of blankets that was my mother spoke quietly. "Just fix some leftovers tonight, sweetheart." She exhaled, as if that handful of words was hard work. Then she rolled over, without even sitting up to look at me. Most mothers would want at least a quick visual check to make sure their firstborn hadn't decided to cover her body in tattoos or dye her hair purple since breakfast. Not mine. She pulled a pillow over her head.

If today was like yesterday, or the days before, I knew she'd been at the hospital for hours, talking to doctors, nurses, counselors. I knew she'd brought a gigantic stack of library books to read to Junie, to distract my sister from the medicines that were making her sick and somehow better at the same time. I knew she'd probably called my dad during his lunch break to give him the daily report on Junie's condition. My mother used her energy all day, for everyone else. By the time the sun went down, she had nothing left for me.

"Mom?"

"Fix . . . leftovers . . ." she said, even softer this time.

"Why? Are they broken?" I thought I might be able to cheer her up with something clever.

"Hmm?" she mumbled from beneath the pillow.

"I can't fix leftovers, Mom. Because they went the way of the dinosaurs. They're extinct." I huffed. "Get it?"

The blankets made a confused rustle.

"You have to actually cook for there to be leftovers," I said a little louder.

She groaned, as if my words were tiny stinging nettles.

I hadn't meant to hurt her; I was just stating the truth. I tried a different approach, making sure my words didn't have any prickly edges. "I found something in the clearing today."

Before Junie got sick, my sister and I loved exploring outside. We quickly learned that the orchard offered a seemingly endless supply of treasures, if we looked carefully. We spent hours collecting chips of bark, colorful leaves, flakes of lichen, and smooth pebbles. Then we'd come home and present our findings to Mom. She would *ooh* and *aah*, then help us arrange everything in an old wooden box that we called our Cabinet of Curiosities. Now it was gathering dust in my room. It didn't feel right to play with it without Junie.

"Did you hear me?" I asked. "I found something. It won't fit in our Cabinet of Curiosities, but it's definitely curious . . ."

"Oh?" she said wearily.

"Don't worry, it's not made of mud," I added, still hoping to brighten her mood. Along with being a master treasure-finder, Junie was an expert mud chef. She liked to test different recipes during our afternoon adventures, blending the slimiest ingredients she could find. Mud cakes and mud soufflé were her specialties. One day, against my advice, she delivered a dozen extra gooey mud cakes right to the kitchen table. Even though Mom wanted to encourage Junie's culinary interests, she insisted that all mud creations stay outside from then on.

Lately, when Junie came home from the hospital between treatments, she was too nauseated or tired to play outside. Plus, the doctors said digging around in the dirt wasn't safe because bacteria could cause an infection that Junie might not be able to fight.

"I know they were awful gross, but I sort of miss those mud cakes," I said. "Spring is the best season for mud-making. All that thawed snow, plus April showers . . ."

"Not now, Isa." Mom pressed the pillow tighter over her ears. "My head, it's pounding."

"My stomach, it's rumbling. Together we could have a pretty sweet band. Rumble, grumble! Boom, bam!" I drummed my hands against my belly.

"Please, baby. I need some quiet. I just . . ." Her voice faded away.

My hands dropped to my sides. "Fine. Is anyone around here going to make dinner? When's Dad coming home?"

One thing Mom disliked more than mud on the kitchen table was whining. She sat up and reached for the lamp next to her bed, pulling the cord with a fierce yank. I jumped back. Her wavy auburn hair wasn't shiny or smooth; it was tangled and wild, piled on top of her head like one of those nests the birds in the orchard were building. Her eyes were the same olive-green color as Junie's, but they didn't have their usual gleam and they were ringed in red. She blinked furiously, as if the light were too bright or as if she were fighting back tears. Or maybe both.

"He's working, Isabel. We're doing the best we can." She cinched her bathrobe tightly around her waist and stared at me. "Your father's completely fried. We all are."

I tried to muster up some words, but they all sounded too cruel to say out loud. Even though I was mad, I didn't want to make Mom's eyes redder or her face puffier. I knew why Dad had to work so hard, and why Mom spent so much time at the hospital. I knew I needed to *hang in there* and *be a good girl*. But knowing something in your head and feeling it in your heart are two very different things. Sometimes I think grown-ups forget how hard that can be.

I turned on my heels and marched down the stairs, intentionally stepping on all the creakiest boards, letting them do the whining for me.

I pulled a box of cereal from the kitchen cupboard. CrunchyFunPuffs! Again. Oh joy. What fun. I swung the fridge door open, then kicked it shut. Empty.

A hollowness formed in my gut where hunger mixed with anger. What would Junie call that? *Hanger?* I sat alone at the table and shoveled milkless spoonfuls of cereal into my mouth. I wondered what my sister was eating for dinner. It was probably hospital mush, but I hoped it was cupcakes. That would make her happy. I pushed my bowl aside and grabbed the telephone. I'd ask her myself. There was no one to stop me. I punched the numbers and listened to the bleating ring tone.

"Delorna Regional Hospital. How may I direct your call?"

Mom and Dad said we were so lucky that Delorna Regional had a special cancer center just for kids. If there hadn't been a good hospital nearby, we might've had to move again.

"Um, the Children's Care Unit, please." I cleared my throat. "Oncology," I added, which did not mean the study of uncles, as Junie had originally thought. "Room 612." Easy to remember. Our ages: six for Junie, twelve for me.

"One moment please."

Soft music warbled. I couldn't wait to hear Junie's voice. She'd love my story about the squirrel and the sapling. She'd probably even be jealous of my dinner. The word *CrunchyFunPuffs!* alone would trigger a giggle meltdown.

"Hello?" An unfamiliar voice. Definitely not Junie.

"Oh. Hi. I'd like to speak with . . . Penelope Hucklesby Fitzwilken, Jr." I don't know why I said her full name. It sounded too fancy, too serious, too everything. Junie was so small that even her nickname needed a nickname: Junie, short for Junior, short for, well, that silly oversize name of hers.

"She's not available right now. Can I take a message?"

"Not available? What does that mean?"

"I'm sorry, may I ask who's calling?"

"I'm her sister. Is she all right?"

A long pause. "I'm really not at liberty to say." The voice was cold and formal. I bet it belonged to someone with a very long name. "We have strict patient confidentiality policies. I could connect you with one of our supervisors."

Missing Junie carved an emptiness inside me that was far worse than hanger. As I hung up the phone, I felt like it might swallow me whole.

CHAPTER 3

Back in November, when the weather began to snap with cold, Junie and I went to play in the orchard. Mom worried we'd catch a chill. She insisted we wear our puffy coats, plus hats and thick mittens. She even wrapped scarves around our necks, the itchy ones in hideous colors that Aunt Sheila knitted for us each year.

As soon as we got to the clearing, we flung those scarves off. Junie climbed onto the swing. I pushed her while she hooted and hollered, her breath leaving little steamy clouds suspended in the crisp air.

"Junie-to-the-moonie!" she sang, soaring higher. Too high. She couldn't grip the ropes with those thick mittens. Before I realized what was happening, she tumbled off the swing, landing like a sack of potatoes in the frosty grass.

"Junie!" I screamed, rushing to her.

After the world's longest three seconds, her eyes opened. "Did you see me, Isa?" she rasped. "Did you see me fly? Wasn't I awesomesauce?"

I breathed a sigh of relief. She was fine. Awesomesauce, even. But when she stood up a few minutes later, she moaned and grabbed her stomach. I carried her all the way home. By the time we got to the front porch, I was sweating buckets and my arm muscles burned worse than if I'd pitched five innings straight.

After that, everything happened quickly. A visit to the pediatrician turned into a trip to the emergency room. I cried in the car all the way to the hospital, even though I wasn't the one who had fallen. I cried because I thought I'd broken my little sister.

After tests and scans and meetings with a whole team of specialists, we learned that the tumble from the swing hadn't harmed Junie, but it did reveal a bigger issue. The doctors called the fall a blessing in disguise. I called it the worstible afternoon of my life.

For weeks leading up to that day, my parents and I assumed the bulge in my sister's middle was the result of too many sweets. Junie even called it her *dessert belly*. At dinner, when her regular belly was too full to eat another vegetable, her dessert belly always had room to spare. Imagine our shock when the tall man with

27

bushy eyebrows named Dr. Ebbens told us the bulge was actually a tumor attached to Junie's kidney.

At first, I thought finding a tumor was like discovering an unwanted raisin in a chocolate chip cookie: something that didn't belong, but could be plucked out pretty easily. I was wrong. It was a lot more complicated.

"Wilms tumor," Dr. Ebbens explained. "Also called nephroblastoma, is the most common form of kidney cancer in children. With prompt and aggressive treatment, it's successfully treated in the majority of our patients." Then he began rattling off a bunch of important-sounding medical terms, but I couldn't get past the word *cancer*. It knocked the wind straight out of me.

My eyes darted over to Junie. She didn't seem fazed. I don't think she understood what it all meant. Frankly, neither did I. But I knew enough to know it wasn't good. As the doctor continued talking, Mom's face crumpled and Dad's shoulders rolled forward. Everyone looked ready to cry. Except Junie. Like the eye of a storm, she was calm while the world roared around her.

Then she interrupted the grown-ups. "Excuse me? Could we call him Willie instead?" She patted her stomach. "Wilmer Nephew Blast-o-Rama sounds too fancy."

28

It was such a Junie thing to do: give a tumor a nickname and find a way to make everyone laugh when life was teetering toward a place almost too scary to bear.

***

A few days after the diagnosis, I asked my parents what I could do to help. I was the big sister, but I felt small. Powerless and confused and unprepared for everything that was happening. I needed something, anything, to keep me from shattering into pieces.

My parents stared at me with wide, confused eyes, as if I were speaking an alien language. They'd been so focused on Junie, I think they temporarily forgot they had two daughters. That's when I started becoming invisible.

My lower lip began doing this annoying wobbly thing. I bit it, hard, just to make it stop. "Junie's job is to get better," I said. "That's pretty obvious. But what's mine?"

Dad leaned over, clasped a hand on my shoulder, and said, "Just hang in there, sweetheart."

Mom patted my back, adding, "You're such a good girl. Keep it up. That's all we ask. We'll get through this."

So I did what they asked, week after week, month after month, the best I could. I paid attention in school. I did my homework without anyone asking. While Junie recovered from kidney surgery and a procedure to implant a port in her chest, I sat by her bedside, cutting and coloring an army of paper dolls and playing a mind-numbing amount of Go Fish.

As Junie's medicine weakened her immune system and germs became enemy number one, I helped Mom scrub and disinfect the house daily—even the toilets, which made me gag. At least I never threw up. My sister wasn't nearly that lucky.

When Junie napped, which was often, I tiptoed around the house and whispered in a voice softer than kitten fur, afraid to disturb her precious rest, and also terrified I might somehow wake the cancer.

I didn't complain when Dad stopped playing catch with me in the evenings. I tried to forget about our half-finished dollhouse project in the workshop. I understood why Mom occasionally picked me up late from school, and I even ate the disgustingly healthy kale casseroles she cooked for dinner without fussing. These were all small prices to pay.

But then things got worse. A series of complications (which is basically a grown-up term for worstibles) sent Junie back to the hospital, for much longer than usual. Mom began to change. Dad too. With each passing week, I felt myself fading away. Heck, the only company I'd had for days was that nutso squirrel. Despite what I'd promised my parents, *hanging in there* was starting to feel like literally dangling off the edge of a cliff without any ropes or harnesses to keep me from falling. I wasn't sure how much longer I could keep it up.

CHAPTER 4

Beep. Beep. Beeeeeeeep.

I hushed the alarm clock and rolled over. The morning sun slashed its way bright and unwelcome through my blinds. My brain started waking up, trying to untangle dreams from dawn, but I wasn't ready to face the day just yet. I wanted to stay in a make-believe world where magic was real, and the absurd made perfect sense. I tugged my blanket over my head and squeezed my eyes shut.

As I drifted back to sleep, I felt blue ropes wrap around my waist, lifting me gently toward the leaves of a giant beanstalk. I reached for Junie's hand and pulled her up too. Together we climbed higher and higher, until the clouds were close enough to touch. They were downy as dandelion fluff and tasted like cotton candy. The beanstalk swayed. We grabbed the blue rope and swung like monkeys onto a floating island in the sky. When huge boulders blocked our path, we pushed them aside, squealing as they bounced away as easily as beach balls. Beneath the boulders we expected to find salamanders and centipedes, but we discovered jewels instead. We filled our pockets until they were bursting with glittering treasures. Butterflies the size of eagles swooped down to greet us, and a squirrel in a tuxedo and high-tops served us a tray of cookies.

BEEP! BEEP! BEEEEEEEP! My clock launched another attack, scattering the dream. I sat up, blinked my eyes, and growled.

My room was nowhere near as exciting as my dream. The most disappointing difference was that Junie wasn't there. In our old apartments, Junie and I had always shared a bedroom, out of necessity. When we moved to the Melwick farmhouse, there was finally enough space for us to have our own rooms. Junie liked to play in her room, but she still preferred sleeping in mine. Each night she'd sneak across the hall and snuggle next to me in my bed.

At the crack of dawn, she'd poke me and try to peel my eyelids open. "Isa! Isa! Wake up! I have to tell you about my dream before it disappears!" she'd say, wiggling like a worm. I used to think it was the most annoying thing in the world. Now I'd trade my alarm clock in a heartbeat for a poke in the eye.

I stood, stretched, then pulled on a cleanish outfit. It wasn't quite warm enough yet for shorts, so yesterday's patched jeans would have to do. I was planning to skip socks altogether, like I had the day before, but that had caused the volcanic blister on my heel, so I rooted around in my dresser for a bit. It was in a sad state. Mom obsessively washed Junie's clothes and sheets and stuffed animals, but my laundry hadn't exactly been anyone's top priority lately. Eventually I found one yellow sock and one green sock covered with tiny snowmen. Certainly not fashionable, but they'd have to do.

I slid my watch onto my right wrist and tightened the purple band snugly. When I looked into the mirror, I saw Junie's face where mine should have been: pudgy cheeks framed by elfin ears and two pigtails spraying fountains of wispy hair so blonde it was almost white. I blinked and she was gone.

Just my face. A pale oval. My eyes were the same steely blue as Dad's. The freckles on my nose were faded. They were always that way after a long winter. I made a mental note to ask Ms. Perdilla if freckles hibernated. A few days of sunshine and they'd be back.

I picked up an elastic hair tie and wrangled my frizzy hair into an acceptable hairstyle. I wished for the billionth time that it could be either curly or straight, instead of some maddeningly untamable combination of the two, then I instantly felt guilty for worrying about something so silly.

In the next room, Mom was still asleep. I could hear her snoring. She usually left for the hospital before the bus picked me up for school, but she seemed extra tired lately, so I avoided the creaky steps, moving through the house silently.

Isabel-Invisible.

I inspected the kitchen for signs of Dad's existence. A half cup of lukewarm coffee on the counter told me that he had, indeed, come home. The faint trail of aftershave lingering by the front door told me he had already gone again.

I peered inside the tin can on top of the microwave where he left my lunch money each morning. Today it was as empty as the fridge. Not even a note. He must have forgotten. He often stayed overnight with Junie at the hospital. Then he'd wake up at dawn, come home to shower and change his clothes, and be off again. Which was one of the reasons he was completely fried, as my mother had put it.

The word *fried* got me thinking about french fries and corn dogs and all the other good-but-bad foods Mom rarely let us have. My mouth began to water. I reached into the box of CrunchyFunPuffs! and scooped up a handful of stale sweetness. Both crunch and fun were long gone.

This just wouldn't do.

I started opening drawers, hunting for coins. If I had to turn the house upside down, I would. When the kitchen yielded a disappointing thirty-two cents, I turned my search to the living room. The couch cushions generously produced one dollar and seventy-four cents. In the mudroom, the pockets of Mom's raincoat offered a crumpled dollar bill and a stick of petrified chewing gum. Not great, but not so bad either. I tucked the money into my jeans and swung my backpack over my shoulder. I stopped. I looked down at my feet. I twitched my toes, making the tiny snowmen on my right foot wiggle. The blister on my heel was still raw, so I ran back to the kitchen and grabbed a Band-Aid from the catchall drawer. I bandaged myself up. As I slid my sock back on, I remembered . . .

My shoes.

That squirrel! That stupid orchard! What had I done?

Between feeling so hungry and grumpy last night, I'd forgotten to remind Mom that I wanted a new pair of shoes. No, not wanted: I desperately *needed* a new pair.

I stomped out an angry tantrum dance. If Junie were home, she'd call me *flusterated*. But that would be the understatement of the century. I steamed and stomped some more. It was strangely satisfying. I felt the same way at softball practice. Each catch, hit, and pitch was a welcome outlet for all those pent-up flusterations.

Feeling calmer, I examined the closet's footwear options: two pairs of Mom's ticky-clicky high heels—almost my size but too flashy and bound to twist one of my ankles; one boat-sized pair of Dad's loafers—perfect, if I was attending clown auditions at the circus; and Junie's jelly sandals—so tiny they'd barely fit my big toes. Mom always said I needed to put myself in other people's shoes, but I didn't think this was what she meant.

I weighed my remaining choices: a pair of ice skates or fuzzy cat slippers. Wildly impractical versus utterly mortifying. I looked down at the slippers. *Meow!* they taunted. I accepted defeat. Bring on the mortification.

Unless . . .

I peered out the large bay window. Fog rose from the rolling hills of the orchard, catching columns of sunshine. Almost like a spotlight. *Here! Over here!* Dirty sneakers with earthworm shoelaces became suddenly appealing. I crossed the backyard and strode up the hill, trampling the dewy grass. By the time I reached the gate at the top, my socks were soaked. I pulled them off and hung them on a branch of the nearest tree to dry.

The orchard was eerily quiet. Usually at this time of day, the birds were tweeting louder than my alarm clock. Wisps of morning mist wove between the apple trees and pooled thick and dense in the clearing. When a breeze rolled through, I caught a faint whiff of that sawdust-cinnamon-leather-strawberry smell from yesterday. Today there were also notes of coconut, wood smoke, and chamomile.

With those smells came another wave of memories: building sand castles at the beach; roasting s'mores by a campfire; afternoon tea parties. I closed my eyes and lifted my chin, letting the sun warm my face. This time, I didn't fight the memories. Like the sun, they warmed me up.

There was a rustling in the trees. My eyes snapped open, expecting to see the squirrel. I looked left. Looked right. He was nowhere in sight. As the sun's rays beat down, the fog thinned, revealing something in the clearing much larger than a squirrel.

I squinted, blinked. When my eyes finally focused, I reeled backward, my bare feet slipping in the wet grass. I caught the outstretched limb of a nearby apple tree and held tight until I regained my balance. I straightened myself up and took a deep breath. I pinched my own arm, just to make sure I wasn't dreaming. It hurt like heck and left a very real, very red welt.

"Hello?" I called out, my voice shaky. I glanced around to check if someone was playing a practical joke on me. "You know April Fools' was yesterday, right?"

No one was there, not even a bushy-tailed rodent. I took a tentative step forward. I could hear the *thrump-thrump* of my own heart. It grew louder and faster as the fog lifted. I climbed over the old foundation stones and rubbed my eyes. I shook my head.

There, in the center of the clearing, stood the sapling, completely transformed.

In a single evening, it had more than quadrupled in size. Now it towered over me, nearly the same height as the nearby apple trees. Its trunk was as thick as a telephone pole, twisting upward like a bundle of ropes. The bark swirled like luminous marble, milky gray and green. A dense ruffle of leaves decorated each branch. The leaves were twice as large as any oak leaf, and almost see-through, with a hint of silvery blue streaked through them. The tree looked both ancient and futuristic at the same time. It was the most beautiful thing I had ever seen.

The leaves shimmered and whispered, beckoning me to come closer. I couldn't resist. I stepped beneath the boughs. A gentle breeze embraced me in a hug. I reached out and pressed my palms against the bark. It was warm to the touch and sent a faint tingling sensation through my body.

As the clouds shifted overhead, beams of sunlight pierced the canopy. The sparkling leaves acted like the prisms Ms. Perdilla hung in our classroom windows, bending light and throwing little rainbows across the meadow.

I laughed. A real, full, hard-to-catch-your-breath laugh. I spun and leaped, chasing the flickering splashes of color. My heart drummed wildly in my chest, in a good way, reminding me that I was healthy and alive and having fun for the first time in months.

The clearing suddenly erupted with noise. Crickets chirped. Chickadees sang. The apple trees rustled and shook. Swallows swooped through the air, equally excited by the strange new addition to the orchard. I wished the squirrel would scamper out to see what had happened.

I twirled like a top, making myself dizzy. The sapling's branches swayed as though they were trying to dance with me. I stretched my hands over my head. Something feathery brushed my palm. At first I thought it was one of the birds, dipping down too low. But then I felt it again. I looked up and gasped.

Dangling from the tree's lowest branch was a cluster of extremely peculiar fruit. When I stood on my tippy toes to get a better view, I spotted several other clusters higher up. They were grouped in twos, like enormous cherries hanging by bright orange stems. Red feathered petals wrapped each fruit—or whatever it was—in a protective pod.

I grabbed the nearest pair. With a tug, the pods broke free from their stems. They were so large that they tumbled out of my hands and onto the ground. My stomach, still waiting for breakfast, wondered aloud if they might be edible. If so, would they taste sweet or sour? Would they be fleshy like a peach or full of seeds like a watermelon? Maybe segmented like an orange or crunchy like an apple?

I began peeling back the delicate petals, one by one.

What I discovered disappointed my stomach, but delighted my feet.

CHAPTER 5

Nestled within the feathery peel was a sneaker. Yes. A sneaker. One in each pod. Believe me, I did a double take, too. Navy blue laces zigzagged between shining grommets, looping into a smiling knot at the ankle. Brand new. Left and right. A perfect pair. Hunter green canvas, crisp white rubber soles. My style. I didn't even care that I wasn't wearing any socks; I slipped the shoes on and wiggled ten very satisfied toes. My size. One hundred percent perfecterrific.

My brain whirred at warp speed trying to make sense of what I was seeing, touching, smelling . . . and now wearing. All evidence suggested that my buried sneakers went to seed and sprouted an entire crop of, well, shoefruits. But something was missing from that explanation. Okay, a lot was missing. Whatever happened was definitely not part of Ms. Perdilla's science curriculum.

I knew chance seedlings had a habit of producing unexpected fruit, but this was ridiculous. Shoes were made. Shoes didn't grow. My sneakers may have inspired this odd new crop, but the sapling had already been there, so what I'd planted wasn't technically a seed. Plus, a tree couldn't quadruple in size in a single night. Could it?

All I knew for sure was that I'd given the tree a pair of old sneakers and, in return, it gave me a glimpse into a world where anything might be possible.

Junie would insist it was magic. I could practically hear her squeaky voice, breathless with excitement. I could feel her fingers, sticky from some sweet she'd been eating, clasping my hand so tightly it almost hurt. I could see her olive-green eyes, wide as teacups and full to the brim with wonder.

But, no. Magic didn't exist. It couldn't. There was no place for magic in a world where a six-year-old gets cancer.

The leaves of that beautiful tree rustled. *Tssk. Tssk. Tssk.* Almost like it was disagreeing with me. Like it wanted to prove me wrong. The branches dipped gently, lowering another cluster of shoefruits within arm's reach. It felt like a challenge I'd be silly not to take.

I plucked and peeled the pods. I expected to find more sneakers, but to my surprise, I discovered a pair of softball cleats. They were sleek black and yellow. Exactly what I needed for the upcoming season. I laid them on a patch of grass and gazed at the tree in disbelief. Branches crisscrossed like arms linked together. Standing beneath them, I felt protected. More than that, I felt seen.

I spied another cluster dangling from a higher branch. I bent my knees and jumped, pulling the pods down with me. Inside the peels were rubber rain boots. Not only were they my size, but they were printed with my favorite polka-dot pattern. I scratched my head, dumbfounded.

The only explanation that made any sense was the impossible one.

"Magic?" I said, testing the weight of the word. It hitched in my throat and I realized how badly I actually wished it could be true. Then I rolled my eyes. How ludicrous. I was acting nuttier than a squirrel. There was definitely no such thing as . . .

The branches lifted up and down ever so slightly. If I hadn't been watching the tree so carefully, I might've missed the gesture. Was it a nod? Or a shrug? Some sort of tree sign-language? Or just the wind, rolling on through?

Suddenly my watch beeped. I looked at its blinking face. I had completely lost track of time. Even at top speed, I probably wouldn't make it to the bus stop in front of our house. I could cut through the orchard, though, and try to catch the bus farther down the road.

I needed to move quickly. I stuffed the cleats and boots into my backpack.

I yanked my good luck key chain, a small brass bell clipped to the zipper. It jangled frantically as I tugged and tugged, until the backpack finally zipped shut. As I turned to leave, I noticed a few more pods hanging from the upper branches, but time was running out. The rest would have to wait. I could hear the bus chugging along the winding country road.

I took off. New sneakers, fast legs, light heart. Across the clearing, through the orchard. For the past few months, I'd trudged through this landscape. Now I devoured it. The tiny bell sang. *Ting-ting-ting!* I chose a shortcut, leaping across a burbling brook. I skidded down a steep slope, past another house, toward the road. The yellow bus curved around the bend. I would beat it. I was unstoppable.

Except . . .

I tripped. Face first. Green grass, mean fall. My overstuffed backpack launched over my shoulders, hitting the ground. The zipper split, scattering textbooks and homework and shoes. One sad little *ting!* escaped from the bell. And I thought I'd avoided mortification

45

for the day. I scrambled to my feet. Had anyone on the bus seen me? Hard to tell. I prayed the neighbor's garage blocked the view. I reached for one of the rain boots.

"Hey, Cinderella. Here you go," a voice said behind me. "It's not exactly a glass slipper, but . . ."

I turned and grabbed the softball cleat from a tall girl with chestnut hair like a horse's mane. Her mother had been our realtor when we moved to Bridgebury, and I was pretty sure they lived right down the road. But I'd never bothered to introduce myself to the girl before. It was part of my don't-need-friends policy.

"It's nice to see you at my bus stop," she said, beaming.

"I missed my regular stop, so . . ."

"A happy accident!"

I gathered up the rest of my belongings, keeping my head down. "Sure, whatever."

"Where'd you get these?" She handed me the other cleat.

I froze, like a criminal in a searchlight. Planting sneakers under a possibly magical tree wasn't illegal, was it? "A store," I lied, holding my secret tight.

"I've never seen cleats like this before. They're so cool!"

"Thanks, I know," I mumbled. The school bus slowed to a halt in front of us. The door folded open.

Perfect timing. I jumped in, clutching my backpack. I landed in the first empty seat.

"You forgot this." The girl plunked down beside me and waved a sheet of paper in my face. "I'm impressed. This assignment isn't due until next week, you eager-beaver-overachiever!" Her voice was so chipper it made me cringe.

"I like numbers." I snatched the math homework away and slipped it into my backpack. "You're in Miss Benítez's class too?"

"Actually, I'm in every single one of your classes." She looked at me squarely. "Nice of you to notice."

I stared back blankly.

"Do you even know my name?" she asked. Her hair was so long it tumbled onto my shoulder. I brushed it away. "Seriously, Isabel. Do you?" Ugh. She was so persistent.

I bit my lip. "Sure I do. You're . . . Jennif . . . Jessic . . . ?" I watched her face for a hint. Nothing. So I played the odds. "Emm . . . Soph . . . ?" And lost.

She didn't look mad, just disappointed. I felt like a world-class jerk.

"It's okay," she said. Her eyes were too nice, all squishy and full of warm, brown kindness. I had to look away. "I know you've been having a tough time lately." She patted me on the arm.

I flinched. I wanted to scream, *Get your hands and your freakishly long hair off me!* The bus stopped again. More kids boarded, equally nameless. I thought about bolting, escaping that torturous ride. Run back to the orchard. My parents would never notice. By the time Principal Tam called home, Mom would already be at the hospital and would never get the message.

But I liked school. It occupied my mind with things other than sickness and tin cans with no lunch money. Plus, I had snazzy new cleats I couldn't wait to use at softball practice. So I stayed on the bus.

I pressed my forehead to the window and tried to ignore the seat intruder next to me. She inched closer and closer, until I could practically smell the orange juice on her breath. I decided this girl was another sort of MIA—Most Intolerably Annoying.

We passed the millpond where Dad and I used to feed the ducks before we played catch in the evenings. Next was Mrs. Tolson's farm, with a feisty flock of chickens that we avoided at all costs because they pecked and scratched anyone who came near. The bus whizzed by a grove of birch trees, pale and slender, wrapped in papery bark like mummies. They were striking and mysterious, but nothing compared to the chance seedling growing in my own backyard. A rock wall snaked between the birches, marking an old property line that nature had chosen to disregard. Not unlike the girl encroaching further into my personal space with each passing minute. Her hair fell across my shoulder again. I resisted the urge to give it a strong yank.

The bus rounded the last bend of Melwick Lane and turned onto Drabbington Avenue, which was completely misnamed, in my opinion. The houses on Drabbington were packed in tight, sort of cuddled together. Square lawns spread out like green table-cloths, and ribbons of sidewalk spooled into a large cul de sac that was always filled with kids drawing with chalk, jumping rope, and riding bikes. If she wasn't so sick, Junie would've loved to play there. And if I hadn't instituted my don't-need-friends policy, I might have, too. Especially since I heard they had pickup ballgames most weekends.

I caught the reflection of the girl next to me in the glass. She was peering at the cul de sac. Her eyes had a funny look in them. A wishing look.

The bus eased up to the curb, welcoming a riot of kids aboard. They burst in like a swarm of bees, buzz-ing down the aisle until the bus driver yelled at every-one to "Sit and zip!" As we drove on, the other kids laughed and chattered. I could feel the humming of friendship all around. The girl next to me kept direct-ing that wishing look my way.

We made a few more stops, nearing the town center. We passed a hardware store, a bakery, a post office. Farther ahead, a brick library, a steepled church, a cemetery, and a few more shops ringed a grassy square. Compared to the cities we'd lived in, Bridgebury was tiny. *Quaint* was the word my parents used, which was typically grown-up code for boring. But after everything that had happened in the orchard this morning, boring didn't fit one bit.

We pulled up to school just in time. I was positively itching to get off that bus. The long-haired girl blocked me. "By the way," she said cheerily, "my name is Kira. And we can be friends." Like it was the simplest thing in the world. The nerve.

CHAPTER 6

I should've played hooky after all. I couldn't stop thinking about the orchard. I was utterly useless in math class, which was usually my best subject. When Miss Benítez asked me the answer to twenty-seven divided by nine, I replied, "Tree. Oh! I mean, three."

In English class, when Mr. Clarke announced our lesson plan for the day, I practically fell out of my chair.

"Everything all right, Miss Fitzwilken?" he asked.

"Yeah, fine. Just, um . . . did you say roots?"

"Latin and Greek roots, yes. They can tell us a lot about the meaning of our vocabulary words. In fact, more than half of the words in the English language have Latin or Greek roots."

"I thought you meant something else," I said.

"No problem," Mr. Clarke replied. "Here, I'll explain. Take the word *bibliography*."

"Like the thing Ms. Perdilla says we have to include

with our science project?" the girl named Kira asked. Somehow she was sitting next to me. Again.

"Exactly. In Greek, *biblio* means books. The second part comes from *graphos*, which refers to writing or recording information. Mash it together and it describes a list of books and articles used for your research. Make sense?"

It actually did. It reminded me of Junie's silly word combinations.

"Let's play a matching game," Mr. Clarke said.

"I love games!" Kira clapped. This girl was too much. I rolled my eyes so hard they just about disappeared into my head.

Mr. Clarke wrote a bunch of words on one side of the whiteboard. On the other side, he wrote several roots with their meanings. "Dissect a word using its roots," he said, "and you'll find its definition. Casey, choose a word, please."

A boy sitting a few rows in front of me pointed to the first word on the list. "Ant-o-what-ah?"

"Anthozoa. Sounds tricky, doesn't it? But if you happen to know that the Greek word *anthos* means flower," he circled the root on the board, "and the word *zoa* means animals . . ." He circled that, too, and drew lines connecting everything. "It starts to make a whole lot more sense."

Casey shrugged. "Sort of."

"Wait!" I said, before we moved on. "Are you saying anthozoa means *flower animals*?"

"Precisely!"

"Flower animals? Really? Do things like that actually exist?" I asked.

"Certainly. Corals and sea anemones fall into that category. I'm sure Ms. Perdilla could give you more specific information if you're interested."

I *was* interested. Bizarre plants were the only things I could think about.

By the time science class rolled around, I still hadn't snapped out of it. And that kind of distraction can be seriously dangerous, especially if Bunsen burners are involved. I didn't get a chance to ask Ms. Perdilla about anthozoa because I was busy nearly torching Kira's mane. It was her own fault, really. She insisted on being my lab partner.

"Lab buddies!" she squealed as soon as Ms. Perdilla asked us to pair up.

Then, open flame. Long hair. An accident waiting to happen. Thankfully, Ms. Perdilla intervened before anything actually caught fire. I thought the whole incident might discourage Kira, but she was more determined than ever to be my friend. Some people just can't take a hint.

***

At noon, the lunch bell rang. Kids flooded the hall-ways, surging in a chatty mass toward the cafeteria. I joined the lunch line, ready to hand over my money in return for a tray of waxy beans, a scoop of some questionable purée, and an unidentifiable hunk of meat. I was so hungry that my standards were at an all-time low. Anything was better than another bowl of stale cereal.

I reached into my pocket. I pulled out the stick of petrified chewing gum. I tried the other pocket, wiggling my fingers. The money was gone. Gone? That's when I felt it: a hole. One Mom hadn't patched. Surprise, surprise. All those scrounged coins and dollar bill must have slipped away when I fell running for the bus. My heart dropped. Down through my chest, through my empty stomach, right on through that hole in my pocket. I was shocked it didn't leave a crater in the cafeteria floor a mile deep.

I needed a plan. I could tell the lunch lady that my dad forgot to give me lunch money. But that might lead to questions. And with one little tug, even well-meaning questions could unravel me quicker than one of Aunt Sheila's badly knit scarves. Before I knew it, I'd be a blubbering mess, going on and on about a battle between a sweet little kid named Junie and a nasty tumor named Willie.

I stepped out of the lunch line, empty-handed. I crossed the cafeteria and veered left through a set of double doors that led to an open courtyard. On nice days, we were allowed to spend our lunch period out there. I sucked in the fresh air, wishing it was chicken soup, or a banana smoothie, or anything to satisfy my rumbling stomach. I sat at an empty picnic table and watched as some boys climbed the big stones in the middle of the courtyard, throwing grapes at each other like miniature grenades. A few girls came outside next, giggling and gossiping, carrying trays of food. Their shoulders bumped together easily as they walked. They sat a few tables away, casting an occasional glance my way.

I didn't usually mind sitting alone, as long as I had something to focus my attention on. A tray of food or a lunch box acted like a shield, telling the world you had a purpose. You couldn't be bothered with petty lunchtime chatter when you were focused on important tasks, like sculpting mashed potato mountain ranges or dissecting a particularly sketchy hamburger patty. Unfortunately, that afternoon I had nothing to fiddle with, no shield. I didn't really want to be anyone's friend, but I didn't want my classmates to consider me a total loser either. It was a delicate balance.

As a last resort, I unwrapped the stick of petrified chewing gum and placed it on my tongue. I would blow bubbles. Big, pink bubbles would be my shield. I chewed once, twice. The gum crumbled and dissolved into sugary dust. I tried folding the wrapper into an elegant origami crane. It looked more like a road-kill pigeon. So much for a shield.

The picnic table shifted. Someone slid along the bench, directly across from me.

My stomach growled embarrassingly loud. I honed in on the crumpled bird with laser focus. I tried to summon my powers of invisibility. *Leave. Me. Alone. Please.*

"On a diet?"

I recognized that singsongy voice. I looked up. It was Kira. Annoying. Until I realized she could be my armor. Just for today. With her sitting there, I didn't feel so exposed and pitiful. I abandoned my origami disaster.

"A diet?" I said. "No. Well, not an intentional one."

"Aha, I know your secret." Her too-nice eyes twinkled.

What was she talking about? What did she know?

"Your mutant pet centipede ate your lunch. Right?

I mean, why else would someone have all those boots and cleats in their backpack, but no food?"

I laughed. For the second time in one day. A new record. I really tried not to, but I couldn't help it. It just crept up on me. Like a centipede, all wiggly and tickly with a hundred crazy legs.

"Here." She opened her lunch box and pushed an orange and a stack of cookies wrapped in wax paper across the table. "Sharing is caring," she said, winking at me like we were actually friends or something. I grimaced. She caught my expression and said, "The cookies are homemade. Try them! They're good."

I could hardly remember the last time my mom had baked something, which was odd for two reasons. First, she used to work as a pastry chef. Second, I was usually really good at keeping track of time. I could calculate exactly how long it'd been since I'd had a dentist appointment or ridden a roller coaster. I loved counting forward too: tracking the months, weeks, days, hours, and minutes until something fun was supposed to happen, like a birthday party or a trip to the beach. I had a teacher once who thought it was an impressive skill, which inspired my parents to buy me my own watch. It wasn't nearly as fancy as Dad's antique gold one, but mine had a purple leather strap and a happy-looking face and I loved it.

I still wore that watch every day, even though I was trying to quit my habit. I'd lost all faith in time. If Junie hadn't gotten sick, I'm pretty sure the past five months and better-not-to-think-about-how-many minutes would've flown by. Quick and happy. Blink of an eye. Instead, they dragged. Slow and heavy. Like drips of molasses. And since no one seemed to know exactly when Junie would get better, I couldn't count forward either.

"Aren't you hungry?" Kira asked, nudging the snacks closer.

I glanced at the cookies, as if my stomach now controlled my eyeballs. They were tied with a ribbon like a present. A note was attached. When Kira saw it, she reached across the table and snapped the paper away. She stuffed the note in her pocket.

"My mom still treats me like a baby. It's so embarrassing," she said. "She leaves notes on my cookies, notes in my backpack. Notes stuck to the bathroom mirror when I wake up in the morning."

I felt a little jab in my stomach. Hunger pain. Or memory pain? I pictured the empty tin can in our kitchen. Not a penny or note inside to rattle *I love you.* Or at the very least, *I may have forgotten your lunch money, but I haven't forgotten about you.*

"Sounds awful," I muttered.

"It's like I can't escape." Kira took a bite of the best-looking turkey sandwich I'd ever seen. "Mothers are the worst like that."

"Like what?" I asked, bewildered. Even when Mom couldn't bring herself to cook, or brush her hair, or clean up her spilled tea, she never made it onto my list of worstibles. Not yet at least.

"Like always smothering you with *Great job!* And *Have a nice day, Pookie!*"

"Pookie?" Another laugh snuck out in the form of a snort. Mortifying.

She nodded, brow furrowed. As if using the name Pookie was a truly serious offense. Kira and I lived right down the road from each other, but it was clear that we actually lived in opposite universes. I decided to play along, because it was almost fun to imagine.

"Or how they always want to spend time with you," I said. I peeled the orange, which wasn't as exciting as peeling a feathery shoefruit pod, but at least this was edible.

"Right! And talk to you about your day. Ugh." Kira sighed dramatically.

I ate the sweet orange slices. "And ask how you're feeling."

"Mmhmm. And take you shopping for frilly dresses you wouldn't be caught dead in."

"And tuck you into bed at night." Out of nowhere, the almost-fun feeling vanished. My mouth filled with a bitter taste. "You know?" I spit out the words and shut my mouth fast, before anything bigger and truer could slip out.

Kira nodded enthusiastically. "Believe me. I know."

But she had no idea. How could anyone else understand what was happening?

My face felt like it was about to crack open like an egg. I slid off the picnic table bench and ran. Not the light, joyful running of the morning. This was an escape. Lead legs, aching heart, almost-cracked egg face. I ran to the only decent hiding spot I could think of, where no one, except maybe the janitor, would bother me.

***

I sat in the last stall of the girls' bathroom for the rest of lunch, and all the way through geography and music class too. I read and reread the graffiti on the wall, where the middle school social order was spelled out in loopy handwriting and i's dotted with hearts. I learned that Vanessa loved Robert, Liz hated Amelia, and Casey smells. I memorized important equations that Miss Benítez must have skipped over in math class, like

R + S = 4eva and AP, SC, MO = BFFS!!! and A <3 F. Fascinating stuff. Really.

When the last bell finally rang, I emerged. Brand new cleats were calling my name. Ready for a happier run. I rejoined my classmates in the hallway, like I'd been there all along, and made my way toward the gym.

The girls' locker room was empty. I was grateful for a moment alone. I unzipped my backpack. The yellow-and-black cleats dazzled. My muscles twitched. I couldn't wait to take them out for a spin.

I changed into my gym clothes and slid my hand into my glove. It had belonged to Dad when he was a boy, and Grandpa Isaac before him. Our nightly tosses had been postponed for a while, but wearing that glove and practicing with the team made me feel close to my father. If I played really well, maybe I could persuade him to leave his office for a few hours and watch our first game of the season.

I was about to slam my locker closed when a piece of paper on the bulletin board caught my eye. Coach Naron's chicken scratches were strewn all over, barely legible, just like her playbook.

Girls' Softball: practice canceled today due to rain.
See you on the field tomorrow! —Coach N

Rain? No way. It was sunny and clear at lunch. Then again, I hadn't left the windowless bathroom stall for hours. For all I knew, the entire town could have been hit by a meteor shower or trampled by a herd of runaway rhinos from the zoo. I left the locker room, jogged past the gym and down the hall, toward the school's side entrance. I opened the door. A sheet of angry water and a smudged sky greeted me. I ducked back inside.

Great. Just great. I returned to the locker room and took off my cleats, trading them for the polka-dot boots. The tree really had known what I might need today. Science couldn't explain that, could it? But magic could. Suddenly the prospect of a rainy walk home felt a whole lot less dreadful.

The bus was long gone by now, and I was positive Mom hadn't heard the news that Coach canceled practice. I pulled an umbrella from the nearby lost and found bin. It was badly busted. When I tried to slide it open, it popped upward like a startled tulip. I opened the door and stepped out under the awning, clutching my backpack with one hand and the crooked umbrella with the other.

Just then, a shiny red minivan pulled up to the curb. *Honk, honk!* The door eased open and an arm waved. Someone hollered, but the rain washed the voice away.

I craned my neck to listen, squinted my eyes to get a better view. The arm waved again, followed by a long swath of chestnut hair.

"Hurry! Get in!" Kira called out. "We'll drive you home!"

"I'm going to walk," I shouted.

The front window lowered and a kind face appeared. "Walk? More like swim, dear. You'll drown out here."

"Really, it's fine."

"It's no trouble at all. We live just up the road from you." The offer was tempting, especially now that rain was falling by the bucketful.

"Mom's right. Get in!" Kira said. Apparently she'd forgiven her mother's crimes of kindness.

"Come along, dear. We won't take no for an answer." Heck. They were both persistent. At least she wasn't calling me Pookie. It could've been worse.

I abandoned the umbrella and sprinted for the car. It was warm and dry inside, with plush seats and a tiny television mounted in the headrest, like a cozy living room on wheels.

Kira clapped and squealed. "Carpool buddies!" She tried to give me a high five, but I left her hanging. High fives were a major violation of my don't-need-friends policy.

"Buckle up, girls. I brought some juice boxes if you're thirsty." Kira's mom smiled in the rearview mirror, beaming so brightly that I had to turn away.

"You want grape or fruit punch? They both have bendy straws. I just love bendy straws, don't you? They're totally silly, but also very convenient." Kira looked cross-eyed down her own straw. "A real contradiction," she said between sips.

"Good word, Pookie!" her mother cooed from the front seat.

"I know! It comes from the Latin roots *contra* and *dicere*." Kira grinned proudly.

Flaunting some stupid vocabulary word we'd learned in Mr. Clarke's class was not going to impress me. Not one bit. Okay, if Junie said a word like that it would probably sound cute. Because she was six years old. And because she was Junie. Kira was neither.

"So?" Kira asked, giving me a little nudge. "Which flavor do you want? You can have both. We have plenty."

Plenty. A word that sounded luxurious, and foreign. Lately, the only thing we Fitzwilkens had plenty of were problems.

"Grape," I said, giving in. "Thanks." The juice hit my empty stomach, sending sugar rushing through my veins.

Kira took a few big gulps, then dragged on her bendy straw, filling the car with a symphony of slurping. The juice box eventually surrendered to her torture and collapsed in on itself. Crushed. Just as we pulled up to my house.

"Thanks for the ride," I said, gathering my things.

"You're welcome, dear." Kira's mom turned to look at me. "I've told your mother over and over, I'm happy to pick you up, whenever you need. It's really no trouble. And I know Kira would love to spend more time with you."

"Carpool buddies!" Kira tried the high five again. I placed my empty juice box in her hand instead. Did that count?

The car door slid open, friendly and smooth. Opening our station wagon's dented doors usually required a swift kick and a couple of bad words. Like I said, we lived in opposite universes.

"See ya later, alligator!" Kira trilled.

"Bye," I said, jumping out of the car. Thankfully, the rain had slowed to a light patter.

"No, you're supposed to say *in a while, crocodile!*" It was the sort of rhyming game Junie and I used to play. The memory stung like lemon juice on a paper cut.

I couldn't bear to answer her. When Kira waved good-bye, her long hair swung back and forth over her shoulder. I almost wished the door would shut on that ridiculous mane. Chop. Good riddance.

"Wait!" she screeched. She scrambled out of the car and ran over to me. She didn't seem to mind the raindrops spattering her face and clothes. "You forgot these at lunch." She pressed the perfectly wrapped cookies into my palm.

"Oh, right. Thanks."

"You're welcome. I hope you like them. I can bring you more tomorrow, if you want."

"Okay." I was grateful for the cookies but eager to escape and check on my tree.

Kira stood and stared at me, a smile plastered to her face. My own face was like a fun-house mirror, reflecting the reverse image.

"You know, it takes sixty-two muscles to frown," she said, squinting. "It only takes twenty-six to smile. You should try turning that frown upside down."

"Maybe I need the exercise," I grumbled.

Kira laughed. "Good one."

"It wasn't a joke."

"Well, it was funny, so I laughed. You should try that sometime too. Along with smiling."

"Thanks for the tip." The truth was, some days it felt unfair to smile when my little sister was so sick. But maybe Kira was right. I forced the corners of my mouth up the slightest bit.

"Much better." Kira nodded. She turned and climbed back into the car. "Bye-bye, butterfly!"

As they left, I felt myself filling up with emotions that didn't quite go together. It was a weird combination, like lima beans mixed with ice cream. I wanted to be seen and heard and cared about. By my family, though, not by some stranger.

My heart started insisting that a stranger could become a friend, and a friend could become like family, if I gave her a chance. My brain rallied against the idea, crying out, *What if you move again? Why suffer more? Why risk one more good-bye?*

No, I didn't want a friend. I really didn't. A friend would just complicate things. Plus, Kira drove me crazy. She was too perky, too loud, too everything.

You sure about that? asked my heart. I'd nearly torched her precious locks in science class. I'd ditched her in the middle of lunch with no explanation whatsoever. And yet she still offered me a ride home. She stood with me in the rain. She made sure I had something to eat and drink. She was excited to see me. She listened when I talked. It was more than my own parents had done for me in a while. My stubborn brain couldn't deny the fact that Kira was kind. Even when I'd been nothing but cranky in return.

I sighed. There were lots of things in life I couldn't change, like tumors named Willie and apple trees that refused to blossom. But I could change the way I acted toward Kira. I wasn't ready to revoke my don't-need-friends policy, but at the very minimum, I would try to be friendly. It was a compromise my heart and brain seemed content with, at least for the moment.

***

I purposefully stepped in every puddle I could find from the driveway to the front door. My new boots splashed and dashed the water, happy for the challenge. The screen door greeted me with its typical croaky whimper, but the rest of the house was as quiet as I'd left it that morning. I stacked my books and home-work on a shelf, then crouched down and unloaded my backpack of its more precious cargo, placing the sneak-ers and cleats along the mudroom wall. I grabbed Dad's golf umbrella and my empty backpack. The weather was just fine for a harvest.

Across the backyard, up the hill, into the orchard. Like pebbles at the beach, the colors of spring were more vibrant when wet. Green green. Yellow yellow.

Then, on the ground, red red. I reached down and touched a fallen shoefruit. It slowly shriveled, then melted into the grass. Leaving nothing behind. Not a stem. Not a shoelace. My chest rose, then sank.

The tree glistened, telling me in its quiet way not to give up so easily. I looked down. The rain boots were a little muddy, but still in good condition. My feet were dry and snug inside them. I kicked one foot out from under the umbrella. I wiggled it around, letting the rain drip all over the polka-dotted rubber. I pulled my foot back in and gave a few big stomps. The boots showed no signs of disintegrating. My spirits lifted.

All around the perimeter of the tree, the remaining pods fell one by one, disappearing as they touched the ground. I stood beneath the black halo of the umbrella. There was nothing I could do.

Except eat cookies and watch. I pulled the wax-paper package from my pocket and inspected one of Kira's cookies. Oatmeal, chunks of chocolate, maybe a roasted almond or two. The first bite: crispy outside, chewy inside. Buttery sweet. As close to perfecterrific as a cookie could get.

Which is why it was really hard—near impossible—not to eat every last bite.

But I didn't.

I saved one cookie.

This time, it wasn't the squirrel that made me do it. It was the thought of our empty refrigerator and another bowl of stale cereal. I plunged my hands into the ground. It was gloopy and squishy—the ideal consistency for Junie's famous mud soufflé. But I was hoping for something much more appetizing.

Maybe it was just the patter of raindrops, but I swear the leaves quivered excitedly as I placed that scrumptious cookie into the hole in the ground. I covered it up and gave the mud a little pat. I wondered if the twisting bluish roots were sending some sort of signal up into the tree.

Heck. If it worked for the shoes, it was worth a shot with the cookies.

CHAPTER 7

I awoke that night to the sound of voices.

"Darn it, Nel. I'm out there breaking my back and you go spend half a week's paycheck in one afternoon? On shoes? What were you thinking?"

"I told you, I didn't buy them," Mom said.

My parents were fighting. Because of me. I lay in bed, my eyes like the puddles in our driveway. Filling up. Spilling over.

"The cleats alone must have cost a fortune. Where could they have come from?" Dad asked.

"Isabel?"

I sat up straight. The sound of my name zapped electric.

"You think she stole them?"

I almost got out of bed and marched into their room. I would tell them the truth about the squirrel and the tree. Everything. Crazy as it might sound. But.

Crazy. If I told the truth, they'd probably haul me off to the hospital to get my head checked. Another medical bill was the last thing we needed. So I stayed in bed.

"Isa? Stealing? I can't imagine her doing that," Mom said.

"She sure as heck didn't buy them. The poor kid didn't even have lunch money today."

"What? Oh no, Nathan."

"I feel terrible. I completely forgot. I didn't realize until this afternoon. I just have so much on my mind." His words were shaky.

"We all do. But it'll get better." There was a long pause. "At least that's what everyone keeps saying."

"I think I know where the shoes came from." Dad's voice rose up, mad. "Lewis."

"Your brother? Why would he do that?"

"Because I refused his pity money."

"He offered? Money?" There was a little hope on the tip of Mom's tongue. She couldn't hide it. I'd seen the pile of bills on the kitchen counter. It grew almost as fast as the chance seedling.

"He always offers," Dad said. "My answer is always the same."

"He's only trying to help. It's generous."

"No, it's insulting. We can take care of our own family, Nel." I didn't like hearing my dad talk that way. Like the weight of the world rested on their shoulders alone.

Their voices faded away. Part of me wanted to press my ear to the wall and keep listening; the other part was scared to hear more. The wind blew outside my window and the trees in the orchard whispered. *Husha, hush.* As if they were trying to soothe me.

I tossed and turned, glancing at the clock beside my bed every few minutes, trying not to count the hours until dawn.

***

When sleep finally came, it brought dreams of a sprawling orchard. Instead of green leaves and juicy fruit, the trees in this orchard sprouted envelopes. I picked one after another, hoping to find nice things inside, like a party invitation, a report card with straight A's, or a drawing from Junie. But each envelope contained a sheet of paper covered with bright red numbers, angry words, and a million exclamation points. As soon as I tore one bill up, two more grew in its place. Instead of whispering *Husha, hush,* these creepy trees snarled, *Hurry, hurry, hurry!*

Thankfully, the nightmare vanished when I opened my eyes the next morning. The eavesdropper's guilt was harder to shake. It followed me out of bed and into the bathroom. A cold splash of water to the face couldn't wash it away. Down the stairs, it clung to my ankles, heavy and awkward. I couldn't unhear the things I heard last night. The tone of Dad's voice haunted me most. I had hoped to see him for a few minutes before he left for work. Just enough time for a quick hug. But I had no such luck. His car rumbled away as I entered the kitchen.

The discovery of a jar of raspberry jam and a loaf of bread on the counter helped improve my crummy mood a little. A gallon of milk, sticks of sweet cream butter, and a dozen fresh eggs in the fridge helped some more. Even if I had to cook them myself.

Butter in skillet, egg in butter, breakfast in stomach.

I hummed, the way Mom used to, as I spread warm toast with a layer of jam almost an inch thick. I traced the shape of a heart with the knife before putting another slice of toast on top. You couldn't see it, but the love was in there. And sometimes you can't see the most important stuff.

I cut the sandwich down the middle. I wrapped one half in tinfoil and put it in the fridge. For Dad, for whenever he came home next. I placed the other on a plate, for Mom. I made a second identical sandwich, wrapped it, and placed it inside my backpack. If I could've drawn a heart in Junie's hospital mush, I would've done that too.

I went back upstairs, careful not to trip or spill. "Good morning," I said as I placed a cup of milk and the half-heart jam sandwich on my mother's bedside table.

She looked up, bleary-eyed. "That's nice of you, Isa."

I sat on the edge of her bed, tracing the lines of color running through her blanket. It used to be white with red stripes, but several trips through the wash had turned it various shades of pink. Now rows of rosy thread were stitched across the hills and valleys of my mother's body, the way our orchard might have looked in blossom. Before the trees decided to give up growing apples, that is.

I waited, hoping Mom would say more. Hoping she hadn't given up yet.

I missed the way she used to flit around the house in the morning, getting everyone prepared for the day. Scrambling eggs, packing lunches, inspecting backpacks for finished homework. Each completed task was accompanied by a kiss to the forehead, like a checkmark on a to-do list. Then she'd straighten Dad's tie, which always seemed to be askew. Our morning routine had been the same, no matter how many times we moved. There was comfort in that sameness. Now every day was a guessing game.

I cleared my throat. "Can you take me to see Junie tonight?"

"We'll see," she said quietly.

Why did grown-ups always say stuff like that? Every kid on earth knows *we'll see* means no. A delayed no, but a no nonetheless.

"Why?" I said, on the brink of whining.

"Junie's not feeling well."

"Um, newsflash: I know. That's why she's in the hospital. If she felt good, she wouldn't be there. She'd be home with us. Where she belongs." I planted my hands on my hips. "So, when can I go?"

"Maybe this weekend."

"Maybe? What do you mean, maybe? She's probably lonely all by herself." Was I really talking about Junie, or myself?

Mom sat up. "She's not by herself, Isabel. I spend all day with her. Your father visits her after work. There are nurses and doctors caring for her 24/7. Plus, she's made some friends."

I felt a stab of pain, a fear of being replaced.

"What do you want us to do?" Mom continued. "We can't take you out of school. You need to maintain your routine and a sense of normalcy. That's what the counselors suggested, and Dad and I agree."

"Well, my routine stinks," I snapped. "And I feel about as normal as a fish with three heads."

"Isabel."

I peeked at my watch. "I haven't seen Junie in five days, four hours, and twenty-eight minutes. In sister-time that's basically eternity. I have to see her, Mom."

My mother sucked in her breath. I could tell she was torn.

"It's important," I pleaded. "She has to know."

"Know what?"

"That I haven't forgotten about her!"

"Don't be dramatic, Isabel. Of course she knows that. She knows you'll always be there for her."

I threw my hands in the air. "How can I possibly be there for her, when I'm *here* and she's *there*?!" My lower lip began to wobble. "What if she forgets about me, Mom?" I turned my back to her and buried my face in the blankets.

"That's not possible, Isa. She talks about you all the time." Mom placed a hand on my shoulder. Her touch was such a surprise that I nearly jumped. "We're not trying to keep you apart." She started rubbing my back in slow circles. I melted into her touch. "We would never, ever do that. I hate that she can't be home with us right now. But Junie's situation is complicated. It's safer for her to stay at the hospital for the moment, where they can give her constant attention, in case . . ."

"In case what?"

Mom coughed nervously, like she'd said more than she meant to. "Her blood counts have been really low lately, Isa. She doesn't have the antibodies to fight off infections." Her hands left my back and settled in her lap. "Remember?"

I did. Junie had recently recovered from a bad respiratory infection. Afterward, she came home for a handful of days before returning to the hospital for chemo. The whole ordeal had scared us silly. I did not want anything like that to happen again.

I turned around. "Couldn't I just skip one day of school? Take a sick day, or something? My attendance is practically perfect."

"Exactly, Isabel. Because you're perfectly healthy," she replied brusquely. "Enough of this, please. Go get ready for school." She'd been so tender a moment ago, but now she just dismissed me, like my feelings meant nothing. I was healthy, therefore not important enough to worry about.

I gritted my teeth. "I promise to make up all my work. I'm sure my teachers wouldn't mind."

Mom exhaled. "We'll see . . ."

I wanted to grab her, shake her, but also just hug her. There were people at the hospital who would understand—child life specialists, social workers, nurses, doctors. I knew they were always available to help, but right now I only wanted my mom.

"Could you bring me tonight after practice? Please?" I begged.

She stiffened. "For one thing, it's nearly an hour drive."

I shook my head. "It's forty-three minutes, tops. Thirty-eight if we speed on the highway. That's nothing! We drove seventeen hours when we moved here from Georgia."

"Listen, it's difficult for her to have visitors when she's sick."

"I'm not a visitor. I'm family!"

"Don't be selfish, Isabel," she snapped.

My whole body prickled, inside and out. Not the tingly sensation I felt when I was near the chance seedling, but the burning sensation of anger.

"I know you miss her," Mom said, softening as she watched the red creep into my face. "We all miss her."

Something inside me cracked. "Don't talk about her like that!" I shouted.

"Like what?"

"Like she's already dead."

"Isabel Abernathy Fitzwilken!" My mother lunged forward and shrieked in a voice I'd never heard before. It exploded out of her without any warning, from somewhere deep inside, pierced with pain and fear and a million other scary things. I nearly fell off the bed, not so much from the ringing in my practically deaf ears, but from shock.

"Don't you dare say that word!" She thrashed at the blankets. "Don't say it! Do you hear me? Don't you dare! Ever!" The hand that had been rubbing my back was raised in the air, like she might slap me. She took a shuddering breath and quickly lowered her arm. She looked down at her fingers, horrified and confused.

I stumbled out of the room. Mom hadn't hit me, but my cheeks throbbed just the same. I ran down the stairs and into the kitchen. I gripped the counter to steady myself. My chest tightened, as if my ribs were constricting my heart and lungs. I waited, afraid and also hoping that Mom would follow me.

The house creaked like old houses do, but that was it. There were no feet on the stairs. No one calling out to apologize, or see if I was okay.

I stared at the telephone. I considered calling Dad at work. I could tell him that I'd upset Mom badly, but that she'd upset me too. He used to be a good listener. When we played catch in the evenings, he always gave me advice and calmed me down if I was riled up about something. But we hadn't had a real talk in ages.

My watch beeped innocently. After yesterday's trip-and-fall fiasco, I'd set a new alarm, giving myself extra wiggle room in the morning. I wiped my face dry with the back of my hand. Even though I'd packed a lunch, I felt around inside the tin can for lunch money. To my surprise, Dad hadn't forgotten. There was even a note written on a scrap of paper.

Sorry about yesterday, sweetheart. Here's a little something extra—think of it as an emergency lunch money fund in case I forget again. (But I'll try really hard not to!) Game of catch soon? Love, Dad

That small promise picked my bruised heart up and dusted it off. I slipped my backpack over my shoulder. My watch gave another warning beep. The bus would turn down Melwick Lane in ten minutes.

I ran to the mudroom, laced up my new sneakers, grabbed the umbrella, and rushed outside.

***

The charcoal sky drizzled and spat. Thick, cottony fog enveloped the orchard. Safe and dry under my umbrella, I approached the tree. The canopy dripped with rain. The bark glowed, colors shifting and melting together like a watercolor painting come to life.

"Good morning," I said. The branches stirred, like they were glad to see me, then proudly displayed several tiny violet buds. They weren't nearly as large or impressive as yesterday's shoefruits. Not yet, at least. Maybe the rain was stunting their growth? Maybe they needed more sunlight? They would bloom when they were ready, I supposed. You couldn't rush these things. I would have to be patient.

Secrets were hard. But waiting for a secret to bloom was even harder.

CHAPTER 8

I made my way carefully down the hillside behind the orchard, retracing yesterday's leaps and bounds and tumbles. I was a little disappointed the tree hadn't bloomed yet, but I was relieved to find most of my lost lunch money. The dollar was plastered to a rock, a slug draped across the president's face like a slimy mustache. I nudged it away and did my best to dry the damp bill. I found a few coins in the grass and made sure to check my pockets for holes before placing them inside.

Kira jogged toward me, her endless hair wrapped into a bun the size of a cinnamon roll.

"Bus buddy!" she sang, waving like a fool beneath her umbrella. "You came to my bus stop again!" A mile-wide grin stretched across her face.

Be nice, my heart reminded me. A lopsided lip twitch was the closest thing to a smile I could muster. At least it wasn't a frown. "I lost something around here yesterday," I said, kneeling down to pluck a dime from the wet grass.

"More shoes?" She giggled. "Which reminds me, did you buy those fancy cleats at the mall? I'd love to get a pair too."

"None of your business," I snapped, guarding the secret of my tree, forgetting to be nice.

Kira made a surprised hiccupping noise like she might cry.

"Hey, I'm sorry," I said. "I'm . . ."

"I know." She sniffled and waved her hand, like my meanness was a fly she could shoo away. She lifted her chin. "It's okay. My mom said I shouldn't take it personally."

It was strange to think of them talking about me. "Take what personally?"

"When you act like that. Mom says it's not because you don't like me. It's just that you're . . ."

"What?" A world-class jerk? An antisocial weirdo? A loner who talks to squirrels and trees instead of perfectly nice humans? I steeled myself for her response.

"Feeling blue?" It was more question than insult.

Up the road, the school bus wound its way toward us. Usually it kicked up a cloud of dust. Today the sky wept, pressing the dirt to the ground. I clutched my umbrella.

"I'm feeling a lot of things, I guess." I tried to picture the colors of all the things in my life.

The ache in my chest. Blue, like Kira said.

Mom's anger. My cheeks. Red.

The buds on the tree. Purple.

The orchard and meadow grasses. Green.

The uncertainty of Junie's health. Gray.

Altogether, a total mess. Blue and red smeared with purple and green and gray. One of Junie's finger paintings gone wild.

"I'm mostly flusterated," I said, for lack of a better word.

"Huh?"

"Never mind. It's a word my sister invented. I just . . . I need to see her."

Kira twirled her umbrella while she brainstormed. "So go see her. She's at the hospital, right? It's not like she's on the moon or something."

Junie-to-the-moonie. I felt a dark-colored pang of something I didn't have a name for.

"My mom said no. Not today at least. Besides, I have no way to get there."

"We could drive you," Kira offered.

"Really?"

"Sure. But my mom would probably tell your mom."

"It's better if she doesn't know," I said.

85

Kira tapped a finger to her chin. "Why don't you take the bus?"

"The school bus?"

"No, silly. The county bus. The 83 goes to the hospital."

"Really?" A little river of happiness trickled into my voice. Mom thought she knew what was best for me and Junie, but she was wrong. I would take matters into my own hands, even if it meant keeping another secret.

"There's a stop across from the post office. I know because I mail a package to my dad each week. I see the bus all the time. You could walk there after school."

My hand was in my pocket, silently counting the coins and rumpled bill. Shining golden yellow, forcing back the blue. With Dad's emergency lunch money fund, I had enough to see Junie.

The school bus came to a stop at the curb. I felt badly for snapping at Kira earlier. She was only trying to help.

"Kira?" I turned to her before I climbed the steps.

"Yeah?"

"Want to sit together?"

A giddy squeal. "For real? Bus buddies?"

I nodded. My heart said, *See? Was that really so hard?*

If I was useless at school yesterday, today I was on fire. And not in a Bunsen-burner-gone-wrong kind of way. I was energized and engaged in the nerdiest and best of ways. I'm pretty sure I aced my math quiz, and I volunteered to read aloud in English class, which always carried the risk of possible humiliation. But I didn't care. I was going to see Junie and that made everything perfecterrific. Also, I wasn't carting around my usual lunchtime dread, since I had a sandwich waiting in my bag, and I was pretty sure Kira and I would sit together.

I was a little surprised when Ms. Perdilla came by my desk looking concerned after science class. I'd taken notes and even raised my hand with correct answers a few times.

"Isabel, could you stay for a moment? We need to talk."

I thought fast. "Ms. Perdilla, I'm really sorry about the Bunsen burner yesterday. I honestly didn't mean to turn it on. Kira's hair is fine. It was an accident and . . ."

"I know."

"You're not mad?"

"No, I'm not mad. Although in general, try to avoid setting your friends on fire."

"She's not my friend," I said out of habit, even though it didn't feel totally accurate anymore. "But, yeah, I'll work on that. The not-igniting-people part. Sorry again." I turned to leave.

"Isabel, that's not why I asked you to stay."

Stay. That word. It tugged, it pulled. Like roots.

Ms. Perdilla's eyes were gentle. "Have you given any thought to your research project topic?"

I could tell it wasn't her real question, just something to say.

"Not really." Then the secret of the tree started smoldering somewhere inside. Hot and itchy. I needed to come up with something quickly, or I might spill the beans. "Anthozoa?" I said, remembering that weird flower-animal word Mr. Clarke taught us.

Ms. Perdilla looked surprised. "Funny you should mention that. Casey already signed up to do his project on anthozoa. Coral and anemone, to be exact. You could partner with him if you like."

"That's okay. I'd rather work alone."

She nodded but didn't say anything else. The silence stretched out long and slow, like a snake uncurling on a warm rock.

"Maybe something about trees." The words snuck out, practically on their own. I slapped my hand over my mouth, horrified.

"Trees? That sounds interesting." Ms. Perdilla perked up. "You live next to Melwick Orchard, right?"

A lump formed in my throat. I nodded and tried to swallow it down.

"Orchards are similar to reefs, actually. Fruit trees and corals create wonderfully diverse ecosystems where an astounding diversity of life can thrive. You're lucky, Isabel. Living near those trees is like having a classroom in your own backyard. I'm sure there are all kinds of fascinating things to study, right at your fingertips."

If she only knew. I pressed my lips together so nothing else could slip past them.

"I used to adore those Melwick apples." She smiled wistfully. "Gave extra credit to kids when they'd bring me one. Something so unusual about them."

"What do you mean?" I'd never paid much attention to the stories about our orchard, but now I was more curious than ever.

"Some were sweet. Others were tangy. Some were even salty."

"Salty apples?" I grimaced. "Yuck."

"Strange, yes. And yet exquisitely delicious." Her eyes closed as she savored the memory. "It's hard to describe. Somehow a Melwick apple could take on the flavor of whatever you were craving at the moment."

"Really?" Thank goodness I'd eaten breakfast, otherwise my stomach would've been making quite a ruckus.

"They were like flavor chameleons. I swear I once ate one that tasted just like a honey-baked ham. Such a shame how those apples stopped growing. Nobody knows why. Do you?"

Her question jolted me. "Me? No. I don't know anything about those trees," I said, which wasn't entirely true.

Ms. Perdilla nodded. "I'm sure you've heard the local lore. Tall tales. The sort of stuff that makes good small-town chatter. Everyone has their theories about the Melwick land. Might be worthwhile to dispel those rumors with some hard science."

Could science explain what was going on? All evidence seemed to suggest otherwise. The secret grew hotter and itchier. I regretted even uttering the word *tree*.

"How about it?" Ms. Perdilla pressed.

Change the subject. Hurry. I scanned the room for something. Anything. Help!

A poster on the wall caught my eye: The tadpole life cycle. "Actually, I might do my project on frogs or toads. Or maybe some kind of salamander. One of *those* animals." Phew. I squelched the secret, for now.

"You mean amphibians?"

"Sure."

The poster had six colorful bubbles connected by a series of arrows. It read: "I am an egg! I am a tadpole with gills! I am a tadpole! I am a tadpole with legs! I am a froglet! I am an adult frog!"

Suddenly I was reminded of Junie, which felt good and bad at the same time, like an apple that tasted both bitter and sweet. "My sister calls them *unfittians*. She loves animals, but she can't stand *them*."

"Why is that? Why doesn't Junie like amphibians?" Ms. Perdilla's voice felt like a gentle breeze at my back, guiding me forward.

"They kind of freak her out. And not because they're squirmy or slimy like you'd expect."

"No? Then why?"

"It's because they don't fit anywhere. Get it? Unfittians?"

"Yes, I get it." Ms. Perdilla walked over to her desk and sat down in her chair. There was a stack of homework on the desk that needed grading, and a paper-bag lunch that probably needed eating, but she was in no hurry to do anything but talk with me. "Your sister sounds like a very clever girl."

"She is. She's young, but she's smart. Not like bookworm smart, but kind of kooky smart."

"I know exactly what you mean. I call it *creative intelligence*."

I liked the sound of that. "Her brain puts all these bits of words together and makes new words."

"Just like Frankenstein."

My mouth crinkled into a squiggly line. My eyebrows scrunched to match. I had no idea what she was talking about.

"Victor Frankenstein took different body parts, put them together, and gave them life. As something new."

"Didn't he make a monster?"

"Okay, yes, technically. But it's the concept that really interests me. And in his defense, the monster wasn't really so bad. Just misunderstood."

I unscrunched everything. I made a mental note to remember Frankenstein. FrankenJunie. She'd think it was hilarious.

Ms. Perdilla leaned back. "Tell me more about why Junie thinks amphibians are unfittians."

"You're a science teacher. You probably already know everything about them." I gazed at the poster again.

"I'm always learning. Besides, I'd like to hear your thoughts. And Junie's. A new perspective is always enlightening."

"Well, they don't really live in one place. They can

be in the water or on land. Junie says they should be here or there, but not both. Because it isn't right. It's not natural."

"What's not natural?"

"Being in between. Like that tadpole with legs." I pointed to the diagram.

"I see. Why do you think she feels uncomfortable with the idea of being in between?" Jeez. Ms. Perdilla should have been an interrogator or spy instead of a middle school science teacher. She could really make people talk.

"Probably because we're always moving around for Dad's work, when all we want to do is stay put." I looked down. "That's also why she doesn't like being sick. Not that anyone likes being sick, but I think it makes her feel out of place. She's constantly going back and forth between the hospital and our home."

Ms. Perdilla nodded, and I kept chatterboxing.

"Also, Mom said being sick forced Junie to grow up quick."

"Making her part child, part adult. Almost like she skipped a few steps. From tadpole right to froglet, without enough time to properly adjust." Ms. Perdilla was smart. She just got it.

"Exactly. And some medicines make her feel part awake and part asleep." Part alive and also part, well,

I wouldn't utter that word out loud. I wouldn't even think that word. Not after the way Mom reacted when I said it.

"That makes sense. In between is a tricky place to be."

I tried to remember the word Dad had used. It was a word I didn't really understand.

"Limbo," I finally said.

"In a way, yes."

"Like shimmying backward under a broomstick?"

"That's one meaning of the word. There are others too."

"Junie and I used to do that. It hurt my back, but not Junie's. She's bendy as a willow branch and she never even took gymnastics lessons. Mostly because Dad said we couldn't afford them. Which is basically his response to anything fun," I said sheepishly. "Which is why we were stuck entertaining ourselves with brooms." I was suddenly embarrassed by how much I had spilled. I wished words were water so I could mop them all back up.

"People with creative intelligence can make just about anything fun. It's a special talent. You and Junie are lucky to have it."

I'm pretty sure she was just being nice. Still, it felt good to get a compliment.

The lunch bell rang. For once, it didn't send a wave of panic down my spine.

"I'd better go."

"Isabel, if you ever need to talk . . ."

"About amphibians?"

"About anything."

I picked up my books and turned toward the door. I could feel the secret warming up again. Getting ready to ignite, like that Bunsen burner, with a will of its own. "Ms. Perdilla?" I spoke with my back to her, afraid the secret might be visible, blazing in my eyes.

"Yes, Isabel?"

"I do have one question . . ." I moved the words around in my head, like a puzzle. Trying to fit the right ones together, without giving too much away. "Do you think there's a scientific explanation for everything?"

"Of course not."

That surprised me. I turned to meet her eyes. I knew I wasn't just a paper doll-girl in her doorway. I had edges and depth. She saw it all. Maybe she even saw my secret.

"You're a science teacher. Isn't that your job? To find the answer to everything?"

She laughed softly, not at me. "Even if I could, I'm not sure I'd want to."

"Why?"

"Life would be awfully boring if we knew the answer to everything. There are many unexplainable things in this world."

"Like apples that taste like ham?"

"Precisely. Like miracles and great mysteries. Good and bad."

Magic trees and sick sisters.

"Can I ask you one more thing?"

"Of course."

I scratched my nose. "It's kind of a dumb question."

"Isabel, there are no dumb questions in my classroom."

"Are you sure?"

"Absolutely positive."

"Posolutely?" I made my very own Frankensteined word. Maybe I really did have a little creative intelligence.

She nodded.

"Do freckles hibernate?"

It was pretty clear from the expression on her face that Ms. Perdilla had not seen that one coming. The serious, caring crease that had been deepening between her brows melted. Her lips tugged up, up, up. She studied me like maybe *I* was one of life's great mysteries.

"I'll have to research that for you," she answered.

CHAPTER 9

The rain stopped just before lunch, but the sun hid bashfully behind soot-colored clouds, trying to decide if it might shine. Apparently even the weather was feeling like an unfittian. Kira and I sat at a table in the cafeteria and discussed my plans for the afternoon.

"Are you sure you don't want me to come with you?" she asked as she unwrapped her sandwich. She might as well have asked if I'd like to cartwheel across the cafeteria in nothing but my underpants.

"No way!" I blurted rudely. "I mean . . . no, thanks." I wasn't ready to share so much, so fast. I was still warming up to the idea of being bus buddies, for goodness' sake. "I have to go by myself. Junie might not be feeling well. And it's tough to have visitors when she's sick." I couldn't believe I was repeating Mom's excuse.

Kira looked a little bummed, but said only, "I understand." I was grateful she didn't keep bugging me about it. She took a bite of her sandwich. "What about softball practice?"

"I'll skip it." I didn't want to, especially with our first game just around the corner. It was my chance to impress Dad. Or, at the very least, remind him of my existence. But I didn't have a choice. Junie trumped pretty much everything.

"Won't Coach Naron be upset?"

"How do you know Coach Naron?"

"Isa! I'm on the team too." Kira nearly dropped her sandwich. "Thanks for noticing," she huffed, stuffing loose lettuce leaves back between the slices of pumpernickel.

My stomach twisted. I understood how she felt. I was Isabel-Invisible, after all. I hated making someone else feel that way. "Right. Of course. I knew that." She might have believed me, if I just stopped there. But like a total moron, I didn't. "You play . . . shortstop?"

"Isa!" This time her entire sandwich launched into the air. She let out a flusterated groan. Maybe because the bread landed mustard-side down. But probably not.

I handed her a slice of cheese that had flown in my direction. "Left field?"

Kira shook her head, loosening her bun and sending hair cascading down her shoulders and across the table. I brushed it away before it swiped a blob of mustard.

"First base?" I said.

"Nice try."

Except I hadn't really tried. That was the problem. Until recently, I'd counted on time instead of people. I looked across the table at Kira, who was wearing an uncharacteristic frown. Ignoring other kids was supposed to protect me, but I hadn't realized it might hurt them. "I'm sorry," I said, apologizing to Kira for the second time that day. "What position do you play?"

"No," she replied calmly.

"What do you mean, no?"

"I mean I'm not going to tell you. You'll have to wait until our next practice to find out."

She gave up on the scattered sandwich and pulled a bag of potato chips and a juice box from her lunch box. There was a long pause filled with chewing and stewing. I couldn't blame Kira for being annoyed at me. Heck. I was annoyed at me.

"It takes sixty-two muscles to frown," I said sheepishly. "Only twenty-six to smile . . ."

She shot me an uncertain look.

"Someone very wise told me that just yesterday," I said.

"Hmmm." Kira fiddled with her juice box's bendy straw. The corners of her lips twitched up a little. I was thankful she didn't hold a grudge for long.

"Is she very sick?" she said eventually.

I blinked. "Junie?"

"Yeah. She's been in the hospital for a while, right?"

"Too long."

Kira waited, giving me space to talk, just like Ms. Perdilla.

Don't be scared, my heart urged.

"She had surgery in November to remove a tumor on her kidney. We thought there was just one tumor, but it turned out to be two. Junie named them Willie and Pablo."

Kira raised an eyebrow. Not in a judgy way, just out of curiosity.

"Naming tumors is totally weird, I know." Surprisingly, the words bubbled up easily, like soda in a shaken bottle. "Along the way, she's had about a billion tests and scans, a port placed in her chest, not to mention several rounds of chemotherapy, which is really strong medicine that's supposed to kill the bad cells. But it also harms the good cells and makes her feel awful." I tried not to think about all the nasty side effects. "She usually stays home between treatments, but lately she's only been able to come back for a few days at a time."

"Why?"

"Complications." I used my parents' standard catchall answer for confusing medical stuff.

"She'll be okay though, right? Eventually?"

My chest tightened. "The doctors keep telling us she has a really good shot at getting better. Ninety percent of kids with Nephew Blast-o-Rama survive."

"Wait, what?"

"It's a name Junie uses for her sickness. The real word is hard to pronounce. It's also called Wilms tumor."

"Oh." Kira took a sip of juice. "Ninety percent is good, isn't it? If I get ninety percent on a quiz, I'm super happy."

I started to get irritated. A stupid quiz at school was nothing like a person's life. Especially a person that you loved and needed more than anything in the world. Part of me wanted to clam up, run away, and never utter another word to Kira. But the other part of me knew she'd never understand unless I helped her. I took a deep breath. "Listen, if you had a basket of ten Melwick apples, but you knew that one of them was poisonous, would you take a chance and bite into one?"

Kira eyed the green apple in her lunch box skeptically. "Melwick apples disappeared years ago. Long before I moved here. But hypothetically speaking," she emphasized the vocabulary word we'd learned earlier that day, "if one in ten could actually kill me, I wouldn't take those odds and eat one. No matter how magically delicious they might taste."

"Exactly." I looked directly at her. "That's why anything less than one hundred percent isn't good enough."

"I think I get it now." She crunched a potato chip and mulled over the idea. "What's it like?" she asked shyly.

A glob of jam stuck in my throat. "Cancer?" I spat out the word.

"No, no!" She blushed, then quickly gathered her hair and twisted it into a bun. Her fingers were nervous and twitchy. "What's it like having a sibling? A sister?"

I stared at her, dumbfounded. That was like asking what it was like to have an ear, or a nostril, or a beating heart. "My sister is . . . a part of me. We're inseparable." Shortly after Junie's diagnosis, one of the child life specialists at the hospital explained that the human body is designed with two kidneys. She told me that if one kidney fails, or gets removed due to a tumor, like with Junie, the other kidney will take over and continue working. But I knew I wasn't anything like a kidney. If I lost Junie, there was no way I could function normally.

"I always kind of wished I had one," Kira said softly. "Not a sick one, I mean . . . Oh. That sounded terrible."

My cheeks flushed deep red. Tinfoil balled up tightly in my hand.

"Isa, wait. Please don't disappear, like yesterday. Stay," Kira pleaded.

Stay. Twice today, that word. Tugging. Our family had uprooted so many times, it was hard to trust that word.

"I just meant being an only child is lonely sometimes." Kira slid a bundle of cookies in my direction. A peace offering.

My heart whispered, *Stay.* I relaxed my fingers. The tinfoil ball rolled across the table. Kira caught it before it fell.

One moment passed, then two. When I finally felt ready, I said, simply, "Thanks."

"For what?" Kira looked surprised.

"For listening." I knew it sounded cheesy, but I meant it.

Kira nodded. "Anytime." She pushed the cookies closer.

I reached out and accepted them. The secret began tingling just below the surface of my skin. I smiled at Kira across the table. If my tree bloomed again, maybe I could return the favor.

CHAPTER 10

I felt like a criminal, ditching softball practice and sneaking off to the bus stop after school. But it had to be done. For Junie. For me. I stood in front of the post office and waited for the 83, just like Kira instructed.

I glanced at the bus schedule mounted to a tall pole. Old me would have studied the routes and calculated the exact number of minutes between stops. Old me would've shut out everything else and focused on numbers instead of names or faces. But after lunch with Kira, I was determined to make some changes.

People moved in and out of the post office, dropping off and picking up mail. Maybe a few miracles and mysteries were hidden in those packages sealed with tape and stamps. My mind drifted back to Kira. What did she send to her father each week? Where did he live? Why had he left? How long had he been gone? Would he come back? I made a mental note to ask her, then give her plenty of space to talk, the way she had done for me.

The bus approached and several people jostled me, lining up to get on. I shuffled my feet in the new sneakers to keep my nerves at bay. I'd ridden plenty of buses and trains with my family in cities before, but for some reason traveling to the hospital alone felt daunting.

When the 83 opened its doors, I boarded with shaky steps. Thankfully, the bus driver didn't yell at me to *sit and zip!* Instead, he gestured kindly to a box next to his steering wheel. He reminded me of a scarecrow, with tufts of straw-colored hair sticking out from under a denim hat.

"Where to, darlin'?" His voice had a honey-dipped twang that I recognized from one of our previous moves. Was it Louisville?

"Um, the hospital," I said.

"This isn't an ambulance," he replied with a wink. "Thank goodness your condition doesn't look too serious." His mustache twitched when he smiled. His accent was like a souvenir. Definitely from somewhere in Kentucky. We'd lived there for almost two years (okay, one year, three hundred days, six hours). A long stint for us Fitzwilkens.

"What do you mean, my condition?" I asked, my face turning its signature shade of mortified tomato.

"A case of the jitters! I didn't go to medical school, but I'm pretty good at diagnosing folks. Isn't that right, Miss Muriel?"

The woman standing in front of me nodded. Her hair was so white it was almost blue. Muriel. I repeated the name in my head, committing it to memory.

The bus driver, whose name was Reggie according to his name tag, took a long look at me. Just like Ms. Perdilla, I sensed he could see more than my paper-doll silhouette. "Don't you fret. Just put your money right here." He patted the box. "Make yourself comfortable. The trip will go by lickety-split. I'll holler when we're at the hospital. Though you won't be needing a doctor. Your condition's improving as we speak."

He was right. My feet stopped shuffling. My face was returning to a normal color. "I'm not going for myself," I said. "I'm visiting someone there. Someone special."

"Isn't everybody special?" Reggie replied with a question that didn't ask for an answer.

"Mmhmm," Muriel murmured as she took a seat, a bright pink smile hoisting up the lines of her face in a hammock of happy.

My coins made a pleasant clinking sound and the box spit out a small slip of paper. I stuffed the ticket into my pocket. Reggie nodded and I scooted down the aisle. Rather than sit alone in an empty row (something old me would have done), I planted myself next to blue-haired, bright-lipped Muriel. She smelled awfully nice, like rosewater, hand cream, and some kind of spice. What was it?

Cinnamon? Yes. Just like I'd smelled a few days ago by the sapling with the squirrel. Just like Mom used when she made her famous sticky buns, a recipe reserved for special occasions. I closed my eyes as the bus sped out of town, letting a cinnamon-scented memory carry me away.

We were celebrating our arrival in Bridgebury. All four of us overjoyed by the possibility of a place to finally grow roots. The real estate agent told us the orchard on our property was defunct, but when Junie and I went outside to explore for the first time, the land felt alive, as curious about us as we were about it.

When we came back inside, the sweet perfume of freshly baked sticky buns greeted us. Mom was in the kitchen, humming as she pulled a tray of warm, gooey, knotted dough from the oven. We sniffed the air and yipped excitedly like a pair of puppies. Dad joined us at the table for a bite. He told Mom she looked more beautiful than ever, even though she had flour smudged across her cheeks.

The bus bumped over some potholes. I opened my eyes. I wanted to ask Muriel what she'd been baking and for whom. But before I knew it, the bus pulled up in front of the hospital. I glanced at my watch in disbelief. The trip had gone by in the fastest forty-seven minutes and thirty-two seconds on record.

I thanked Reggie as I hopped down the steps. He waved and seemed pleased that I knew his name.

"You were right," I said, tapping my wrist. "Lickety-split."

"As promised, darlin'."

"Mmhmm," Muriel nodded from her seat, releasing another dash of cinnamon into the air.

"Go on inside," Reggie urged. "Something tells me a visit from you will help more than any medicine for your special somebody."

I hoped he was right. I walked toward the hospital feeling fuller, or taller, or maybe both. Taking the bus by myself hadn't been so bad after all. The fear of doing something new was worse than actually doing it. I just had to try.

***

When the automatic glass doors opened, the smell was the first thing I noticed. Not delicious spices, but bitter lemon and bleach, mixed with Band-Aids, cotton balls, and worry. An unwelcome sucker punch that made my eyes water. Every time I entered the hospital, I fought the urge to sprint in the opposite direction, even though I wasn't the one about to be poked or scanned.

I pushed a button on the wall and waited for the elevator. Glass, metal, and serious grayish-blue paint washed the main floor lobby, but Junie's wing was totally different. As soon as I stepped off the elevator, bright colors and smiling faces welcomed me. A giant mobile dangled above the front desk, with airplanes and rocket ships spinning above the receptionist's head. Orange and yellow tiles danced across the floor, while murals of animals adorned the hallways. There was even an aquarium full of fish, and an activity room with craft supplies, computers, books, and comfy stools shaped like jellybeans. If Junie had to be stuck somewhere until she got stronger, at least this part of the hospital was cheerful and sunny.

I walked down the hall, stopping at a hand sanitizing station to get rid of any germs that could make Junie sick. The door to Room 612 was open. I peeked inside, feeling that lima-beans-and-ice-cream-mash-up of emotions. Anxious, happy, excited, scared.

Junie was propped up in her bed, surrounded by pillows and stuffed animals. Her favorite patchwork blanket was draped across her legs. Photographs and drawings were taped to the wall. Coloring books and crayons lay on a table nearby. If I ignored the lemony bleach smell and the countless machines ticking and blinking behind the bed, I could almost pretend she was in her room at home.

Her hospital room also had a private bathroom, a television, and a long couch that turned into an extra bed where visitors could sleep. The couch was covered in plasticky green material that squeaked whenever you moved an inch. No wonder Dad looked so tired lately. I couldn't imagine getting a good night's rest on that thing.

Junie hunched over a sheet of paper, eyes squinting, tongue out, deep in concentration. Those once-pudgy cheeks looked a little deflated, but still cute. Her purple knit cap was pulled down low, pom-pom flopped to one side. She picked her nose because she thought no one was watching. I loved her something fierce.

"Hi, stranger," I said.

Her eyes flitted up. "Isa! It's about time!"

I rushed over to her.

"Wait! Stop!" She held up a hand, halting me in my tracks. "Did you get the squirts?" she asked seriously.

"Eww. What?"

"The squirts! You can't touch me until you get 'em."

"Junie, what on earth are you talking about?"

"You know, the germ-busting squirty-squirts!" She pointed to a wall-mounted dispenser of hand sanitizer.

"Ohhh. Yes, I'm clean as a whistle. Don't worry. I know the drill."

"Phew! I love you, but not your cooties." She scooched over in bed, and patted the space next to her. I sat down. She seemed smaller than I remembered. Like I had grown and she had shrunk in the few days since we'd been apart. I found her knobby knees under the covers and gave them a little pinch.

"What are you, a crab?" She snorted. "I don't want a pinch."

"No?" I laughed. "What, then? A squirt?"

"A squg!"

"Of course!" A *squg* was a hug so full of love that it nearly squeezed the breath out of you. The kind of hug that would make a boa constrictor jealous. Thankfully, Junie didn't have any tubes attached to her this afternoon. Some days she was positively tangled in them, like a cyborg robot or something. I wrapped my arms around her. I knew she was strong, but she felt so fragile, delicate, and brittle. I loosened my grip and rocked her, like a baby, just for a moment. Before she got a case of the wiggles.

"We have work to do," she said.

"We do?"

"Yes, and I need your help. Look." She held up a sheet of paper. Wobbly intersecting lines formed a grid with seven squares. "I'm making a calendar."

"To count the days until you come home?" Maybe she had inherited some of my time-counting habits.

"No. It's for the nurses." She lowered her voice to a conspiring whisper. "They don't even know the days of the week."

"I'm pretty sure they do."

"Nope. And they're lazy. They never even get dressed. They wear pajamas to work. Like it's a slumber party." She rolled her eyes, something I'd never seen her do before. "Look." She pointed to the doorway. A nurse walked by pushing a cart of supplies; she stopped to wave and smile at us. "See?" Junie rasped. "Pajamas!"

"Ja-hooonie," I pulled her name out long, like a horn. She giggled. Mission accomplished. "Those are called scrubs. That's what the nurses are supposed to wear. You know that! It's like their uniform."

She clicked her tongue. "Uniform, shmuniform."

What would she think of our own mother, who held it together during the day, only to collapse into a sea of bedsheets and sadness (and that ratty bathrobe) the second she came home each afternoon?

113

Junie shook her head. "Lazy. And clueless."

A half-empty bag of clear liquid hung from a tall metal contraption on wheels near her bed. It was no longer attached to Junie, but I wondered what was inside the bag. Probably a strong dose of feisty juice, because my little sister was sure full of something today.

"It's true," she said, scowling. "Don't you think so?"

I didn't. Everyone on Junie's floor had been nothing but kind and helpful since her diagnosis.

"They're only trying to take care of you," I said.

She grumbled. "They're nincompoops."

I tried not to laugh. "That's not nice, Junie."

Another uncharacteristic eye roll. "Isa, are true things always nice?" Her voice sounded older than it should. Her chest rattled when she breathed. My own chest tightened with worry.

"Are true things always nice?" she asked again, though it wasn't really a question.

I stared at her, just a little kid in a hospital bed. Nope, true things were not always nice.

True things were sometimes unfair. And confusing.

Then I saw the sneakers on my feet and remembered the mysterious buds on the tree. True things could also be good. Wonderful, even.

"Junie, I have to tell you something!"

"First we make the calendar. It's important. Days of the week. Seven days. See?" She pointed at the wobbly squares.

"But, Junie—"

"Isa!" She wiggled impatiently.

"Fine."

"Good. Now tell me, what day is today?"

"Friday."

"Here, write it down. Please." She handed me the pencil. "Fryday. F-r-y-d-a-y. The day Junie gets to eat french fries."

I could see where this was going. "Let me guess, Mom wouldn't let you have any?"

A scowl. "No french fries. Not a single one. Know what I got instead?" Her hands curled into tiny fists. "A bath!"

"Oh, the horror." This time I rolled my eyes. Baths, a worstible in Junie's opinion, could only be tolerated once a week. Unfortunately for her, hospital rules stated she needed to stay extra clean, to minimize risk of infection.

"It's not funny, Isa!" She jabbed the paper. "Write it down. Right here. Baths only allowed on Wetsdays."

"You know that's not possible."

She ignored me. "After Wetsday comes Thirstday. The day Junie gets to drink chocolate milkshakes. Or pink lemonade. If I'm thirsty. Mom keeps trying to make me drink green juice that tastes like vegetable water. Blech! The only green drink I want on Thirst-day is lime soda. Did you write it?" She peered over my shoulder. "Good. Then comes Fryday. You already wrote that one. Next is Saturnday, when I get to play on the swings."

"What do the swings have to do with Saturn?"

"You know. I like to swing high, high, high!"

"Junie-to-the-moonie high?"

She was all seriousness. "Higher. All the way to Saturn high."

"Got it. Okay, then Sunday."

"Obvious one. Junie gets to eat an ice-cream sundae. Banana split. With extra whipped cream. And don't forget the sprinkles! Sprinkles make everything better. Yummy." She rubbed her stomach. She might've only had one kidney left, but her dessert belly was still intact, even if the chemo often wiped out her appetite.

I wrote it all down. "Next comes Monday," I said.

"Momday. When Mom visits me."

"I thought she visits you every day."

"She does. But on Momdays she has to bring you. And we have to have a tea party. All the girls together. Plus Daddy. He's the only boy allowed. Just like we used to." She smiled. "With cookies and milk. And tea, of course."

"Junie, speaking of cookies, I have something to tell you."

"We have to finish, Isa! There's only one day left."

"I know, but this is really important!"

"So is Tuesday," she said earnestly.

"All right." I sighed. "Tuesday . . . how about Shoesday?" I was desperate to tell her about the tree.

"Nope. Chooseday," she corrected. "Junie gets to choose anything she wants."

"That sounds nice."

"Did you write it? All of it?"

"Yup. It's all here. Seven days of Junie. Nice and clear."

"Good. Now those nurses won't get confused." She growled angrily, "A bath on a Fryday . . . the nerve." She tugged the strings of her knit cap. She started wearing it back in December, around the time I began finding hair on my clothes, in my food, in my bed. Everywhere but Junie's head. I'd seen her without the hat plenty of times at home, but she always wore it at the hospital, even though there were several other bald kids on her floor and it was nothing to be embarrassed about.

A nurse named Paulette stepped into the room. "Ladies, it's almost time for one of Junie's tests. Another five minutes or so, and then it's time to say your good-byes. Okay?"

Good-byes. A thousand bee stings, prickling.

"But my sister just got here," Junie protested.

"I know, honey. But the doctor ordered a follow-up, and it needs to be done this afternoon."

"Follow-up to what?" I asked, but Paulette didn't seem to hear me. Either that or she chose not to answer.

"And you really need some rest," she said to Junie.

Paulette crossed the room and filled some paper cups with an assortment of pills. I was always shocked by how many different medicines Junie had to take. When Mom went to the pharmacy, the bag she returned home with was so full it looked like it contained a belly-buster special from the local burger joint. "Don't worry," she said to me after Junie swallowed the pills with some big gulps of water. "You're welcome to come back with your dad later tonight."

Easier said than done, I thought.

Paulette picked up a chart and looked it over. "Is your mother in the waiting area?" she asked.

I froze. "Umm, she dropped me off. She had some errands to run." I hadn't planned on lying. It just sort of happened. "She'll be back soon, I think."

Paulette nodded. She didn't seem to question my

story. "No problem. I'll get Junie prepped. We're used to busy schedules around here."

"Hmph. Speaking of schedules . . ." Junie waved her calendar.

"Right! You better not be coming back to give her another bath!" I said, jumping to my sister's defense.

Paulette looked confused. "No, she needs some bloodwork, not a bath." She double-checked the chart. "I'll be back in a few minutes."

"I agree," I whispered to Junie once we were alone again. "About the nurses. I used to think they were so nice. But now I don't like them either. Not one bit."

"See? Nincompoops, all of them! I told you so!" Junie clutched the calendar. "That's why we had to make this."

She pushed her stuffed animals aside. She was wearing a striped pajama top, and as she eased out of bed I noticed she was also sporting a purple tutu and rainbow leggings. It was quite the ensemble, but who was I to give fashion advice? And besides, unless she was in the ICU for some reason, the team at the hospital had encouraged Junie to wear whatever she felt most comfortable in, even if it was a little unconventional.

Junie stretched her thin arms and legs. She whimpered. I wondered if the treatments were making her feel achy again. The drugs had all sorts of side effects, ranging from inconvenient to downright dreadful. Aside from bath frequency and lack of fried food, Junie rarely complained, so sometimes it was hard to tell how bad things really were. The doctors often said a good attitude was almost as important as medicine in the healing process.

Today Junie was slower and stiffer and crankier than usual. It scared me.

"Do you want help?" I said as she shuffled across the room. I moved to her side, ready to catch her if she fell.

"Nope. I can do it." She snatched a roll of medical tape from a drawer and stood on her tippy-toes. "There. Perfecterrific." She stuck the calendar to the wall, just below a photograph of us at the beach a few summers ago. Mom had buried us up to our waists, then sculpted the sand around our legs to look like mermaid tales. Junie and I were squinting and grinning, our noses slathered with a coating of sunscreen as thick as cream cheese. We looked like part-girl part-fish unfittians. Next to that photo was one of Mom and Dad dancing at Uncle Lewis and Aunt Sheila's wedding. They looked relaxed and happy. I missed that version of them.

Junie climbed back into bed. As soon as I joined her, she cuddled close to me. "See?" she said, admiring the calendar on the wall. My eyes drifted toward a drawing of a blue house nestled into a green hill. Four stick figures held hands on the front porch, next to a bushel of red apples. The letters H-O-M-E were scribbled across the top of the page in Junie's handwriting. A whole bunch of emotions stabbed me at once. I winced.

"What's wrong?" Junie asked.

"Nothing," I said, shaking away the feeling.

Junie pointed to the calendar. "That wasn't so hard to make. Easy peasy, right?" The words whistled through the gap between her front teeth. If she still had eyebrows, they would've danced a jig across her forehead.

"I see what you're up to. Easy peasy, lemon squeezy," I said. "Game on."

"Popsicle freezy."

"Nacho cheesy."

"Honey beesy." She pinched my knee.

"Flying trapezey. Ha!" I nudged her playfully, but also extra gently. "Bet you can't beat that!"

Junie's face turned green. She reached for the package of blue barf bags that usually sat on the bedside table, but it was empty. Eyes wide, she scrambled out of bed, surprisingly fast for someone who'd been wobbling around minutes earlier. The bathroom door slammed shut.

"Junie! Junie!" I jumped up after her.

I pressed my ear to the door. She was throwing up. I'd heard the sound many times before, but I never got used to it. It was terrible and always made me feel helpless. I knew Junie preferred to be alone when she was sick like that, but I couldn't resist calling out to her. "Please let me in. Are you all right? Should I call Paulette?"

"No! I'm awesomesauce, Isa. Really."

"You don't sound awesomesauce," I said.

"Fine. I'm more like . . . barftastic."

"Lovely," I said, relieved to hear her make a joke.

The toilet flushed, water rushed. I heard her shuffle around, then brush her teeth, spitting loudly. "Junie?"

Finally, the door opened. I resisted the urge to give her a bone-crushing hug. Instead, when she stretched her arms wide, I carefully picked her up and carried her to bed. I tucked her in and handed her a stuffed animal. She stroked the rabbit's gray fur. It was matted and well-loved. The left ear was tattered, just like the squirrel in the orchard.

I would have to save that story for another day. Junie needed to rest. I kissed her forehead, then squeezed my eyes shut. I wished with all my might that our life would go back to looking like the drawing on the wall with the smiley stick figures. I needed my sister to get better and come home, for good. Enough was enough.

"Isa?" Her voice was gravelly.

"Yeah?" I touched the floppy pom-pom on her hat.

"Easy peasy . . . chemo queasy," she said, peering up at me. A minuscule smirk darted across her pale, tired face. "I win."

***

Good-byes were always awful, but leaving the hospital without Junie definitely topped my worstible list. I flopped down on a bench at the bus stop outside and sulked. I wondered how Dad might react if he found me there. Would he be mad that I'd taken the bus by myself? That I'd skipped softball practice? I wanted his attention, but not in the form of an angry lecture. It was probably for the best that he didn't know what I was up to.

The sun ambled toward the horizon, a late afternoon stroll in the sky. The bus was nowhere in sight. I swung my feet in my new sneakers. I waited, just like those magical buds on my tree waiting to bloom. I tried to pass the time watching people.

A lady with a very large belly and a very nervous

husband made her way toward the hospital entrance. The lady paused every few steps to huff and puff. If I didn't know better, I would've thought the man was the one about to give birth, the way he was practically hyperventilating and yelling, "Baby! Baby on the way!" It was kind of funny and sweet how much he cared. Sometimes caring makes people do strange things.

A few more steps, and they disappeared through the doors to become a family. A thought popped into my brain. Maybe hospitals weren't just for sickness and endings. They were for beginnings too.

A man in a suit came out next, looking flusterated. He wrung his hands. His jacket drooped from his shoulders. He kicked a nearby lamppost and scuffed one of his shiny shoes.

"I'm sorry," he said.

Was he talking to me? The lamppost? His shoe?

Then he looked at me. "Waiting for a ride?" he said gently.

"Uh. Yeah. 83. The bus." For some reason I wasn't able to string together a full sentence.

"I hate to be the bearer of bad news, but that route ends at four o'clock."

I blinked. "What? It can't."

"Unfortunately, it does. Four o'clock on the dot."

"It can't!" If only I'd paid attention to that stupid schedule! But no, I was making changes for the better. Better? Ha! Old me would not be stuck in this situation. Old me would've paid attention to important things, like numbers instead of people.

"Tell me about it. Everything seems to end at four today. Especially good luck. I'm waiting for some lab results, but the tech says they won't be ready until tomorrow." He kicked the lamppost again. Now both shoes were scuffed. He could really use a new pair from my tree.

I don't know why, but I started to cry. In front of a total stranger. I knew it wouldn't solve anything, but I couldn't help it. I bawled like a newborn baby.

"It's all right. Here." A tissue, a kind face. "This place will do that to you."

"The bus stop?" I sniffled.

"The hospital," the man with the scuffed shoes said. "Believe me. It happens to me sometimes too."

"You?" The thought of a full-grown man crying was unsettling.

"Yup. Everyone does from time to time." He handed me an extra tissue. "I'm James, by the way."

I wiped my face dry. "Hi. I'm Isabel."

"Nice to meet you, Isabel. Let's find a way to get you home, safe and sound." He drew a silver cell phone from his pocket. "Is there someone you can call?" He slid his finger across the screen. A photograph of a little boy with a bald head and a huge smile beamed up. He was sitting at a piano, his fingers proudly spread across the black and white keys.

"Who's that?" I asked, blowing my nose.

"My son, Gregory. He's nine." So he was a dad who cried and kicked lampposts. A dad who shared his phone and his tissues with a total stranger. "He loves music. He's not very good. Not yet at least. But he adores it. That's his piano. I took this picture after his last recital. He hasn't been able to play in a while."

"Because he's in there?" I pointed to the hospital.

"Unfortunately, yes. For now."

"My little sister's there too. She's six. Her name's Penelope, but everyone calls her Junie." I paused. "I hope Gregory gets better and can go home soon."

"Me too. Speaking of home, who do you want to call?" He handed me his phone.

"You don't mind?"

"Not at all."

"Thanks." I dialed our landline, even though I doubted anyone would pick up. It rang and rang. So did my mom's cell phone. I didn't want to bother Dad at work. "Can I try someone else?"

"Of course."

I bit my lip. There was only one other person I could think of, but I didn't know her number. "I might need a phone book," I said.

"These days, it's right here." He tapped the phone. "Tell me the name and I'll do a quick search."

Right. Of course. That stuff was all online now. **Kids were supposed** to be more tech-savvy than grown-ups. Except I was basically a cave girl from the era of total loserdom. Add cool gadgets to the list of fun stuff the Fitzwilken family couldn't afford.

"What name should I search?" James asked, interrupting my self-pity session.

"Um . . ." Did I even know Kira's last name? Come on. Think. Stupid bad habit. "My neighbors. They live on Melwick Lane."

"Melwick, huh?" He looked intrigued. "Such a curious place. I always wished Gregory could taste one of those crazy apples." He closed his eyes for a moment, just like Ms. Perdilla had done. "Yum." He shook his head, then blinked. "Sorry, you got me daydreaming about fruit. You know, there's an old expression that says an apple a day keeps the doctor away. My great-aunt swears a Melwick apple cured her fever once. She told me it even tasted like chocolate pudding. Can you believe that?" He chuckled. "A pudding-flavored miracle apple? Nonsense, right?"

"Right," I stammered. If only there was an apple that could help Junie and Gregory, and everyone else inside the hospital.

"So?" James said, waving the phone.

I tried to remember Miss Benítez taking attendance earlier that day. Kira was toward the end. There was Anjali Atkins, Jordan Brancusi, Amelia Egleston, me . . . a whole bunch in the middle . . . then Casey Lorkin, Leo Martins, Nikki Patel . . . a bunch more, then Kira. Kira Ritter. "The Ritter family!" I practically shouted.

James typed the name into the phone and tapped the screen a few times. "Here you go. It's ringing."

I held it to my ear. Please pick up.

"Hello?"

"Hi, Kira?"

"Yes? Who's this?"

"It's Isabel. I'm sorry to call, but—"

She squealed. "Phone buddy! I am so happy you called. You don't even know. Like soooo happy. Elated! Jubilant!" Sometimes she used weirder words than Junie. "What's up?"

"I need some help."

"Drama! What happened? Where are you? How was the bus ride?"

"That's the problem. The 83 stopped running half an hour ago."

"Oh. My. Gosh. You're stranded?"

"I'm fine. I just need to get home . . ." I lowered my voice. "Before my parents notice I'm gone." As if they would.

"Okay. I've got it under control. We'll be there soon. Are you all right to wait a bit longer?"

"Sure." It was odd to have someone care so much about my well-being. I wasn't used to being fussed over. It felt nice. "Kira?"

"Yeah?"

"Thanks. I really appreciate it. I owe you. Big time."

"No problem. It's what friends do." I didn't even mind that she said the word *friend*.

***

James stayed and waited with me at the bus stop. We didn't talk much, but it wasn't uncomfortable. Sometimes you meet people that you can sit with in silence and it's not awkward at all. The air between you feels full and you can be there, together, sharing the quiet. Like you both just know, but you don't have to say. It's rare, but it's nice when you find it.

In forty-five minutes on the dot, the red mini-van came roaring down the road to my rescue. Kira spilled out the door, a mess of lanky limbs and endless hair. She untangled herself and then re-tangled herself around me. In a big hug. Almost a squg. Which I was not prepared for. At all. While I tried to extract myself from her grip, Mrs. Ritter got out and spoke with James. Their voices were hushed in that grown-up way. Then I saw them exchange small smiles, so I figured I wasn't in too much trouble.

Kira dragged me inside the car and shoved a juice box in my face.

"Drink this! You must be parched. Stress is dehydrating!" She sounded like an old mother hen, clucking and flapping. "Drink up!" She tipped the juice box, encouraging me to take a sip.

"It's okay, really. I've waited a lot longer than that for a ride before."

"You have?"

"Lots of times. Junie got sick and *poof!* Isa disappeared." I shrugged. "It stinks, but I'm sort of used to it by now. When you're busy trying to keep one family member alive, everything else takes a back seat." I drained the juice box in one long gulp. I was thirstier than I'd realized. And it wasn't even Thirstday, according to Junie's calendar.

I noticed the corners of Kira's eyes crinkle ever so slightly. "When my parents got divorced," she said, her voice less chipper than usual, "the opposite happened.

I couldn't disappear if I tried. Instead of having two people in the house to bug, now my mom only has one: me."

"You mean Pookie," I said, trying to cheer her up.

"Ugh, don't remind me. Bug, bug, bug. All. The. Time." She was sort of joking around, but I could tell there was more underneath. More to the missing dad and weekly trips to the post office.

Mrs. Ritter got back into the car and Kira clammed up. I didn't ask any more questions because I didn't want to make her uncomfortable.

I rolled my window down. "Thanks again, James. For waiting with me. And letting me use your phone."

"Anytime. Take care, and best wishes to Junie. No one should spend their childhood in a hospital."

I leaned out the window. "True. But guess what's also true?"

"What?" he asked.

"Good things can happen in there too. Happy things. New beginnings." If I hadn't watched that pregnant lady and her husband earlier, I might never have discovered this little nugget of wisdom. I felt a teeny bit proud.

James squinted his eyes. I hoped it was just the setting sun, and not something I said. Even if he had admitted to crying, I sure as heck didn't want to be the cause of any tears.

"You're right." He kicked the lamppost, this time in a joyful way, like a dance move. "Here's to happy beginnings!" Another flick of the foot. "I just needed a little reminding, that's all. Thank you, Isabel."

"You're welcome!" I hadn't felt this wise since explaining nuts and trees to that wily squirrel. Paying attention to people wasn't so awful after all.

CHAPTER 11

Kira chattered about softball practice the entire way home, which saved me from having to talk about the hospital visit. My mind was already wandering back to the orchard. When we pulled up to my house, Mrs. Ritter promised she wouldn't tattle to my mom, as long as I promised not to take the county bus alone again. At least not until I memorized the route schedule, so I wouldn't get stranded.

"Easy peasy," I said. "Thanks again."

That didn't seem to be enough for Kira. She stood beside me in the driveway, shifting back and forth, waiting for something. I offered a high five, but she still dawdled.

"Do you . . ." Before I could finish my sentence, Kira interrupted.

"Want to come over? Yes! Totally!"

"Wait, what?" I'd meant to ask if she'd like to sit

together on the bus tomorrow morning. An unscheduled hang-out was not what I had in mind. There was only a little daylight left to see what had bloomed. All I wanted to do was run, full sprint, to my tree. Alone.

"Mom! Isa invited me over! Can I go? Please, puh-lease?"

"Isabel, is that all right with you?" Mrs. Ritter asked, probably sensing my hesitation.

I wanted to say no, but I couldn't. Not after everything Kira had done for me. "Um, sure, I guess."

"Wonderful. Go ahead, Pookie. Be back in time for dinner, okay?"

Kira didn't even grimace at the nickname. "I will! Awesome. Splendid!"

"Splendid?" I raised an eyebrow.

"Totally. This is going to be the best."

"Better than a bendy straw?" I teased. Heck, if I had to postpone my visit to the tree, I might as well try to have a little fun.

"Way more. Exponentially more."

Kira looked like she might try to hug me again, so I ducked. "Let's go." I led her behind the house, past the shed, up the grassy hill. I grabbed a stick and dragged it across the pickets of the fence that separated the backyard from the orchard. Kira followed me as I hopped over the gate.

A gust of wind nudged me toward the eastern part of the orchard. I pushed against it, moving in the opposite direction and steering Kira as far as possible from the clearing.

"What's that? A sock tree?" she said.

I froze. "What did you say?"

"There." She pointed at one of the apple trees.

Two socks dangled from a nearby branch. One sock was yellow, the other was green with tiny white snowmen. "Huh," I laughed nervously. "Those are mine. I hung them up to dry a few days ago. My feet were wet from walking in the orchard. Nothing special." I grabbed the socks, stuffed them into my pocket, then took a sharp turn. I darted toward the stream where Junie and I used to sail little rafts made from twigs and string.

Kira scrambled after me. "What an adventure!" she puffed. "You know, I've lived down the road for almost two years, but I've never been over here. It's really pretty. I don't understand why everyone in school says this place is haunted or cursed or something."

"They say that?" I asked, slowing down.

"Sure, but it's obviously not true. Right?"

I paused, then reeled around and shouted, "Boo!"

Kira jumped back. "Ha ha. Very funny," she said, unamused. "Hey, where exactly are we going?"

"Just around. We could skip rocks in the millpond, I guess." I didn't really have a plan, other than to stay away from Mrs. Tolson's chickens and to keep Kira from discovering my tree. The secret grew hot and itchy, but I wasn't ready to share it. Not yet.

The sun dipped down orange, moseying toward the horizon.

"Wow. Look at the sky," Kira said.

"Sure, it's splendid," I said, barely looking up, thinking about the tree instead. If the new pods fell to the ground and dissolved before I could get there, I'd never know what had grown. What a waste.

We climbed over a tall rock wall. Kira paused at the top. "Oh. My. Gosh."

"Yeah, yeah. Haven't you ever seen a sunset before?" I kept walking, head down.

Kira didn't answer. She was quiet.

Too quiet.

Then she was running. Too fast.

I took off after her. Honey-colored sunshine spilled through a few lavender clouds, drenching the orchard below. Setting one tree in particular ablaze in light. Like a beacon.

Kira was headed straight for it.

I chased her, the small bell keychain on my back-pack ringing alarm. I was fast, but Kira had longer legs. And a head start. Thankfully, when she neared the clearing, it was like she hit an invisible force field. She stopped at the edge of the meadow, breathless. Her lips opened and closed, like a fish pulled from water. Gaping. *Oh. Oh. Oh.*

When I followed her gaze, my lips did the same.

Oh.

Oh.

Oh!

The seedling had grown several feet taller, and its trunk was now as thick around as a sumo wrestler's stomach. No wonder Kira had been able to spot it from the top of the rock wall.

"Whoa!" I said, amazed.

The greenish-gray bark brightened at the sound of my voice. The crystalline leaves stretched to the size of dinner plates. They shimmered and fluttered like hundreds of hands waving hello. The tree didn't seem to mind that Kira was there at all. In fact, it appeared to welcome her with open branches. A breeze wound around my shoulders, encouraging me to do the same.

"This is Kira," I said, figuring an introduction might be in order.

Kira's head whipped around. Her ponytail struck my shoulder with a sharp *whap!* She eyed me like I was out of my mind. "Are you talking to that tree?"

"I am." It was hard not to laugh at myself. It did seem ridiculous.

"You barely talk to people, but you talk to trees?" She scratched her head. "I'm so confused. What's going on here?" She studied the swishing branches. "Wait, what kind of a tree is this anyway?"

"I'm pretty sure it's a chance seedling," I said. Just days ago, it had been nothing but a dinky gray-brown stick. Now it was mighty and strong. Pride welled up inside me. I knew I wasn't completely responsible for the tree's transformation, but I was certain I'd helped a little. The more I believed in it, the more magical the tree seemed to become. Maybe there was some truth to the Melwick myths after all.

Light filtered through the canopy, scattering thousands of little rainbows across the grass. The leaves parted. My pulse raced. Long purple pods shaped like giant string beans hung from the boughs. Some were the size of my forearm. A new crop was ready for picking!

The most divine fragrance drifted our way. Not flowery, but . . . *floury*—like walking into a bakery. My nostrils sucked it in, devouring the smell.

Kira teetered backward. I was afraid she might fall, but then she rocked forward, nose-first, in a slow, trancelike walk toward the tree, following the heavenly scent. Mom used to call it the alchemy of the oven—a kind of kitchen enchantment that happened when someone baked sticky buns, or cupcakes, or a loaf of bread, or . . .

Dozens and dozens of cookies.

Kira drew closer, sniffing the air. She stopped at the trunk and stared up in wonder.

"Watch this," I said, moving beside her. I pressed my palms to the skin-soft bark. When I pulled them away, glowing handprints remained for a few seconds, then disappeared.

"What? How?" Kira's chin was practically hanging down to her knees. "I need to sit." She turned and slid her back along the tree's trunk until she landed in the grass. "The rumors about this place . . ." She touched the ground with shaky fingertips. "I thought it was just some fairy tale meant to spook kids."

I sat down beside her. "I don't know what happened in this orchard before we moved here. All I know is that there's something special here now."

The branches of the nearby apple trees stirred. *Go on. Go on*, they seemed to murmur.

"Okay," I said to the trees. "If you insist." I told Kira about the squirrel. The sapling. The shoes. As I spoke, the hot, itchy secret cooled. It was refreshing to share a story, to share the truth. Telling Kira the secret didn't mean there was less magic for me. In fact, the opposite seemed to be true. With each word, the tree brightened, as if lit from within.

"How the heck could you keep this to yourself?" Kira asked, taking it all in.

"It hasn't been easy, that's for sure."

"I bet," she said, still wide-eyed, watching the flickering rainbows dance across the ground.

"Please don't say anything though. I'm afraid of what people in town might do if they find out."

"Like study it, or chop it down?"

"Exactly."

"I get it." Kira nodded. "You have to protect the things you love. You were right to keep quiet. I won't utter a peep."

That seemed like a tall order for a chatterbox like her. "You swear?"

She held out her pinky finger and linked it with mine. Just like Junie and I did. Sister-code for *I promise.*

"No one else knows," I said. "Not even Junie. I wanted to tell her today, but it wasn't the right time."

"She might not believe you."

"Of course she will! She knows I wouldn't lie to her. Besides, she's six. She has an active imagination."

"Honestly, if I wasn't here right now, seeing with

my own eyes, smelling with my own nose, I wouldn't believe you. No offense or anything. It's just a little far-fetched."

"That's basically a nice way of saying completely insane."

"Pretty much. Yup." She giggled.

I rose to my feet. "Then I'll just have to bring her some proof!"

There were no pods within arm's reach, so I grabbed the lowest branch and did a chin-up. I kicked my legs, wrapped my ankles around tight and twisted my body upright until I was straddling the branch. From there, I could climb to a set of branches heavy with fruit.

"Be careful up there! Watch out! Don't go too high!" Kira clucked below.

I scooted toward the nearest pod, balancing my weight evenly. The bakery smell grew more intense, like the way Muriel smelled on the bus, only one hundred times stronger. My mouth watered, my stomach growled.

"Slowly, Isa! Easy does it."

"Quit distracting me. I've got this." Just then, the clouds shifted overhead. Bright sunlight refracted off the tree's leaves, blinding me. Without thinking, I lifted a hand to shield my eyes.

I lost my balance and tipped. And slid.

Falling.

In slow motion.

Kira's nervous cluck spiked to a scream.

Tumbling, flailing.

I braced for impact.

But I didn't hit the ground. Someone caught me. Something.

I was cradled in the crook of the tree's lowest branch. The glassy leaves weren't sharp at all, but gel soft. Like huge open palms, holding me up. Keeping me safe.

"I think you should come d–down from there," Kira stuttered, backing away. "And I should get home. It's almost dinnertime."

"Wait!" I said. "Don't go."

Thud! A long purple pod dropped at Kira's feet. It didn't disintegrate into the grass.

"Ha! Ha!" My voice burst like firecrackers. "See? That's practically an invitation. Even the tree wants you to stay."

Kira picked up the pod, inspecting it carefully. "It doesn't look normal."

"Of course it's not normal. That's what makes it so incredible! Does it smell sour or rotten to you?"

She lifted the pod to her nose and inhaled,

closing her eyes. "It smells ahhh-mazing. Magnificent. Scrumptious."

"Open it already!"

"What if it's poisonous? What if ten percent of these pods are poisonous?"

The tree's bark flared fluorescent yellow, as if it were offended by the accusation. The upper branches shook, sending another pod plummeting downward in my direction. I snatched it out of the air, which felt a whole lot like catching a pop fly during softball practice.

"I know this sounds really weird, but I trust this tree." As soon as I said the words, the pod in my hand split down the middle. "I'll try the first one, but only if you come up here." I patted the branch I was sitting on with my free hand. The branch moved. "Whoa, there!" I steadied myself as the branch tilted. Soon its tip rested in the grass at Kira's feet like a ramp.

She stared, dumbstruck, then slowly climbed onto the outstretched bough and sat next to me. The branch began to rise. It was better than any ride at the amusement park. Kira gripped the branch with white knuckles. I shrieked with delight. Up we went, until we were perched about six feet above the ground.

I couldn't wait another minute. I peeled back the pod's skin. It was thick and leathery with a waxy film. Nothing like the feathery shoefruits.

Kira peered over my shoulder and gasped. Inside, half a dozen pecan shortbread cookies were stacked neatly. I removed one and held it between my fingers. It was still warm. I brought it to my lips. I took a bite.

I sputtered and coughed. "Poison!" I clutched my throat.

"No! I warned you!" Kira screeched, until she saw me laughing, crumbs cascading down the front of my shirt.

"Got ya." I smirked, then shoved another cookie in my mouth, crunching loudly.

"I want to call you a lot of mean names right now!" She pouted. "That's not nice. I almost had a heart attack. Are you trying to send me to the hospital?!"

That was the last place I wanted to send anyone. "Of course not. Here. I apologize. I really do. Truce?" I passed her a pecan peace offering. "Eat it. It's perfecterrific."

She pouted some more, just for effect. But she couldn't resist. She took the cookie and chewed noisily, savoring the buttery sweetness. "I hate to say this, but it's better than my mom's recipe. Don't you dare tell her I said so!"

"I won't. I swear." I held out my pinky finger to prove it. Then I reached for another pod, yanking it off its stem. A roll of dark chocolate fudgies was waiting to be devoured. We finished them all, wiping streaks of chocolate from our mouths with the backs of our hands.

The tree readjusted its branches for us—a moving ladder of leafy limbs—making it easy to climb higher and higher and giving us a gentle boost when we needed it. Together we collected and tasted the harvest. Pod by pod. Cookie by cookie.

We discovered bite-sized gingersnaps, with just the right amount of spice, just the right amount of snap.

"These are the best yet."

Then we found peanut butter crisps.

"I take it back. These are the best. By far."

Kira agreed, until she peeled open a pod stuffed with pillowy vanilla snickerdoodles. "So good!" she shouted, sugar spraying from her lips.

Another branch. Another pod of freshly baked, or grown, cookies.

"Wait, wait! You have to try these."

Pistachio creams. Butterscotch chip. Cherry biscotti.

As the sun waned, we stuffed ourselves silly.

"My mom will be furious. I totally spoiled my appetite." Kira climbed down and rested against the tree's trunk, arms and legs splayed, stomach sticking out. "But it was *soooo* worth it."

"Do you think if we eat enough cookies, we might actually turn into one?" I asked, plopping down beside her.

"Like a giant kid-sized cookie?" Kira cracked one last pod in half and pulled down the waxy peel, revealing a row of raspberry macarons. She popped one in her mouth. "After witnessing and tasting *this*—" She finished the cookie with a satisfied crunch. "It seems like just about anything is possible."

Anything is possible, my heart echoed. The words coursed through my body, more potent than sugary grape juice on an empty stomach. I liked the way those words made me feel: brave and excited and curious. I didn't want to let go of that sensation. "Anything is possible," I repeated aloud.

Kira offered me a macaron. I took it and nodded thanks. "If you do turn into a cookie, I promise not to eat you," she said solemnly.

"Ditto." I took a bite. "Unless you turn into one of these, then all bets are off."

"Cookie cannibal!" She threw the peel at me and laughed.

I decided Kira and I could be friends after all. Real friends. Maybe even best friends. Hey, anything *is* possible.

***

Before leaving the orchard, we filled our backpacks with as many cookies as they could carry.

"I'll give some to Junie tomorrow," I said, zipping up my pack.

"You're going back to the hospital?"

"Hopefully my dad can take me, if my mom isn't feeling well."

"Is she sick too?" Kira asked.

"No, well, yes. A different kind of sick."

"Like the flu?"

"Not quite. More like her heart is sick." It was hard to explain something I barely understood. "We should go home, before it gets any darker."

Kira shifted her weight back and forth. I could tell she had something else to say.

"What is it?" I asked.

She stared at the tree. "Aren't you going to plant anything else?"

I suddenly felt careless. Kira was right. We needed to take advantage of the magic, or whatever it was, while it lasted.

"What should we plant?" I purposefully said *we*. We shared this secret now, together. "Do you have anything in your pockets?"

Kira pulled out a ball of lint and an elastic hair band.

My pockets were equally disappointing. All I had was a crumpled bus ticket.

Kira picked up a pebble from the ground. "This?"

"Why would we want a crop of rocks? And how the heck would we harvest a bunch of boulders?"

"Good point. What about this?" She reached into her backpack and pulled out a sheet of paper.

"Homework! Are you crazy? You seriously want to plant a homework tree? Like we don't get enough from Ms. Perdilla and the other teachers already?!"

"Whoa! My mistake. We definitely do not want a homework tree!"

I turned my backpack over in the grass. The tiny brass bell jingled.

"Aha!"

"A keychain?"

"I won't plant the whole thing. Just this," I said, unhooking the bell.

Kira's lips went sideways.

"It's the best we've got. Unless you have a better idea."

She shrugged. "Go for it."

I dug a hole and dropped the shining bell in the ground. A single note of music escaped. Root tendrils extended, blue and twisting. My heart pulsed, giddy with hope. Kira and I filled the hole back up and packed the moist earth with our hands.

"When will it bloom?" Kira asked.

"When it's ready. Could be a day, could be more. We'll have to wait and see."

"I hate waiting." Kira stood up, brushing dirt from her hands.

"Tell me about it. It's the worstible."

"What?"

"Worstible. Worst-most-horrible. Two words smashed together. It's a Junie thing." I hadn't been able to share the secret with her yet, but my sister was all around. In the words I spoke, in the swing that swayed in the breeze across the clearing.

"I thought you were referring to some kind of sausage. Like bratwurst or something. Not that I can even think about food right now." Kira moaned. "Which reminds me. It's almost dinnertime."

We walked through the orchard, down to the place where our paths split. Soon dusk would cover us like a blanket. A chorus of spring peepers peeped and a few fireflies flickered. Kira's mom would be waiting anxiously, pacing the floor of their warm, well-lit house. I imagined a gourmet meal on her table, set with real silver, fancy crystal glasses, and a bouquet of flowers. Okay, that was probably an exaggeration. Still, I knew I was headed to an opposite universe. At least I had new shoes on my feet, a full stomach, a hopeful heart, a whole lot of cookies . . .

And a new friend too.

Things were looking up.

CHAPTER 12

I threw the screen door open and filled the house with light, switch by switch.

As expected, Mom was still MIA—Making Infrequent Appearances. Something I was determined to change. I turned the knob on the stove, sending a flame licking at the bottom of our kettle. I found Mom's favorite tea in the cupboard and dropped one bag into a sturdy-looking mug. I didn't dare use the china cups, since she'd managed to smash one last time.

The kettle whistled.

I retrieved some oatmeal cookies from my backpack and arranged them on a plate. I carried everything upstairs. The door to my parents' room was ajar.

"Mom?" I pushed the door open. "Mom?"

"Issaaa?" Her voice reminded me of the slow hiss of a punctured balloon.

"Yes. It's me. It's so dark in here. Can I turn on the light?"

"Please don't. My head's aching. The light bothers my eyes." She sounded sadder than usual.

"What's wrong? Did something happen?" I asked, fears gathering like gray clouds before a storm.

"Everything's fine, baby. We'll talk more tomorrow."

I shuffled across the room. I banged my knee on the dresser and yelped.

"Shhh."

"You can't shush pain, Mom." I thumped and bumped around some more until I reached the edge of her bed.

"What are you doing, Isabel?"

"I thought you might be hungry. I brought you some cookies and tea. Chamomile. Your favorite."

I felt like the mother now. Like when Junie and I used to play house. She always insisted on being the baby and I would be the mom. It was fun. I would fuss over her, rock her, groom her. Say *ba-ba-ba* and *goo-goo*. I would feed her candy, pretending it was medicine. I would take care of her. But that was make-believe.

This wasn't. And it wasn't fun.

"Remember the tea parties we used to have in the afternoons? With Junie? When you'd bring home treats from the café or bakery where you were working? Let's do that again soon. It'll be nice. Just like old times."

"We'll see, Isa."

I placed the tray on her bedside table. The mug rattled. I almost hoped it would tip over. Make some noise. Make a mess. *Wake up!* I wanted to shout, loud as the kettle on the stove, whistling and wailing for attention.

Instead, I whispered. Releasing trembling words into the room. Hoping they might take seed and grow in her heart too.

"Mom, anything is possible."

✳✳✳

A faint clattering shook me from sleep. Dishes in the sink. My eyes popped open. *Scrape, clank, clang!* I rocketed out of bed, despite a stomach still heavy from last night's cookie gluttony. The stairs creaked—no, they sang—*good morning!*

The shape of my father greeted me, his back to the door. A six-foot silhouette carved in pale yellow light. Memories of our old routine flooded my brain. Lazy weekend mornings, all together. I'd whisk the eggs. Junie would lick batter from the spatula. Mom would twist oranges until they cried sweet juice, and we'd cheer as Dad flipped pancakes with reckless abandon, a circus performer entertaining his adoring fans. Mom tsk-tsked if the pancakes flew too high or too crazy, landing on the floor with a *fwap!* Junie called those ones *fwapjacks*. Dad claimed they were still edible, citing the five-second rule. But Mom insisted we feed them to the neighborhood birds instead.

Then there was the bacon, fried to salty perfection on the griddle. Mom would hum and tap a slippered foot while we waited for the first crispy nibble, like a pack of drooling hounds. If we got too close, she'd swat us with the spatula that Junie had licked clean. We'd explode with laughter.

I ran across the kitchen and flung my arms around Dad's waist. I nuzzled my face into the shallow of his back. I squeezed. A real squg. I inhaled, waiting for his Saturday smell to fill my nostrils: a comforting blend of clean laundry, smoky bacon, and musky dad-ness. Instead, the biting scent of aftershave hit me. The soft flannel shirt he usually wore was replaced by something starchy. The weekday fabric scratched my cheek, told me to back away. Nothing sizzled on the stovetop. The cast-iron griddle sat on the shelf, gathering dust.

"Isa." He reached around and mussed my frizzy hair. His hand was as big as a cluster of bananas; my whole head could probably fit in his palm.

I loosened my grip, but kept my arms around his waist. In case he might try to fly away, like a pancake tossed too high.

"G'morning," he said.

"You're not . . ."

"Going to work. Yes." He nodded, unclasping my hands from his waist. He knelt down so his eyes, steel blue like mine, looked at mine.

"But . . ."

"I know. I know," he said.

It was hard to find the right words. "But . . . bacon." Seriously? That was all I could come up with? I had about a million things I wanted to say. To shout. And all I could come up with was *bacon*? Pathetic.

His hand cupped my cheek. I tilted my head, resting my face in the cradle of his palm. I closed my eyes. A single, fat tear ran through the creases of his skin.

"I have to go to the office. Just for a little while. I'll try to come home early. We'll play catch tonight, okay?" He patted my head, like I was an obedient puppy. "Remember, be a good girl."

Except I wanted to bark. And run. And howl!

"We have to see Junie today," I said frantically. "All of us. Together."

"Mom will take you this afternoon."

"Will she? Really?" My eyebrows crinkled. "Because I haven't had much luck with that lately."

He let out a deep breath. "She'll get better soon. They both will."

"When?" I grumbled.

"Someday soon."

"Someday? Someday is not a day of the week, Dad!" At least not according to Junie's calendar.

"Isa, I'm sorry. I have to go to work."

"Why?"

"You know why."

I glanced at the towering pile of mail on the counter. "Bills?" I said.

Dad loosened his collar, as if the word made him itch. He took a swig of coffee and tucked in his unfriendly shirt. Suits didn't suit him. They never had. On weekends, when he was outside trimming hedges, building swings, or playing with us, he was happy and free in jeans and flannel. The more patches and grass stains, the better. I wished he could find a job with a dress code like that.

"We could try the lottery," I offered. "Then you wouldn't have to work so hard."

"And play with chance? Gamble with our future? That's out of the question."

"Let's buy a scratch ticket. Just one."

"Enough, Isa. I refuse to throw away a single hard-earned penny on something like that."

"But . . . Dad." I paused so that he would stop packing his briefcase and pay attention to me.

"What is it?" he said impatiently.

I waited seven more seconds, just to make sure he was really listening.

"Dad, anything is possible."

He turned away from me. He placed a hand on the counter.

"Dad?" I took a step forward. Was he crying? That's not what was supposed to happen at all.

He straightened up, wheeled around. He clutched his briefcase. His face was made of stone. Not a tear to be found. He cleared his throat and strode past me toward the front door.

He didn't say a word. He didn't even look at me. I'd become invisible again.

CHAPTER 13

I sat on the front porch, hugging my knees to my chest. I wasn't made of stone like my father. I couldn't bury myself in bed and ignore the world, like my mother. There were only two things that could make me feel better. One of them was miles away at Delorna Regional Hospital. The other was a lot closer. I wiped my wet eyes with my sleeve. I rose to my feet.

The fields were already unruly, and it was only early spring. At this rate, it would be a summer of chaos in the orchard. Grasses needed mowing, weeds needed taming, fences needed mending. Everything was desperate for a little TLC—Tender Loving Care. Especially me. A daughter, feeling like a TLC—Totally Lost Child. The morning light touched everything, warming every blade of grass. And yet I still felt chilled.

I was surprised to discover Kira waiting at the edge of the clearing, sitting on the swing. She didn't notice me because I'd perfected the art of walking ninja-quiet. I watched as she braided her chestnut hair. Three strands. Over. Under. Over. I'd tried to braid Junie's hair once. Once and never again. It was a disaster. All I accomplished was one gigantic knot. It was tangled so badly that Mom had to use olive oil just to run a comb through it. Poor thing looked like a greasy mutt for about a week. But Junie didn't mind, as long as we didn't have to cut it all off. At least back then, it was her decision to make.

Kira looped an elastic band around the end of her braid. Once, twice, nice and tight. Everything in its place. Smooth and orderly. It's funny how looking at someone else can make you see yourself more clearly. I was suddenly aware that my own hair was about as wild as the meadow grasses. My life was equally messy. Why would someone like Kira even want to be friends with someone like me? Maybe this was all a big mistake.

I thought about retreating back home using my ninja-stealth, as if I'd never been there in the first place. Kira still hadn't seen or heard me. I was getting really good at this invisibility thing. But that would be another TLC—a Truly Lame Copout.

Instead, I forced reluctant words out of my mouth. "Hey there."

"Tree buddy!" She jumped off the swing, waving like a lunatic. "A few tiny buds have sprouted, but they don't look ripe yet." She ran in circles around the tree's fat trunk, talking a mile a minute, thrusting her arms in the air and pointing up at the branches like some kind of wacky disco move. She could be put together and perfectly braided one minute, but klutzy and silly the next. A contradiction, to use her own word. And I liked her that way.

"Don't worry," she sputtered, her eyes popping. "We won't miss a thing. I've been watching."

"For how long?"

"Since about six this morning. I couldn't sleep last night. I was just thinking and wondering. You know?"

"I do."

"I even drank some of my mom's coffee to stay alert. I probably braided and re-braided my hair fifteen times. I'm prepared. In case something happens. You can count on me! I'm ready!"

I chuckled. "I can see that."

"Now what?" She was still running and pointing and flailing. The opposite of ninja-stealth.

"I think you should calm down a little."

"Oh, okay." Her body relaxed. "Good idea, tree buddy. You always have good ideas."

"Maybe next time skip the coffee."

"Definitely. Another good idea. Caffeine not necessary. Magic is exciting enough on its own."

"Very true." I walked up to the tree and patted it. The leaves glittered.

"Aren't you going to the hospital with your parents today?" Kira asked.

"I was. Now I'm not. Until later, at least. My dad has to work."

"Bummer."

"My thoughts exactly."

"We could take you. I mean my mom could. Because I can't drive yet. Obviously."

I looked up at the tree. Mom always said a watched pot never boils. If the same was true for the tree, then there was no use hanging around all day. Not when Junie needed me. "Do you still have any cookies?" I asked.

"Of course. I ate a couple for breakfast, but there are tons left. All different flavors. Why? You hungry?"

"They're not for me. They're for Junie. We're going to bring them to her."

"You are?"

"*We* are." It's a small word, really. Two letters. Even the sound is tiny. But it's not nothing. Actually, it's a big something. One plus one equals we. And that's huge. "I mean, if you want to come, that is."

"I do!"

"Okay, I'm going to run home, pack a bag, and leave a note for my parents."

"Sounds great! I'll talk to my mom. We'll swing by to pick you up soon. Yay!" she cheered, as if going to the hospital were a trip to the amusement park. If only.

CHAPTER 14

Kira hovered in the hospital hallway, doing that shifting thing. Nurses and doctors moved past her fluidly, like she was a pebble in a stream.

"Come in with me," I said.

Back and forth. Left foot, right foot.

"You do know that Wilms isn't contagious, right? You're not going to catch it from Junie."

"I know that!" A bruised mumble. "Jeez. I'm not a total moron."

"You're not a moron at all. But you are acting a little weird." I wanted to make the most of every minute with Junie. It was Saturnday and there were swings and cookies and secrets to tell.

Kira kept shifting. Left. Right. Left.

"Look, we don't have all day. What's up with you?"

"You should go in first. Have a couple minutes, just the two of you, to do, like, sister stuff."

"You sure?"

"Yeah. I'll wait here for a bit. Check out the aquarium in the lobby. It's no problem." She studied the tiles on the floor like they were the most interesting things in the world.

"Okay."

"Don't forget these." She handed me the bag of cookies.

I opened the door to Room 612. A nurse in pink scrubs stood by the bed, tapping buttons on some alien-looking machine and jotting notes in a chart. She must have been new, because I didn't recognize her. We spent so much time at Delorna that we were on a first-name basis with most of the people who took care of Junie.

"Come in," the nurse said warmly. "She's almost finished."

I did not appreciate her choice of words. The machine beeped. A few lights flashed. Junie's eyes were closed. Some medicines turned her face round and puffy, but today she looked paper-doll flat and kind of grayish. Worse than yesterday. It frightened me.

I wrung my hands. "Is she asleep?" I whispered.

"No, just resting. Right, Penny?" The nurse rubbed Junie's arm gently. Her eyes opened. She looked like she needed a dose of feisty juice.

"Junie," I corrected. "Her name's Junie. Not Penny."

The nurse frowned. "Her chart says Penelope. I just assumed . . ."

"No one calls her that." My voice became fierce. I was Isa, Protector and Defender of Sick Sisters. Hear me roar!

"My mistake. I just transferred to Delorna from another hospital. I'm still getting to know everyone here. I'll make a note in her file, so I don't forget." The nurse scribbled in the chart, smiled, then straightened her scrubs. The ones Junie thought were pajamas.

"How're you feeling?" I asked, leaning over Junie's flatter-than-normal face. I tugged the frayed strings on the cap hiding her hairless head and gave her a tiny kiss on the forehead.

"Crumbuckets," she croaked.

The nurse raised an eyebrow. "Your sister is quite a little wordsmith."

"Smith? My last name's not Smith. It's Fitzwilken." Junie propped herself up in bed, color slowly creeping into her cheeks. "That makes me a wordwilken. Not a wordsmith."

The nurse chuckled. "My point exactly." She glanced at the clock on the wall. "I'll be back in an hour to give you the next dose. Okay?"

Junie stuck out her tongue. "Crummy crumbuckets!" Maybe there was a bit of feisty juice left in her after all. "Give it to that Penny Smith girl instead. I don't want it." She glowered. "Ugh. My tongue already feels scalched!"

"You mean scalded. Or scorched," corrected the nurse.

"She means both," I said. I knew that some of Junie's treatments had side effects like causing numbness and sores in the mouth.

"I won't be able to taste my ice cream with a scalched tongue. And tomorrow is Sundae, right, Isa?" Junie pointed at her calendar, now adorned with a frame of crooked Band-Aids.

"Posolutely. Sundae will be a funday." I would make sure of it.

"You mean Yumday," Junie replied firmly. Ice cream was serious business. "That reminds me. I'd like to place my order for a banana split."

"Do I look like a waitress to you?" The nurse planted her hands on her hips and gave a little wink. "I don't have any banana splits at the moment, but in an hour I'll have a dose of your medicine."

"That's so not an even trade! Give it to that Penny Smith girl instead."

"No. It's for you, Miss Junie Fitzwilken of Room 612."

"Maybe if I sneak into another room, she'll give it to someone else," Junie whispered to me.

"I heard that," the nurse said. "I know you don't like it very much, but that crawpucket medicine, or whatever you call it, is going to help make you better."

"Crawpucket? Crawpucket!" Junie thought that was just about the funniest thing she'd ever heard. She looked at the nurse's nametag: Edith Minkey. "You're a wordinkey, Nurse Minkey!"

"You can call me Edith," she replied, trying not to laugh, because Junie's silliness was infectious.

"But Minkey-wordinkey is much more fun to say. Plus it rhymes with stinky and Slinky!"

A giggle meltdown was a bit like an avalanche: a single goofy-sounding word could set off a chain reaction, gathering momentum until Junie was giggling uncontrollably. Normally, I would egg her on, feeding her new words until both our tummies ached with laughter. But I could tell that her body wouldn't be able to handle that kind of shuddering, shaking silliness. Not now. She was too weak. I was afraid she'd get hurt. You knew things were bad when laughing was a dangerous activity.

Unfortunately, I was right.

Junie's eyes grew wide. She started wheezing. It was an awful sound.

"Calm down. Junie, calm down." I felt like I was falling, again. But with no special tree to catch me. I watched her gasping for air.

Her grayish-pink face turned purple and I screamed. Nurse Minkey moved lightning fast. She pushed some buttons. She attached a space mask to Junie's mouth and nose.

Whoosh! Hiss. Some urgent beeping.

Then, a sigh of relief.

Junie closed her eyes. Her chest rose. And fell. Up and down. She was breathing. Or the machine was breathing for her, I couldn't tell. At least she wasn't purple anymore. She was okay.

But I was a total wreck. I felt like I'd aged at warp speed. From twelve years old to an ancient, tired one hundred in a few seconds. My skin hung from my bones. My heart was exhausted from beating so wildly, from caring so hard. I wanted to crawl into bed and not get out until everything was better.

Just like Mom when she came home each afternoon.

The thought pricked like a needle.

I lay down next to Junie. I forgot about the nurse and the beeping machines. I forgot about the backpack filled with cookies. I forgot about my new friend waiting in the hallway. I just watched Junie breathe. Her chest rose and fell. You'd think it would be boring, like watching paint dry. But it wasn't. When it's some-one you love, you stare like the world depends on each breath. Because it does.

After four excruciatingly long minutes, Junie's eye-lids cracked open and fluttered like moths fresh out of their cocoons. She squinted. Like she was expecting to see heaven or something.

She saw my face instead. I can only imagine how bad I looked, all rumpled and crooked with worry.

She reached a hand up and touched my cheek. "Better than an angel," she wheezed.

"This ugly old mug?" I made a face and gently pinched her bony knee under the covers. She nudged me back. Sisters speak all kinds of languages. Many of them don't require words.

* * *

The nurse continued checking machines and pushing buttons. From time to time, she would poke at Junie or attach some tube here or there. She scribbled in her chart.

Finally, she removed the mask from Junie's face. "Everything looks stable now. Feeling better?"

Junie took a breath on her own, then stuck out her tongue.

"All right. A little attitude is fine with me. Shows me the spirit is strong." Edith stuck out her own tongue. "See? Two can play at this game."

Junie grinned, but didn't dare laugh. She took a few more deep breaths instead. I helped tuck some pillows behind her head. My sister closed her eyes. Within seconds she began to snore.

Edith watched her for a minute, then pressed some kind of remote control into my hand. "If anything happens, you push this immediately. Got it?" She spoke quietly, so she wouldn't wake Junie. "Her vitals look good. But she needs rest. Please don't do anything to rile her up."

Which pretty much ruled out stories about a magical orchard.

She rested a hand on my shoulder and gave it a soft squeeze. "It's hard to see someone you love get sick. If you ever need to talk, there are people here to help. The child life specialists, counselors, doctors. And me too."

I swallowed and nodded.

"Junie is strong. And so are you. I can tell."

I felt the exact opposite of strong. Junie looked the opposite of strong. We were like two sticks of petrified chewing gum about to crumble into tiny pieces. I didn't want to disappoint Edith, so I made a pathetic fist and raised it in the air. What a joke.

She seemed convinced. "All right. I'll check back soon." She patted me on the head. Just like Dad had earlier that morning before he turned into a gargoyle made of stone. *Good girl. Be strong.* Compared to what Junie was going through, my life was a walk in the park. So why did it feel so hard sometimes?

"Thanks," I mumbled. My fist softened into a wave. I turned to Junie. She snorted and rolled over, nuzzling next to me. I closed my weary eyes. Just as I drifted off, one of my eyelids peeled open. A tiny finger poked me once, twice.

"Quit it," I said, swatting the hand away. In my drowsy state, I temporarily forgot we were in the hospital.

Another poke. "I have to tell you about my dream before it disappears," Junie's voice was scratchy. My other eyelid peeled open.

"Ouch." I sat up, remembering where I was. The lemony bleach smell hung in the air. The too-bright lights hurt my eyes.

"Rise and shine, Sleeping Beauty," Junie said.

I looked at my watch. Junie had been asleep for less than ten minutes. "That was quick," I said groggily, wishing for more time.

"Power nap. I'm a pro at those." She yawned and I saw sores inside her mouth. She cuddled close to me and we looked at each other for a very long time. Memorizing. Breathing. Staying quiet and being still.

"Are you reading my mind?" Junie eventually asked.

"No. Are you reading mine?" I pressed my forehead to hers.

"Nope."

"Would be cool if we could."

"We could chat all day long." Junie eased back against the pillows. "And we'd never be lonely."

"Are you lonely?" I felt myself aging, worrying, growing old again.

"Not really," Junie said matter-of-factly. "I've got oodles of visitors. Mom, Dad, you. The other kids down the hall. And now I've got Henry."

I felt a pang of jealousy.

"Who's Henry?"

"My tumor."

Great. I was jealous of a tumor. This was officially a new low.

"Hold on, your tumor's name is Henry? I thought it was Willie. Or Pablo?"

"Duh, Isa. Henry is Willie's brother. Pablo was their cousin."

"I'm confused. Didn't the doctors make them go away? During your operation?"

"They did. Except everyone was so worried about Willie and Pablo that no one noticed Henry."

Apparently, this tumor and I had a lot in common. Awesome.

"How come you never mentioned him before?"

"How come you never mentioned *her* before?" Junie pointed. Kira stood in the doorway, her long braid draped over her shoulder.

My cheeks flushed. I didn't want Junie to think I'd replaced her. Thankfully, Junie's big eyes and equally big smile told me I had nothing to worry about.

"You never told me you were friends with a princess," Junie said.

"Princess?"

"Rapunzel," she said, eying Kira's endless tresses with awe and a little bit of envy.

I made an awkward introduction. "Junie, Kira. Kira, Junie."

Kira fiddled with her braid the way I usually fiddled with the contents of my lunch tray. I suddenly got the impression her hair was her shield.

Junie glanced at me. "You did tell her I'm not contagious, right?"

"She knows," I said. "Kira, come in."

Kira didn't budge.

"And you told her I don't bite? I don't smell, either.

I swear," Junie's voice trilled. She seemed excited to meet Kira. I was glad I'd invited her to come with me. "The nurses give me baths way too often. I couldn't even stink if I wanted to."

I sniffed and smirked. "You sure about that?"

She elbowed me and made a face.

"Seriously, Kira. Please come in," I said.

She slowly crossed the room and perched on the foot of the bed. She continued to fidget, braiding and re-braiding her hair.

Junie was transfixed. "Can I try?" she asked.

"Huh?"

"She likes your hair," I explained.

"Aw, thanks! Here." Kira moved closer, then extended the braid, thick as rope, and placed it in Junie's palm.

"It's so long!"

"I haven't cut it since my dad left," Kira said. "That was a couple years ago, not that I'm keeping track or anything." I wondered if that was true. Maybe I wasn't the only one who counted time? "He used to tell me it was pretty."

"It is. Pretty and beautiful. Prettiful. If I had hair like this, I wouldn't mind taking a bath. I'd shampoo it really well. I'd condition it, comb it, style it." Junie studied the braid, tracing the pattern with her fingertips. "Could you teach Isa how to do this?"

"I could teach both of you. It's easy."

"Hear that, Isa? Easy peasy. Ha! More like hairdo greasy." She snorted, recalling my prior failure and the olive oil that followed.

"Very funny." I opted not to engage in our regular rhyming rally for fear of needing the remote control Edith had given me.

"I'll teach you right now. Watch." Without realizing what she was doing, Kira pulled the purple cap from Junie's head.

There are lots of problems with hospitals: they smell weird, there are no comfortable places to sit, and the lights are always too bright. So bright that you see things you shouldn't. Or don't want to. Things that are hard to forget.

I don't know which was worse, the look on Junie's face or the look on Kira's. I considered pushing the remote's red button. *Help! Emergency!* I almost grabbed the oxygen mask for myself because I couldn't breathe.

Then the fierceness welled up in me. I'm pretty sure I yelled something mean. I ripped the cap from Kira's hands and tried to put it back on Junie's bare head as fast as I could. I kept fumbling with the strings and the floppy pom-pom got in the way. Instead of making anything better, I was making everything worse.

"Stop, stop. Isa! It's okay!" Junie pulled the cap from my clumsy hands.

"No! It's not!" I shrieked.

"It is." Surprisingly, Junie didn't sound mad. She didn't put the cap back on either. She just held it in her lap. Here I was freaking out, and she was cool as a bald cucumber.

When she spoke again, her voice was calm. Hairless and slightly hunched, she was like a very cute version of Yoda. "She didn't know any better." It was something Mom used to say a lot when Junie was younger and would smash my sand castles or break my toys by accident.

"It was a mistake for me to come," Kira faltered. "I'm so . . . I'm so . . ."

"It's fine," Junie repeated. "Really."

Kira looked up. "When will it grow back?" she asked hesitantly.

"Someday," I answered for Junie, mostly because I wanted it to be true. I needed it to be true.

Junie's eyes darted to the calendar on the wall. "Someday is not a day of the week, Isa."

It was the same argument I'd made to Dad that morning.

"But someday could be any day. That's the whole point," Kira said. "Someday could be tomorrow."

We soaked in that idea for a moment. Then Junie beamed, and I couldn't be mad at Kira anymore. I resisted the urge to hug them both.

"She's right. Someday really could be any day," I said. "Because anything is possible."

Kira's eyes sparkled. "Oh! Did you tell her?"

I wished again that I could read people's minds, or at least send Kira a silent brainwave message to *sit and zip!* If we told Junie about the tree, she would get all riled up. I knew it. Edith would have to come back and re-inflate her with that machine and maybe needles or other scary stuff from the worstible list.

"Tell me what?"

"Nothing." It was agony, not telling my secret—our secret—to the one person I wanted to tell most in the world.

A loud clashing and banging interrupted our conversation.

Kira cupped her hands over her ears. "What is *that*?"

"Sounds like a riot," I said, cringing. "Maybe the nurses are on strike?"

"Music it is," Junie said, still all tranquil in Yoda mode.

"That is not music. It's a cacophony." Kira flexed her vocab muscles, but the wordwilken was too focused on the noise to be impressed.

"Listen!" Junie sat up taller. "They're coming to serenade us!"

"You say serenade, I say torture." I stuck my fingers into my ears and exchanged a look with Kira.

"It's Gregory and his band!" Junie clapped and wiggled to a nonexistent beat.

"Orchestra," someone said. The noise stopped. I rubbed my ears. A boy with big, white teeth stuck his head in the door and grinned. He looked vaguely familiar. "We're an orchestra. We're very serious musicians." He drummed an overturned bedpan with a spoon, as if that supported his position. "I play percussion. Maisie plays wind." An older girl tooted a whistle. "Wallace and Cal are on strings. Gemma on brass." Two boys strummed tissue boxes tied with elastic bands. A girl in a wheelchair clutched a funnel attached to a loop of plastic tubing, apparently serving as a makeshift trumpet. A boy about Junie's age shook a bottle of pills like a maraca. "And Derick plays . . . whatever that is."

"Thanks for coming by," Junie said. "This is my sister, Isa. And our friend, Rapunzel."

"Nice to meet you. I'm Gregory. I'm also the conductor."

I realized why he looked familiar. "Hey, I know you. I mean I know your dad, James. I met him waiting for the bus. He showed me a picture of you playing the piano."

"Ah, my keys," Gregory said wistfully. "Too bad he can't bring them here. The nurses said a piano won't fit in the elevator. The child life specialists are working on getting us some better instruments, though. They say music can be a form of medicine." He thumped the bedpan. "In the meantime, I'm stuck with this." He shrugged. "Could be worse."

I forced a cheerful face, even though my ears were still ringing.

"Hey, you want to play with us?" Gregory asked. "If you can find some instruments, you can join. The more, the merrier. We've been trying to get more kids, but it's slow going."

I resisted the urge to tell him why they were having recruitment issues.

"Thanks, Gregory." Junie smiled brightly. "But we're going to stay here for now."

"No worries. If you change your mind, we'll be down the hall, rehearsing for our next gig."

"You have a gig?" I asked skeptically.

"Sure, every week. For the folks on the ninth floor. The audiological patients are big fans. They love our sound."

"I bet they do," I said. *Because most of them are deaf,* I thought.

"Time to practice. See ya later. And Junie—"

"Yeah?"

"Nice dome." He pointed to her bald head. "It's a good look on you."

She blushed. From pride or embarrassment, I wasn't sure.

✳✳✳

We gave Junie a dozen cookies before leaving. To avoid discussing the tree, I claimed that Kira's mom had baked them. The bug-eyed stare I directed at Kira kept her yappy mouth closed. Thank goodness. Junie was ready for another power nap, and didn't have the energy for extra questions. If she didn't quite believe our story, she didn't show it.

We left another dozen cookies at the nurses' station and gave the rest to Gregory's misfit orchestra down the hall. They gladly put down their noisemakers so they could enjoy the treats. A doctor in a white coat walked by and gave us a wave of gratitude. The brief quiet was almost as delicious as a raspberry macaron.

CHAPTER 15

I was happy to tag along with Kira for the rest of the afternoon, not only because Mrs. Ritter promised us grilled cheese sandwiches and milkshakes at the local diner, but because I enjoyed their company.

On our way to lunch, we ran errands around town, visiting the bakery, the hardware store, the bank. While Mrs. Ritter stopped at her real estate office, Kira and I sat on a bench outside in the sun, chewing gumballs and blowing gigantic bubbles that splat across our cheeks like sticky face masks. It was a miracle the gum never ended up in Kira's long hair. The sound our gum made when it popped reminded me of Junie's balloon tradition. I thought of the lost wishing pin, but I wouldn't let myself count the time until her birthday. There were just too many unknowns between now and then.

***

It was early evening when Kira and her mom dropped me off at home. I was pleasantly surprised to find an unexpected treasure waiting for me. A pepperoni pizza sitting in a box on the kitchen counter, still molten lava hot. I knew better. But I couldn't resist. I raised a slice to my lips and took a bite.

"Ooooww!" I dropped it back into the box.

My father rushed into the kitchen, fast as Nurse Minkey in an emergency. A moment later, he handed me a glass of ice water. My mouth pulsed with pain. I thought about the side effects of Junie's medicine. Is this what it felt like?

"There you are!" Mom appeared in the doorway, hands on her hips. I did a double take. I wasn't used to seeing her downstairs in the daylight, dressed. Okay, it was only yoga pants and a cotton sweater, but compared to the bathrobe she was usually wearing when I came home, this outfit was practically a ball gown. Her hair was combed and she was even wearing lip gloss. She looked almost normal. It was nice, but also weird. Like she was wearing a costume of her old self. "Where have you been all day?" she snapped. Not exactly the warm welcome I would've liked, but at least she was noticing me for once.

"I was hanging out with Kira." Not a lie. Just not a whole truth.

Mom frowned. "You said you wanted to see Junie and then you just ran off. I looked everywhere!"

"Everywhere?" Had she checked in the orchard?

"You cannot just do that!"

"Do what?" My insides lurched.

"Disappear, Isabel. You need to be more responsible. You need to think about other people and not just yourself."

I couldn't believe what I was hearing. I wanted to shout the exact same words right back at my parents. A wave of heat rolled through my body. More than just my tongue burned. "I left you a note," I said. "I told you what I was doing." Well, mostly. "You could've called Mrs. Ritter if you were really so worried about me."

"Nel," Dad said gently. "Don't take this out on her. It's been a long day. It's not Isa's fault the wind blew the note off the table." He glanced over at me sympathetically. "It took a while to find it," he explained. "Next time, try sticking your notes to the fridge with a magnet. Okay, sweetheart?"

I nodded, relieved that his face was no longer made of stone and that he was actually taking my side. "Sure, easy peasy," I said, eying my mother wearily. She had turned her back to us and was wiping down the already spotless counter. "Can we eat now?" I asked, trying to break up the awkward tension. Luckily, my tongue was recovering from the molten pizza encounter, and I was starving.

"Yes, let's," Dad said, setting plates and napkins on the table. "Nel?"

Mom stopped scrubbing and joined us. She began extracting slices of pizza from the box. Three out of the four spots at the kitchen table were occupied. Better than usual. Still, something wasn't quite right.

"We need to talk," Dad said, then coughed like the rest of the words were stuck in his throat. I passed him my cold water. He gulped it down. "Thanks."

I took a tentative bite, watching their faces for clues. "What's going on?"

Mom ran her hands through her hair, making a mess of it. She inhaled, exhaled. "Something is . . . growing." She looked across the table, directly at me. My stomach somersaulted. I hadn't had time to check on the tree when I got home. Both cars in the driveway and the smell of pizza lured me right inside. Had my parents discovered the most recent crop? Would they be mad? Could they be mad? What *was* out there? Bells? Or something else?

"Growing?" I resisted the urge to look out the window toward the orchard.

"I suppose we knew this was a possibility," Dad said.

They did? Everyone in town told stories about our strange property. It made sense that my parents would eventually hear the chatter.

"It's confusing and overwhelming for all of us." Mom peered down at her plate, searching the pattern of pepperoni for some kind of logic. She shook her head.

I tried to keep my voice steady. "Ms. Perdilla says it would be boring to have a scientific explanation for everything."

Dad looked up. In a split second, his face shifted, hardened. He slammed the table with his fist. The plates rattled. It was the first time I'd seen him hit anything, other than a nail with a hammer or a ball with a bat. The wooden table legs shook, knock-kneed scared as I was.

Mom rested a hand on Dad's fist. "Clearly your father and I were very upset to learn about this new growth." Now that she was downstairs in the light, I noticed several hairs, as white as Muriel's, on my mother's head. After my visit to the hospital, I understood about worrying. Aging at warp speed. It was taking its toll on my mother. Not just inside, but outside too. "Very upset," she repeated.

What on earth had the tree sprouted this afternoon that could be so terrible? Shoes and cookies had been relatively harmless. What sort of threat could some tiny brass bells pose?

"The growth," I said, using their term, "might not actually be bad. Maybe it's just misunderstood?" Like Frankenstein's monster.

"Don't be ridiculous, Isabel," Dad barked.

Great. I was doomed.

Mom touched her fingertips to her temples, which meant a splitting headache was probably brewing. "What your father means is we have to get rid of it."

Correction: my tree was doomed.

"No!" I yelled, slamming down my own fist. Poor table. It occurred to me that it had once been a tree. Probably not a magical one, but nevertheless my heart ached. "Please, no." The clock on the wall ticked. The kitchen faucet dripped into the sink. My parents wouldn't, or couldn't, respond. "Why?" I asked that stupid question for the billionth time.

"We need to remove it quickly. In case it spreads."

"Spreads?" The chance seedling had grown at an alarming rate. Perhaps new trees could sprout equally fast. But I still didn't understand why that was bad or dangerous. It sounded wonderful to me. Too wonderful to destroy. I bit my lip and forced back tears.

"Your sister needs the surgery," Mom replied.

If my brain could've made noise, it would've sounded like brakes screeching.

"Wait, what?" I dabbed my leaky eyes with a napkin. "Hold on—we're talking about surgery?" Not selective deforestation?

"Junie's most recent scans showed a new tumor. We didn't tell you at first because we didn't want you to worry. The doctors needed to run some extra tests, just to make sure they had the full picture. We met with Dr. Ebbens and his team this afternoon to go over our options."

All I could say was, "Henry." That jerk.

"Who?"

"Never mind." I couldn't believe I hadn't put the pieces together sooner. No wonder my parents had been acting extra weird lately. They'd both been suffering from *scanxiety*—the mess of emotions that followed a CT scan, MRI, X-ray, and other tests that Junie had to endure.

"Wait—" My brain screeched again. "You went to the hospital today? When?"

"Around one o'clock," Mom said.

"Oh." I must've just missed them. I was equal parts bummed and relieved.

"We looked for you, Isabel. But we couldn't wait around all day."

"Are you sure the tumor's not benign?" I asked. Benign, or *B-9* as Junie called it, was a fancy way to say harmless.

Dad's face softened. "We're sure, unfortunately. It's troubling that it wasn't detected sooner. But sometimes these things happen."

Now I felt like an unfittian. Stuck someplace between relief that my tree would be spared and fear that my sister wouldn't. Junie was right. An unfittian was a crummy thing to be.

Dad straightened up in his chair. "Junie's had her fair share of complications. Nothing is ever straightforward. But everyone agrees this is the best course of action. Assuming her blood counts are stable and she seems strong enough, the surgery could happen as early as Tuesday."

I almost spit out my food. So much for Chooseday. I'm pretty sure that was not what my sister had in mind for that day of the week.

"After the surgery, she'll finally be better? She'll come home for good?" I held my breath, waiting. I wanted answers, but part of me only wanted those answers if they were the right ones.

"She'll need time to recover, but then she should be able to come home. Of course, we'll still need to go back to the hospital for follow-up treatments.

There will be careful monitoring. Tests. Ongoing check-ins . . ."

Translation: more scanxiety plus a worstible list a mile long. I could feel worry creep into my body, see it reflected in my parents' faces. Settling dark and heavy beneath our eyes. Weighing even darker and heavier in our hearts. Pushing and shoving, bullying the fledgling seeds of hope I'd been trying to nurture.

"I'm going back to the hospital tonight to stay with Junie," Mom said. "You and Dad will meet us there tomorrow. Okay? We'll all spend the day with her. She really needs us now."

"She needs us *always*." I shouldn't have to tell them that. It annoyed me.

Something resembling guilt slid into Mom's tired eyes, joining the pooling worry. "This whole situation has been challenging. But we'll get through it." Her voice was unconvincing. She looked ready to crawl back to bed and never get out.

Dad put his hand on her shoulder, maybe to keep her from retreating upstairs. "First, let's finish dinner," he said, as if a slice of pizza was the answer to all our problems.

"You're right," Mom replied.

"Speaking of eating, we need to bring Junie something tomorrow," I said.

"What's that?" Dad asked.

"Ice cream. Plus bananas, whipped cream, cherries. And sprinkles. Lots of sprinkles."

"That's not a very healthy option," Mom said. "She barely has an appetite these days. And even if she were hungry, all that sweet stuff might not be good for her body."

"It's good for her soul," I replied.

"I don't know . . ."

"Well, I do. Junie might need medicine and surgery, but she needs a sundae too. I know it will make her feel better." I left out how I knew. About sneaking to the hospital and all that. Details shmetails.

Mom halfheartedly plucked at a glob of cheese.

"It's important," I said firmly. I took pity on the table and resisted slamming down my fist.

"All right." Dad reached for another slice. "We'll figure something out."

"Good." I picked the remaining pepperoni rounds off my pizza and arranged them into a smiley face on my plate.

Junie might not have a choice on Chooseday, but I would make sure Sundae happened.

CHAPTER 16

"Grab the bones and meet me at the millpond!" Dad hollered from the porch after Mom left for the hospital. Despite the news about that jerk Henry, the thought of some quality time with Dad perked me up. "And don't forget your glove!" he added.

I laced up my sneakers, then ran back to the kitchen. We always saved our pizza and bread crusts—which Junie nicknamed *bones*—to feed to the local birds wherever we lived. In New York City it'd been pigeons. In Louisville, crows. Magpies in Calgary. Geese in Philadelphia. Swans in Atlanta. Seagulls in San Francisco. And here in Bridgebury, ducks. Without Junie around to contribute her portion, the millpond mallards would have to make do with a lighter meal tonight.

"Got 'em!" I said, racing out into the yard.

Up ahead, Dad was peering through the cracked

workshop window at the dusty tools and unfinished projects inside. He turned and marched up the grassy hill. He paused to inspect the paint-flecked pickets of the fence at the top. He shook his head, then began to turn right.

"Let's take the back way!" I shouted, trying to catch up with him. I wished my new sneakers were imbued with a little extra magic. A turbo booster would've been real handy.

I ran to his side just as he reached a break in the fence where two footpaths diverged. Both routes met again down by the pond, but one led up the sloping hillside to the east, within eyeshot of the clearing. The other would steer us along the western perimeter of the orchard and a safe distance from my tree.

He took another step to the right.

I grabbed his shirt, nearly tearing the sleeve off. "The back way!"

"Whoa! Okay. The back way it is. But why?"

My mind spun. Letters shot out of my mouth. "PTCD! PTCD!"

"What?"

"PTCD!" I shrieked.

"Isabel! What on earth are you saying?"

"Post-traumatic chicken disorder! Remember?" I lifted the cuff on my jeans to reveal a scar on my leg. "The back route avoids the henhouse." When we first moved to Bridgebury, Junie begged me to take her to Mrs. Tolson's farm to see the animals. Big mistake. We'd barely gotten around to petting the sheep and piglets when a flock of crazy hens swooped in and chased us out, flapping and squawking and pecking at our ankles.

Dad tapped me gently on the head with his glove. "Good thinking. You're always looking out for us."

Yes, indeed. I was Isa, Protector and Defender of Sick Sisters and Distracted Fathers! Nincompoop nurses and cruel poultry, beware!

We set off westward, toward the sinking sun and safely away from the clearing, because I was also Isa, Protector of Magic Seedlings.

***

The ducks quacked happily as we tossed chunks of crust into the water. I wished we had more to feed them, but they didn't seem to mind. They were just grateful for the attention. I glanced over at my father. I felt the same.

Dad gave the last piece of crust to the smallest duckling. A runt, maybe, who kept getting pushed aside by the larger ducks. "Everyone deserves a chance.

Especially the little ones," he said quietly. Then he turned to me. "What do you say we throw something else?" He held up a softball. "A few window-breakers, perhaps? Without the destruction, preferably."

My heart swelled so much it just about busted through my ribcage. It had been such a long time since Dad and I played catch together. Since anything felt close to normal. Now I wanted to drink in every second, the way Kira drained a juice box to the last drop with her bendy straw.

"Is your team ready for the season?" he asked, tossing me a pop fly.

It sank into my glove with a satisfying *thump*.

"I hope so." I threw a curve ball, which curved the wrong way. He still managed to catch it and toss it back, arrow-straight. "Practice was canceled this week because of rain, so we're behind on some drills." The fastball I threw next lazed through the air, anything but fast. I didn't tell him I'd also skipped practice to see Junie. "Our opening game is against a team called the Carolton Minnows. Wimpy, right?"

"Minnows don't sound very intimidating, but that doesn't mean you shouldn't prepare."

He ripped a grounder across the grass. It was called a *wormburner*, a word that could trigger one of Junie's giggle meltdowns without fail. I crouched to scoop it up.

"Names can be deceiving, Isabel. Don't underestimate your opponents. Whatever happens, you always have to try your best."

I wished I could tell him about taking the bus by myself, about being brave. About making changes, like remembering names instead of numbers. About making friends. I was trying. I wanted him to see that. To see *me*.

I threw the ball.

He caught it and shook his head. "If you don't take practice seriously, those minnows might become piranhas." He started reciting his pitching pep talk. "Remember, don't pay attention to the batters. They're just distractions. Focus on home plate. And don't forget to watch your catcher. Trust her. Even if you think you know better. She can see things you can't."

"I know, Dad." A full-blown lecture was brewing and I just wanted to enjoy this time with him. "Our first game is in three weeks. Will you and Mom be there?"

He looked out at the horizon. "There's a lot going on right now, but we'll try."

Not the answer I wanted. I lobbed the ball, nice and straight. Finally. Maybe a little harder than necessary. "You'll try your best?" There was a tiny note of sarcasm in my voice.

"It's all we can do." He stared at me without

blinking, then turned and studied the orchard in the distance. "We should get going."

"Just a few more," I pleaded.

"It's getting dark."

"Please."

"Come on, Isa. Time to go. We'll play again soon."

"Soon?" I didn't have much faith in that word. Lately its definition could be as stretchy as a rubber band. I was standing right in front of my father, but I could feel him slipping out of reach.

"Wait," I said. "Did I tell you? Coach Naron is going to start me!" I blurted desperately.

He looked at me. "She is?"

I hadn't meant to tell a lie that big. I needed to fix this mistake, quickly. But then his eyes brightened and my throat tightened.

"Wow," he said. "A Fitzwilken starting on the mound again! Hasn't happened in a while. Since . . ."

"Since you, Dad."

"Right."

I could see the lie taking root. "So you'll be there? To watch me pitch?" Instead of backtracking, I watered that seed of dishonestly. I let it grow. It was reckless and downright stupid. But there was something in his expression that I couldn't let go of. "Dad?" I waved the ball. Tossed it.

"Opening game. Wouldn't miss it. I promise." He caught the ball and sent it back as a high arc in the plum-colored sky.

My heart followed. Soaring up, then down. The ball landed perfectly in my glove, like an egg in a nest. But my heart landed somewhere on the ground with a smack. I grimaced and swallowed hard, trying to make the bittersweet taste of the lie go away.

"You all right?" Dad asked.

"Bug flew in my mouth," I fibbed. Again. Heck, might as well go for a new record.

"Let's go back to the house and get you some water. Need to keep my star pitcher hydrated." Dad took off his glove and tucked it under his arm. I did the same.

We walked home, side by side, grazing the tips of the overgrown apple branches with our palms. A chorus of peepers began warming up for their evening recital, a far cry from Gregory's misfit orchestra. By the time we reached the break in the fence, constellations sprinkled across the sky. Standing on top of the hill, the moon looked so close. I wanted to reach up and pluck it from the darkness and cradle it in my leather glove.

Dad knocked a crooked fence picket upright with his knuckles. He yanked out a few pesky weeds. He tightened the loose gate latch in the moonlight. "Lot of fixing to do," he said. Then he reached out and clasped my hand. He squeezed it three times.

I. Love. You.

I should have told him the truth, then and there. I wasn't the starting pitcher, not yet at least. I'd visited Junie by myself. I'd made a new friend. Two, actually, if you counted the chance seedling. Three, if you counted the squirrel.

But I didn't say anything. I only held on tight and squeezed his hand back. One, two, three. Too afraid to let go. Too afraid of ruining the moment, and becoming invisible again.

CHAPTER 17

Hours later, that same milky moon flooded my room, washing everything in a thick coat of pearl. But that's not what woke me up. It was a noise. Not peepers or raccoons banging around by the trash cans or the haunting hoots of an owl.

It was music.

Strange humming and ringing, carried by the night wind in soft breaths. I bolted upright in bed. Was I having another one of those weird dreams? I pinched my arm. No. I was awake and the sound was real.

I scanned my bedroom, searching for the source. The alarm clock next to my bed was quiet. I got up and pressed my ear against the wall to see if the music was coming from my parents' room. Nope. Just Dad snoring.

My backpack lay in a pool of moonlight on the

floor. My eyes went right to the zipper. To what *wasn't* attached to it. The bell.

A wonderful realization: The tree had bloomed!

A not-so-wonderful realization: If I didn't shut it up quick, this crop would wake the entire neighborhood. And the secret would be a secret no more.

***

I didn't bother with shoes or ninja-stealth. I just ran. The dew was surprisingly cold. My toes may have been numb, but my mind was sharp, my legs quick. Approaching the clearing was like diving headfirst into an orchestra pit. The wind swept notes into the air like brush strokes on canvas. I never realized sound came in so many colors.

As my eyes adjusted to the darkness, I spied hundreds of buds along the tree's branches, clustered in rows like lily of the valley blossoms, only bigger. As they ripened, papery casings split open and bells emerged. Ringing, tinkling, chiming! I spun around, wet toes in tall grass. Drenched in song and moonlight and hope. The tree swayed with me, its leaves pulsing and glowing like the bioluminescent jellyfish Ms. Perdilla once showed us in class.

My ears were so full they didn't hear Kira approach.

I nearly leapt out of my skin when I felt her hand on my shoulder. She was wearing a fuzzy robe and slippers soggy with dew. And a smile from ear to ear, just like me. We let the tree sing for a few more minutes, dancing together and adding our own chorus of laughter, in perfect harmony.

"I could hear it from my bedroom," Kira shouted.

"Me too. Which means if we don't start harvesting now, the whole town will be out here wondering what's causing such a ruckus."

I was thankful we didn't live on Drabbington Avenue or in one of those sardine-can developments where you shared a backyard the size of a postage stamp with your neighbors. Still, one call from ornery Mrs. Tolson, and we were done for. She'd probably sic her evil chickens on us as punishment for waking her up.

Kira pulled two plastic grocery bags from her pockets.

"At least one of us came prepared," I said gratefully.

We started picking the lowest-hanging bells, filling the bags quickly.

"I think they call this a bumper crop," Kira said, reaching for a fresh cluster of silver bells.

As soon as we'd silence one bunch, another would bloom. We hadn't even started climbing yet. This was going to be a long, loud night.

"At this rate, we'll never get them all. Someone is bound to hear."

"Well, I can't move any faster!" Kira's long arms windmilled frantically as she picked and stuffed, picked and stuffed.

"Me neither." I paused to wipe sweat from my brow.

The wind grew stronger, amplifying the music.

"Shhh!" I commanded. "Shhhhhhh!"

Another gust. The wind refused to be hushed.

"What are we going to do? We can't keep up like this!" Kira squawked.

Then the tree sort of shivered and the music hit a crescendo. I dropped my bag to the ground. The branches shook, and the bells fell. All at once. Every one.

An enormous silence followed. Clouds moved across the sky, swaddling the moon and wrapping us in a soundless and pitch-black night. I wished the seedling would start glowing again, but it had turned as dark as the sky. I couldn't see a thing. I wanted to call out to Kira, but the words wouldn't budge. Finally, the clouds shifted, and the moonlight illuminated the orchard below.

"Phew. There are." I glanced over at Kira. She was standing, frozen, a few feet away. The sudden darkness must have spooked her a little too. "I was worried you'd disappeared," I said, sort of half laughing. "Usually I'm the invisible one."

Kira didn't laugh back. She turned to face me. "You've said that a few times before. But you know, Isa, you're not invisible to me. I always see you."

A little lump formed in my throat. It was quite possibly the nicest thing anyone had said to me in a long time. "Thanks," I mumbled, determined not to cry. "I, um, I see you too."

A twig snapped and we both jumped. Something moved along the edge of the clearing, shaking the branches of one apple tree, and then another.

"Hello?" I called out. The seedling's bark flared bright green and yellow, like a warning. The meadow grasses quivered. Another twig snapped. "It's coming toward us," I said.

"Maybe we should climb the tree? To get out of the way?" Kira whimpered, huddling against the trunk.

Suddenly the grass in front of us parted and a tiny head popped up. Not a fearsome beast or creepy creature. Just the scrappy little squirrel with the notched ear. His glassy black eyes blinked at us.

"Seriously?! We thought there might be a monster out there, and it was just you?" I wagged my finger in the squirrel's direction. "Ugh! You scared us, you sneaky rascal!"

The squirrel stood up on his hind legs, aghast. *Who, me?*

Kira groaned. "Just when I thought things couldn't get any weirder, you start talking to a rat."

"He's not a rat. He's a squirrel. And he's partially responsible for this." I turned around and gave the tree a little pat. "Remember the story I told you? Planting the old sneakers was his idea."

The squirrel puffed up his chest proudly. It was impossible to stay angry at him; he was too cute.

"Did the music wake you up?" I asked, kneeling down.

The squirrel scratched his notched ear, then nodded his head. He pawed a few bells lying in the grass, sniffing around for something to nibble.

"Sorry, no nuts today." The squirrel looked up, disappointed. A moment later, he turned and dashed away through the orchard, snapping twigs and rustling leaves as he went.

"Um, okay. Nice to see you too," I called after him. "Jeez. I didn't even get to say thanks."

"For what?" Kira balked. "Scaring us silly?"

"No. For helping me believe in . . . you know . . ."

"You mean magic?" Kira said, using the word with ease.

I eyed the glittering harvest scattered in the grass.

It had taken me a while to warm up to the idea, but now I embraced it. "Exactly." I reached down to grab one of the bells. It shriveled and disintegrated. Only pale, silver dust remained. Kira gasped.

"This happened before, with the shoes," I said. All around us, bells were starting to disappear. I tied up my bag so no others would fall out. It jangled nicely. "I think we have plenty. We don't really need thousands of bells anyway."

"You're probably right." Kira looked into her own bag. She retrieved a round copper bell as big as a softball. "Come to think of it, what are we going to do with the ones we have?" She took a few steps backward, then tossed the bell in my direction. It soared through the air with a tinkling whistle.

I caught it, then lobbed it back.

"You've got a good arm," she said, making the catch.

"Thanks. You too." I suddenly felt uneasy. I hadn't guessed her softball position before, and we hadn't had practice together since then. There was a chance we might be in direct competition for the opening game. "Kira, are you a pitcher too?"

"No way! Are you crazy?" she bellowed. "I could never stand up there on the mound like you. Everyone watching me. Way too stressful. Pitching requires serious focus. Plus bravery. And consistency. Not to mention talent. And strength. Mental and physical. And . . ."

"Wow. Thanks for that boost of confidence." If I was going to be our team's starting pitcher, I was going to need a lot more practice.

"I'm the catcher, silly," Kira said.

"Oh! That's awesome." I remembered Dad's lecture from earlier that evening. Pitchers and catchers needed to work together. Kira and I could do that. I took a few steps back and threw a curveball, or curve-*bell*, in this case.

To my dismay, the bell turned the wrong way, rising upward. It vanished into the tree's underbelly. I thought it was lost for good. Then the canopy made some crinkly, crunchy sounds, and the bell, chiming softly, sailed back down, directly into Kira's open palm. "Huh?"

"Was that you, or the tree?" I asked.

"I think it was a little of both. Let's try again." She pitched the bell straight up. For a split second, I was worried it might break the tree's crystal leaves, but the branches quickly shifted and stretched. In the moonlight, it was hard to tell exactly what was happening, but it looked as if a cluster of leaves cupped the bell, then released it back down toward me. I caught it.

"Nice throw," I said, staring up.

"Just when I thought we reached peak weirdness talking to a squirrel and harvesting bells in the middle of the night, we start playing catch with a tree!" Kira said gleefully.

"Hey, anything is possible."

The tree pulsed with color, showing us that it agreed.

"That gives me an idea," Kira said. "Let's make up some pitching hand signals. If we're paired together during practice, we'll have an edge."

"I love that idea! Plus, I need all the help I can get."

We tossed the copper bell back and forth, with the tree fielding some of our wilder throws now and then. Soon we developed a secret language. We had signals for fastballs, changeups, curveballs, and even my specialty—the window-breaker.

When our arms grew tired, Kira tucked the bell back into her bag. "We still need to decide what we're going to do with the rest of these."

I wanted to share their beautiful music, without completely giving away the secret of the tree. But how?

Then it was crystal clear.

"The hospital!" I cried. "We have more than

enough bells for every kid on Junie's floor. Gregory's orchestra is about to get a whole lot bigger and a whole lot better sounding!"

"That's a great plan," Kira said, biting her lip. "But I'm just skeptical about the execution."

"I'll bring them tomorrow when I go with my parents. Easy peasy."

"Except how do you explain a bagful of mystery bells? They're noisy. Not exactly easy to smuggle." She began twirling a strand of hair around her fingertip. "I guess you could bring one at a time. Attach it to your keychain or something? No one would suspect anything."

"Hmm. That would take way too long. Those kids will be in the geriatric wing before I have time to deliver each bell. This might be trickier than I initially thought."

"What if we shipped them?" she said.

"In the mail?"

"Why not? We'll say it's a donation."

"An anonymous donation for musical enrichment." I nodded. "I like it. It just might work."

Kira touched the end of her ponytail, like it reminded her of something. "I mail a package to my dad every week. I'll tell my mom I need to send him a big one this time."

"Will she wonder why you're sending him a box of bells?"

"I'll say it's a school project or something." She let go of her hair. "Since the divorce, she doesn't want anything to do with him. I doubt she'll investigate the contents too closely."

I thought about what Kira said earlier, about seeing me. I wanted to show her that I saw her too. "Do you get to visit him often?" I asked, sitting down in the grass, leaning my back against the tree's warm bark. I knew how it felt to miss a parent. I could still feel the gentle squeeze of my dad's hand from earlier that evening.

Beside me, the tree's twisted trunk shifted, forming a space like a backrest, inviting Kira to sit too. Maybe even trying to comfort her. She nestled into the hollow. "Not really. I used to visit him once or twice a year when he lived a few states over. But then he moved all the way across the country. Near Seattle. I've never flown that far by myself. I'm not sure my mom would actually let me."

"Seattle is one place I've never lived," I said. "Which is impressive, since we've lived in eight different cities so far. Actually, Bridgebury is the ninth."

"Nine? That is a lot."

"Tell me about it. Sometimes it feels like we've lived everywhere and nowhere." I thought about all the moving trucks, all the apartments, all the new schools and packing and good-byes. "Nine moves for me. Two before Junie was born. This is number seven for her."

"Lucky number seven?"

"Some luck." I closed my eyes, remembering what my parents had told me during dinner. I felt the scar on my tongue from the pizza burn. The ache in my heart, the clawing worry. "She has another tumor."

"What?" Kira sat up. "Junie? No."

"Yup. She calls this one Henry." Every word hurt.

"Oh, Isa." Kira reached an arm over and wrapped it around my shoulders. "Why didn't you say something sooner?"

"My parents knew for a little while, but I just found out tonight. Actually, Junie mentioned Henry briefly yesterday, but I got distracted and forgot all about him." The tree grew warmer as I spoke. I knew it was listening too. Tears pressed behind my eyelids, but I wouldn't let them out. If I did, I was afraid they'd never stop.

I didn't resist Kira's hug. I even hugged her back. It wasn't quite a squg, but it did feel a bit like one of the softball signals we'd just invented—a way to send an important message without words.

Kira let go of me and leaned back against the tree. Her face turned serious.

"What are you thinking about?" I asked.

She didn't answer right away. "I'm just thinking that it's probably good you never lived where my dad does." She started fiddling with her hair again. "Apparently it rains all the time there. That's what he wrote in his last postcard. But that was months ago, so who knows what the weather is up to now." She shrugged. "Anyway, it doesn't sound like a place I'd really want to visit." Except everything in her voice and her moonlit face said the opposite.

"Couldn't he come to Bridgebury to see you instead?" I asked.

"He keeps saying he will. But we've been here for two years already and he hasn't come once." Kira fidgeted uncomfortably. She reached into her bag and cupped several small bells in her hand. "Listen to these," she said, changing the subject. Avoiding the conversation and the feelings that went along with it.

I knew how that felt. So I gave her lots of space and quiet, in case there was more she wanted to say.

She sighed, letting the bells roll across her palm. "Such glorious tintinnabulation."

I giggled. "Is that one of your fancy vocabulary words?"

"Indeed," she said in a smarty-pants voice. "It

means the ringing of bells. A perfecterrific word for this occasion, I think." Kira looked down. "They're so small and they look so delicate, but they make such a big sound."

I knew all about that idea too. Sometimes little things could be incredibly powerful. My sister was proof. So was the tiny acorn that the squirrel had buried months ago.

Kira yawned. "We should get back home. It's late and I'm sleepy." She returned the bells to the bag, then stood up and stretched her legs. "You know, I'm a little relieved."

"Why?" I didn't want to leave the tree's warmth, but I rose to my feet, shivering as the cool spring air hit my skin. I wished I were wearing my cozy flannel pajamas instead of my cotton nightgown.

"It's dumb, really. I mean, you planted a bell, so it makes sense. But we had all sorts of cookies. And the shoe harvest was pretty diverse, right? You got boots and cleats and sneakers. So I wasn't really sure what to expect this time." She shrugged. "This might sound crazy, but I actually imagined clarinets and cellos and French horns drooping from the branches."

I laughed at the image. "How about a tuba? Or bongo drums!" I drummed my hands against my thighs and stomped to the beat.

"A didgeridoo would've been funny," Kira said.

"Anything's an improvement over instruments made from bedpans and pill bottles. Imagine *that* symphony." I wheeled around and pointed at the tree. "Don't get any ideas!" The tree's bark turned deep magenta, like it was blushing, which made us laugh all over again.

CHAPTER 18

There's a reason sprinkles, whipped cream, and cherries are called *fixings*. They'll fix a bad mood or a worried heart real quick. Maybe they'd even fix a case of Nephew-Blast-o-Rama, as Junie called it.

Dad pushed a cart down the freezer aisle at the market, while I filled it with pints of our favorites: rocky road for Junie (which seemed to accurately describe our life lately), pistachio for Mom, strawberry for Dad, and mint chocolate chip for me.

The whole time, Dad kept saying, "Anything for my girls!" with a smile pulled across his face. But when the cashier packed everything into a cooler, I could see Dad cringe as he handed over the credit card to pay.

As we drove out of town, we passed my school and the softball diamond. I was itching to get out there and practice on Monday. Dad was quiet, deep in his own thoughts. I missed Kira's chatterboxing. And the stash of juice boxes her mom kept in the back seat. My throat was dry, probably from nerves. All four of us Fitzwilkens would be together, which was fantastic. I just wished our little reunion wasn't taking place at the hospital.

✳ ✳ ✳

Inside Delorna Regional Hospital, I led the way, now comfortable taking the elevator and navigating the corridors by myself. Dad trailed behind, lugging the cooler.

When we arrived on Junie's floor, we greeted the receptionist at the front desk. I watched the mobile with clouds and rocket ships rotate around and around while Dad checked us in. We stopped to disinfect our hands, then made our way past the colorful murals, toward Junie's room.

I opened the door. "Look what we brought!" I sang, brimming with excitement.

Junie and Mom weren't there.

"Ooph." Dad placed the cooler on the floor and rubbed his back. "That thing is heavy! I hope your sister's hungry."

"Me too." I really hoped she was feeling more awesomesauce than barftastic today.

"I'll go see if I can track down our favorite ladies," Dad said. "I bet they're in the activity room."

As soon as he was gone, I reached into my pocket and pulled out a silvery iridescent bell the size of a golf ball. It shined so brightly that it practically glowed. A minute later, I heard the heavy clomp of Dad's stride down the corridor, followed by the ticky-click of Mom's heels. Without a second to spare, I tucked the bell under Junie's pillow.

"Special delivery for my Junebug!" Dad entered the room and lifted the cooler over his head like the heavyweight champion of the world.

Mom appeared next, pushing Junie in a wheel-chair. She must have felt too weak to walk, which was not a good sign. But when she saw me, she rose to her feet. I swooped in for a sisterly squg. The purple cap was back on her head and she was wearing uni-corn pajamas paired with a green sequined tutu. The sparkling ruffles reminded me of the seedling and its crown of glittering leaves. When Junie smiled up at me, her nose, chin and cheeks had to scoot and squish, just to make room for all that happy. I returned the smile, wishing I could bottle up the look on her face and save it for a rainy day.

Dad set the cooler down and hugged Junie next. We all knew she was light as a feather, but he made a fuss about how big she was getting, how strong, how healthy. Everything that was true was the opposite. We played along, and it didn't feel like lying. It felt like hoping.

Dad carried her over to the bed, still pretending she weighed as much as a bag of bowling balls. Junie chanted, "Hooray, hooray for Sundae! Yumday! Funday!"

I joined in, praying no one would rearrange the pillows on her bed and reveal the hidden bell.

Mom set up an ice cream buffet on a table and pushed it against the edge of Junie's bed. She peeled and sliced ripe bananas, then arranged them artfully inside paper bowls. Junie smacked her lips and pointed to the flavors and fixings she wanted.

"Whipped cream. Don't skimp. Extra sprinkles, please. Good. And a few more blue-flavored candies, too." She clapped her hands excitedly.

"Junie, blue isn't a flavor," I said, covering my own sundae with a drizzle of caramel sauce.

"Sure it is. If red is a flavor, then so is blue."

"Red's not a flavor either," I said, which made my mom laugh. "Cherry is a flavor. So is strawberry. Those are usually red colored."

"Shows how much you know." Junie snorted. "Mama, can you crumble some cookies on top too?"

"Sure, baby." She picked up the plate of cookies

that Kira and I had left behind yesterday. "Did you buy these at the market the other day, Nathan?"

"Nope," he answered. "Don't know where they came from."

Mom dropped pieces of the chocolate hazelnut delights into Junie's bowl. She snuck a taste. "Mmm. They're even better than the ones we used to make at the bakery. Who brought these?"

"Isa—"

"Sure, I'll take some!" I interrupted. "Nurse Minkey, er, Edith made the cookies for you, right?" I did my best to wink at Junie without our parents seeing.

Junie stared at me. My eyes practically bugged out of my head. This would be so much easier if we were mind readers, or at least had some sister-code signal for this type of thing.

"No, not Edith," Junie said.

Come on! Work with me here! I made my eyes even bigger.

"It was another nurse," Junie said, frowning at me. "She baked them for the whole floor. Gregory and his orchestra got some too."

"That's a nice gesture. I should ask her for the recipe. I've never tasted anything quite like it." Mom took another bite. "Nathan, could you pass the pint of pistachio, please?"

Their curiosity about the cookies seemed satisfied for the moment, but Junie studied me, like she couldn't figure out why I wanted her to fib.

"Dig in!" Dad said, plunking a cherry on top of his own towering sundae.

For a few delicious minutes, we almost forgot we were in the hospital. Junie and I took turns sporting silly whipped cream mustaches. Dad entertained us by tossing candies into the air and trying to catch them with his mouth. He was much better at catching things with a baseball glove. Like his fwapjacks, most of the candies ended up on the floor. Mom sliced more bananas and probably didn't even realize she was humming. The fixings did their job, at least temporarily.

But our cozy family bubble was just that—a bubble. The moment Dr. Ebbens came into the room, it popped. The doctor nudged his glasses up the bridge of his nose and examined the scene. I thought he might scold us, until he said, "Ah, yes. Just what the doctor ordered."

"Would you like some?" Mom offered, looking guiltily down at the sweet spread.

"That's kind of you, but no thank you."

Junie held up her bowl. "Ice creamo-therapy, Doc."

"Clever as always. You might be missing a kidney, but your funny bone is still in working order," he replied with a hearty chuckle. He turned to my parents. "Mr. and Mrs. Fitzwilken, could I speak with you alone for a moment?"

"Of course." Mom and Dad looked like they'd been called into the principal's office.

"There's a consult room available down the hall. We can meet in there."

"Will you girls be okay here for a little while?" Mom asked, placing her bowl on the table and wiping her lips with a paper towel.

We nodded in unison.

"Good. Don't make yourselves sick eating too much sugar, understand?"

As if sugar was the biggest of Junie's worries.

***

"I think I might be a real princess," Junie announced in a raspy voice as soon as the grown-ups left the room.

"Why's that?" I added another scoop of mint ice cream to my bowl.

"I could feel this! All the way through one, two, three pillows!" She dug her hand behind her back and retrieved the bell I'd stashed there.

"It's not exactly pea-sized, Junie. But, sure, you probably are a real princess. I think that's what the doctor wanted to tell Mom and Dad. Maybe one of those blood tests finally revealed your royal heritage."

"It's about time. I always knew it." She inspected the bell. "What I don't know is why you put it there. And why couldn't I tell Mom and Dad that you visited with Kira and brought me cookies?"

"Because Kira's mom didn't bake those cookies." I paused. "And because Mom and Dad don't know I snuck here to see you."

"Sneaking, huh? Sounds a little dangerous."

I wiggled my eyebrows. "You're worth it."

"Because I'm a real princess?"

"Even if you weren't."

"But I am," she said, completely serious.

"I know."

"So, who did bake these?" Junie extracted cookie chunks from her melting sundae.

I'd waited so long to tell her the secret, and here was my shot. I paused for effect, and then I said, "A tree." My whole body buzzed with delight, and also lots of sugar. I waited eagerly for my sister's reaction. I pictured imaginary fireworks exploding with color above us, confetti cannons blasting, trumpets blaring.

Instead, Junie stared at me blankly. Her eyebrows had fallen out months ago, but the place where they should have been lifted up so high that the patch of skin almost disappeared beneath her purple cap. Then she put down her sundae and laughed in my face.

"Ha! Ha! Riiiight." She rolled her eyes. "You're telling me blue's not a flavor, but trees can bake cookies? Good one, Isa." She practically cackled. "I think somebody needs to go for a ride in the donut machine and get her head checked." The donut machine was what she called the CT scanner, because it was big and round with a hole in the middle.

Kira warned me that Junie might not believe the story. I couldn't really blame my sister—the truth did sound pretty strange. "The tree didn't exactly bake the cookies," I explained. "The tree *grew* them!" I sat back and waited for her to erupt with wonder and amazement. "It grew that bell too."

She peered at me skeptically, then she clicked her tongue along the roof of her mouth. "Suuuure. That makes so much more sense."

"It's true! You know I'd never lie to you. Don't tell me the doctors took out your imagination when they removed Willie and Pablo?"

"I don't think they did." She took off her knit cap and scratched her head. "You're saying trees can grow cookies and bells?"

"And shoes!" Before she could roll her eyes again, I added, "It's not just any tree, Junie. It's a chance seedling." I took her hand in mine. "Do you remember the stories about our property? The wacky things people would whisper about our orchard whenever we said we lived in the old Melwick place?"

She shifted in her bed. "One girl in my class told me the apples would turn your skin purple if you ate one."

"I never heard that, but okay. My point is, the stories are true. At least a part of them is true."

She reached over and lifted up the sleeve of my shirt. She inspected my arm. "You don't look purple to me. If the stories were true, you'd be purple, wouldn't you?"

"No. No. No. I didn't eat an apple. There are still no apples. But there is a new tree. It's unlike anything else in the orchard. It sprouted right in the middle of the clearing. That funny squirrel with the notched ear planted an acorn there in the fall. Remember? We used to watch him burying nuts all over the place."

"Sure I do. That rascal stole a nut straight out of our Cabinet of Curiosities!"

"He did? When?"

"In the fall, before I got sick. I had the wooden box on the front porch one afternoon. I found some speckled pebbles, a red maple leaf, and this really pretty acorn. I arranged everything in the box, with the acorn smack dab in the middle. Then I went inside to get a spoon to mix up some mud pies. When I came back, the acorn was gone. I looked everywhere. Then I saw that squirrel's furry little behind making a run for it down the driveway."

"Huh. Well, who knows if it was the same acorn, but whatever that squirrel planted in the clearing grew into the most beautiful thing I've ever seen."

"What? I thought I was the most beautiful thing you'd ever seen!" She batted her eyelids, smooshed her nose up like a piglet's snout, and stuck out her tongue.

"Lovely," I said. "I suppose the tree is a close second."

"Better answer." Junie grinned. "What does it look like?"

"It's taller than the apple trees, and the bark swirls. The trunk is huge and twisty. The leaves sparkle, almost like your tutu." I jumped up and grabbed a crayon and a sheet of paper from the little desk in the corner of the room, but nothing I sketched could do the real tree justice. I crumpled up the paper and threw it away.

"How does it work?" Junie asked, her cheeks pinker by the minute. She was starting to believe, I could tell.

"If you plant something in the ground, right at the base of its trunk, these blue roots wiggle down through the dirt like tiny snakes."

"Blue roots?"

"Yup. They curl around whatever you plant. And then fruit grows."

"Fruit?" Her nose wrinkled. "I thought you said there were no apples."

"Not normal fruit. They're more like pods, with these bizarre peels. Wrapped up inside are versions of whatever you planted. Like shoes. Or cookies. Or bells. Sometimes it takes a day, sometimes longer for them to ripen. Which is crazy, because most trees take months to produce fruit."

Junie tugged the strings on her cap. Her expression changed. "Isa, are you trying to tell me that this tree is . . . magic?"

I bit my lip. "What else could it be?"

"But you don't believe in magic."

I shook my head. "I didn't at first. But then I saw it, smelled it, touched it, tasted it, heard it. It's real, Junie."

She sank into the pillows. She sighed. "As soon I go away, all the fun stuff happens. Phooey." Then she sat up and clasped one of my hands. Her skin was warm. Her eyes twinkled. "Tell me everything!"

So I did, and Junie gobbled up every detail. I wondered if her heart was racing as quickly as mine. I described the glowing bark, the shifting branches. The way things blossomed, then dissolved into the grass. I shook the iridescent bell and filled the hospital room with music.

"I wish I could see it. I mean, meet it." She was excited, but I could also see exhaustion setting in. Her eyelids began to droop. She'd probably need a power nap soon.

"You will. As soon as you get better and come home."

"What are you going to plant next?" She yawned, reaching for the bell. She tucked it under her pillow, as though it were a seed for dreaming.

"I don't know what to plant. Any suggestions? Or requests?"

Her voice dropped low and serious. "Whatever it is, be careful what you wish for. That's what all the fairy tales say." She rested her head on the pillow and pulled her quilt up under her chin.

"A very wise princess you are."

"Oh! I know!" Her face lit up. Just as she was about to tell me her brilliant idea, Mom and Dad walked in. Mom's face was long, Dad's eyes stormier than usual.

"What did the doctor say?" I asked, bolting upright, alarmed by their expressions.

"Nothing," Mom replied. She started cleaning up our sundae buffet. "Nothing for you to worry about, that is." Her words were paper-doll flat. Dad stood in the corner, talking on his cell phone with someone from his office. His voice was prickly.

"Dr. Ebbens must've said something," I pressed.

"Everything's fine." Maybe Mom thought we were still playing the opposite game.

Junie and I stared at each other. We still hadn't figured out how to read minds, but I'm pretty sure we both agreed our parents had been replaced by zombie robots. Or maybe Dr. Ebbens had given them brain transplants in the brief time they'd been gone. Not even Gregory's musicians clanging and banging down the hall could snap them out of their trance. I plugged my ears and winced.

Then a smile flickered across Junie's face and mine, too, as we enjoyed our shared secret. Soon the little orchestra would sound a whole lot better.

CHAPTER 19

I was afraid my parents would make us pack up and leave right away, but after Junie took a power nap Mom pulled a stack of cards from her purse and dangled it like bait in front of Dad's face. He put his phone away and joined us for a few games of Go Fish. I'd started to wonder if my parents would ever relax and be silly with us again, but as we played, we fell into an easy rhythm, teasing each other like we used to.

Paulette came by to take Junie's temperature and blood pressure and whatever else needed checking, and then we were all ready for a change of scenery. As we wheeled Junie down the halls, she waved at everyone—kids, nurses, doctors, even a janitor. Unlike me, Junie made friends wherever we went. She was warm and bubbly and easy to love. Everyone on her floor seemed to know her name, which made me feel happy and then incredibly sad. Over the last few months, she'd spent more time in that hospital than at home.

Mom proposed joining some other families in the activity room for a craft project, but Junie said she was too tired. She must've been truly wiped out, because I'd never seen that kid turn down glue and glitter. When we got back to her room, Mom gave Junie some water to drink. Dad helped her into bed. I made sure the gray rabbit with the torn ear was tucked under her arm. She fell asleep quickly, snoring like a miniature warthog. When she used to sleep in my bed, her snoring drove me absolutely bonkers. Now I thought it was the cutest sound in the entire world.

Mom asked in a quiet voice if I wanted to go home. I told her I'd rather stay and keep Junie company for a bit longer.

"Okay, baby. Do you mind if Dad and I grab a coffee in the cafeteria? We'll just be gone for a few minutes. You want something? A soda?"

She never let us drink soft drinks, but apparently today was an exception to all the rules. "Sure," I said. "A Coke?"

"You got it."

I looked at the clock on the wall. I resisted counting the minutes until they returned. I crossed the room and curled up on the couch by the window. The sun was starting to set. I closed my eyes, thinking about the day we'd spent together as a family. I wanted more of these days. I wanted this to be every day, minus the hospital and cancer part, of course.

I must have drifted off to sleep, because when I woke up my parents were back in the room, speaking in hushed voices. I was facing the window, so they hadn't seen me open my eyes. Junie was snoring away. I kept still and listened carefully. I knew it was wrong to eavesdrop, but I needed to know the real story behind their meeting with Dr. Ebbens, not some candy-coated version.

Mom's shoes clicked as she walked toward me. I shut my eyes. "She's out," Mom said softly. She covered me with one of Junie's extra blankets. "I don't blame her. It's been a long day." She walked back across the room.

"It's been a long year," Dad replied.

"Tell me about it." Mom sounded drained. "So? What about Lewis? I know it's a matter of pride, but we don't have many options. We're running out of time to figure this out."

Running out of time? What did they need to figure out?

"I already spoke to him. He'll help as much as he can. But he has a family of his own to support. This is more than any of us ever expected." Dad's words were unsteady. "We have the mortgage, utility bills, groceries. We're still behind on our payments from the last round of treatments, not to mention all these recent scans and tests. Plus the upcoming surgery." He exhaled a heavy breath. I could tell he was making calculations in his brain—not minutes and hours like I did, but dollars and cents. "Even with our insurance, this could bankrupt us."

I knew it. Everything was not fine.

"I'll speak with the billing department again," Mom said. "Maybe we can work something out. The social worker offered to help us apply for some aid packages as well."

"It's worth a shot, but the health care system is so complex."

"The system is broken," Mom snapped, a little too loudly.

I heard Junie rustle in bed. Mom and Dad stopped talking. A few seconds later, Junie was snoring again. I opened my eyes, just a sliver. I could see my parents' reflections in the window. Dad's arm was wrapped around Mom's shoulders. Her head was buried in his chest. He squeezed her gently, three times. I. Love. You. "We'll figure this out," he said. "In the meantime, I'll pick up more shifts at work. We can sell one of the cars."

Mom sat up. "Why don't we sell a few acres of the orchard?"

I felt queasy. I couldn't let them do that.

"I've looked into that too. Turns out our land is more of a liability than an asset. People are superstitious about the Melwick trees."

Mom huffed. "That's just small-town gossip. There's no truth to those ludicrous stories, Nathan."

If they only knew.

"Well, no one can farm those trees, but no one wants to cut them down either. Better to just forget they're there at all."

My hands tightened into fists. I sure as heck didn't want some developer cutting down the orchard to build shops and parking lots, but the trees didn't deserve to be forgotten, either.

"There's value in the house, of course," Dad continued, "but that would mean . . ."

"I'll call the hardware store in town," Mom interrupted, like she refused to entertain whatever Dad was about to say. "Helen Ritter said they're hiring."

That hardly seemed like a good solution either. Mom poured all her energy into caring for Junie, then basically collapsed each afternoon. I couldn't imagine her juggling a new job too. Especially one involving hammers and nails instead of whisks and measuring cups.

"But if we're both working all day, who will take care of Junie and Isabel?" Mom added, her voice ragged. I ached listening to them, but I was also reassured to know I wasn't a TLC—a Truly Lost Cause. "What's the point of all this, if it forces us to abandon the girls when they need us the most?"

Dad coughed. "We're not abandoning anyone."

"This hasn't been easy for either of them, Nathan."

"I know," Dad said wearily. "At least Isa's channeling her energy in positive ways." My heart plumped up. "Did she tell you? Coach Naron is going to start her in the opening game. It's a big deal. I promised her we would be there."

Ugh. My poor, guilty heart shriveled like a raisin.

"You did? But if . . ."

"We have to try our best, Nel."

Paulette walked in to check on Junie again, and the conversation abruptly came to a halt. A few minutes later, Mom came over and rubbed my back. "Wake up, Isa. Time to go."

I opened my eyes slowly. "I don't want to go."

"I know, but it's a school night. Dad's going to take you home. I'll stay with Junie. You need to get a good night's rest. I'll see you tomorrow after school."

"Okay." I yawned as though I'd actually slept through their entire conversation.

"Here, baby." She handed me a can of soda. "Just don't drink it now. Otherwise the caffeine will keep you up all night."

Caffeine was the least of my worries. There were plenty of other things guaranteed to keep me up worrying until the wee hours.

CHAPTER 20

I buckled my seatbelt and stretched my legs across the back seat as the car's engine rumbled to life and we left the hospital.

Good-bye, good-bye. Repeating like a catchy but annoying song on the radio that gets stuck in your head for days.

Good-bye. Good. Bye. Nothing good about it.

As we merged onto the highway and picked up speed, my mind raced.

Dad turned up the radio and sang along to the lyrics. "You can't always get what you want. But if you try sometimes, well you might find, you get what you need . . ." He played the steering wheel like a drum, and hit some high notes that hurt my ears but made me laugh. "You can't always get what you want," he sang as the song ended, "unless what you want is a hamburger."

"Was that a question?" I giggled. "Or your attempt at songwriting?"

Dad smiled at me in the rearview mirror. "There aren't enough songs about hamburgers, if you ask me."

"Now you're making me hungry," I said.

"Then you're in luck. There's a fast food place off the next exit."

"That sounds good." I couldn't believe I was actually hungry again after that gigantic sundae.

Dad signaled and changed lanes. "I think Junie really enjoyed our visit today," he said.

"Me too." I tried to sound upbeat, but it was hard to pretend I didn't know what was really going on.

The car jolted to a stop at the drive-thru window. Our station wagon was pretty old and clunky; surely it wouldn't fetch enough money to pay all our bills. Besides, if we did sell it, we'd be left with just one car. Between trips to the hospital, the pharmacy, school, work, softball, and all the other places we needed to go each week, I couldn't figure out how my family would function without it. Things would've been a lot easier if we still lived in a city, with public transportation options like trains and buses. Bridgebury did have the county bus line, but there were only a few routes and those ran infrequently.

Selling the car just didn't make sense. There had to be another way to find the money we needed. While I ate my french fries in the back seat, I brainstormed a plan and got to work.

I began rooting around for coins, which was like an archeological dig. I wedged my fingers between the seat cushions and unearthed a few ancient Crunchy-FunPuffs! Next I discovered a crayon, a chunk of pre-historic pretzel, and a tag from a dress Mom bought at a thrift shop. I reached deeper.

I pulled out a paper doll. We could never afford the fancy ones in the stationery store that Junie wanted, so I'd made this one, and many others, by hand. I inspected the doll. She was about ten inches tall, made from faded yellow cardstock and missing all her paper accessories. No purse, tiara, ball gown, or slippers. Even her paper hairdo was gone. Stripped down to nothing but the polka-dot bathing suit Junie insisted I draw on her body to save her from total nakedness. Poor thing had been stuck back here all alone for a very long time.

I laid the rescued doll down on the seat next to me. I would use the tree to solve all our problems. But first I needed to find the right seed.

✳✳✳

237

When we got home, Dad immediately set up his computer in the study. While he worked, I ransacked the house, searching for money. I hadn't excavated a single dime from our station wagon's seats during the drive. Unfortunately, the tin can above the microwave was empty, and the couch cushions had long since been looted.

"Isabel, what on earth are you doing in there?"

"Turning the house upside down."

"I hope not!" Dad hollered. "The last thing your mother needs is to come home to a gigantic mess."

"I'll clean everything up, don't worry." Then I had an idea. I poked my head into the study. "Hey, Dad?"

"Yes, Isa?" His patience was wearing thin. "I'm trying to get some work done. What is it?"

"Could I get my lunch money now? One less thing to remember tomorrow morning."

"Let me see." He reached into his pocket and pulled out his wallet. He flipped through the compartments. "Sorry, sweetheart. I'm out of cash. Used up my last few bucks on dinner. Jam sandwich it is, I guess." He nodded toward the kitchen. "Do you need me to make it for you?"

My shoulders dropped. "Nope. I can do it. Thanks."

I went into the living room and flopped down in the overstuffed armchair to think. A photograph on the mantel above the fireplace caught my eye. It was similar to the one taped to the wall beside Junie's bed at the hospital, with Mom and Dad dressed up in fancy clothes for Uncle Lewis and Aunt Sheila's wedding. Mom wore a string of pearls around her neck. Earrings dangled from her ears. My pulse quickened.

If I couldn't plant money, I could at least plant something valuable, like jewelry.

Mom's jewelry box sat on top of the tall dresser in her room. I jumped out of the chair and dashed toward the staircase. Dad stopped me halfway up.

"Wait a second, young lady. You need to clean this disaster zone before going anywhere. You promised, remember?"

Ugh! I went back to the living room and replaced the couch cushions and pillows as fast as I could. I put all the books back on the shelves. I stuffed countless knick-knacks back into drawers. I hung each coat back on its hook in the mudroom. Just as I was finishing, I heard my dad shut down his computer and climb the stairs.

"I'm going to bed," he called out. "I'm fried. You should get some rest too, Isa."

"Yup. Coming soon." I groaned. "Just going to make that sandwich for lunch tomorrow."

My mission would have to wait until morning. After he left for work, I'd try again.

CHAPTER 21

All night, bizarre dreams and nightmares wove together. There were trees with clawed branches, clouds that rained copper pennies, chickens with devil horns, ice cream avalanches.

"Rise and shine!" Dad said, poking his head into my bedroom.

I rubbed my eyes, trying to shake the disturbing images out of my mind. I glanced at my clock. "Shouldn't you be at work already?"

"I wanted to make sure you got off to school okay."

It was nice to be noticed, but of all the days for him to finally pay attention, why did it have to be now? I needed him to leave so that I could sneak into his room and take a piece of jewelry.

I got dressed quickly and ran down to the kitchen where I scarfed a piece of toast and guzzled some juice for breakfast. I grabbed my books and homework, plus my lunch and softball glove, and zipped up my back-pack. I'd clipped a brand new bell to the keychain and it sang beautifully, filling me with hope. "Bye, Dad!" I called over my shoulder.

"Wow! That was speedy." He peered over the banister from the upstairs landing. "Have a good day!"

I waved, then dashed out the door. The sooner I got out of the house, the sooner he would too.

I almost stepped on Kira, who was sitting on my front porch. She was holding the large copper bell that we'd played catch with. In the daylight, it was blindingly shiny with a faint bluish-green patina. "Ring-a-ling! Bell buddy! Happy Monday!" She jumped up and tossed me the bell. It sounded like glass raindrops on a tin roof.

I caught it and hissed, "Shhhh!" I stuffed the bell into my bag.

"What? There's no one around."

"My dad's upstairs. Keep a lid on it." I grabbed her arm and pulled her around the house and behind the workshop.

"We had so much fun the other night. What's up with you today?" She wriggled free.

"I need you to cover for me. I'm not going to school. Not yet."

"Where are you going? The hospital?"

I glanced over my shoulder. "No, I'm going back inside. I just have to wait until my dad leaves the house."

She frowned. "You're going to break into your own house?"

"Not break in. I have a key. I need to find something. Something to plant."

"A seed! Fun!" she shouted, then clamped a hand over her mouth. "Sorry. Can I help?"

"It would be too suspicious if we're both missing from school. Your mom would get a call from Principal Tam and then the whole plan would be shot."

"True. We need to be . . ." She bit her lip. "Inconspicuous! That's the word!"

"Sure, call it whatever you want." My watch beeped. "The bus will be here soon."

"What should I tell the teachers? They're going to wonder where you are."

"Just make up some excuse. But don't mention my sister, okay? The teachers know what's going on with my family, but none of the other kids do. I'd rather keep it that way."

"Got it," Kira said.

"I should be there by third period." I looked up at the house. Dad seemed extra pokey today, or maybe I was just extra impatient.

"I'll take care of it. Don't worry. It's kind of cool. Like we're on this secret mission, and there's intrigue and adventure and . . ."

"Kira."

"Yeah?"

"The bus." I tapped my watch.

She nodded. "Right. Going now."

"Oh! One more thing—"

She turned. "What?"

"I need you to help me at softball practice today." I scratched my neck. "I sort of have to start in the opening game." I tried to act like it was no big deal.

She blinked. "Start? Really?"

"Don't look so skeptical!"

"I'm not. It's just . . . well . . . you've missed some practices and there are other girls on the team." My face fell. "Don't worry. You'll be great. We'll figure something out." She patted my arm. "Besides, we have our new hand signals. Those should help." She offered a high five. I returned it reluctantly.

The bus chugged down the hill.

"Later gator," I said.

Her eyes brightened. "To the bus, octopus! Good luck with the super secret mission." She took off running, her hair flying wildly behind her.

"Thanks. I'm going to need it."

***

I hid behind the workshop until Dad's car rumbled away in a plume of dust. Then I crept around the yard and tiptoed onto the porch. I pulled the key from the little red pouch in my backpack. Since Junie's diagnosis, I'd gotten used to coming and going by myself, but when I unlocked the door that morning, I felt like an intruder in my own home. My plan did involve a little thievery, but I preferred to think of it as borrowing. Borrowing that would pay serious dividends. Hopefully.

I scaled the staircase in a few ninja-quick bounds and ducked into my parents' bedroom. The jewelry box sat on the dresser. I opened it and searched for the perfect item. Unfortunately everything looked dingy and tarnished. The bracelets were missing beads, the necklace chains were tangled. I couldn't find the strand of pearls or the fancy earrings from the photograph. Maybe Mom had borrowed them for the occasion? Or maybe she'd already started to sell our valuables to help pay the bills? Except for sentimental value, the remaining jewelry looked fairly worthless. Great. That's just what we needed growing in our backyard: a sparkling junk tree. Almost as appealing as a homework tree. I thought I might find Junie's lost wishing pin in there, but I had no luck with that either.

I sat on the bed in a swath of sunshine to think. The house was quiet, waiting to see what I might come up with. But it wasn't totally silent. It took me a few minutes to recognize the faint *tick-tick-tick*.

I followed the sound. I opened a drawer in the bedside table. My father's antique wristwatch lay inside. Just like my leather glove, the gold watch had originally belonged to my grandfather, Isaac Arnold Fitzwilken. I knew the watch was special because Dad only wore it on important occasions. The soft ticking almost sounded like purring. Its delicate golden hands were set at ten and two, like a smile. I picked it up and turned it over. Inscribed on the back were the initials IAF. Which also happened to be my initials. A sign. That I should take it. That I was meant to have it. I felt a tiny tug of guilt, but that disappeared completely when I thought about my sister, the towering pile of bills, and everything my parents had said in the hospital.

***

I bolted through the orchard and into the clearing at record speed. I skidded to a stop at the base of the tree. Several brown buds studded the tips of the branches like miniature fists. This was very odd because Kira and I hadn't planted anything after the bell harvest. And then I remembered . . .

That squirrel! I bet that greedy little rascal planted some sort of nut in the ground after we left. I was so annoyed that I stamped my foot on the ground. The tree shook, its bark shifting from luminous sage green to flat gray. The veins that ran through the crystal leaves darkened.

I gripped the watch in my right hand. I'd never planted a new seed while something else was ripening, but this couldn't wait. I bent over to dig a hole near the base of the trunk. The ground was cold. The branches flinched and writhed, like the entire tree wanted to get away from me. A smell like vinegar mixed with bitter orange peel burned my nose. My eyes watered. The bark rippled. Tiny prickles emerged, the thorns sending a clear message: *Stay away!*

I stumbled backward, scowling at the tree. Then I stood and stomped my foot in the grass once more. "Fine," I said, returning the watch to my backpack. "I can take a hint. But I hope you know what you're doing." I stormed away. "I'm depending on you."

CHAPTER 22

I walked to school, still fuming. I usually loved the tree's unpredictability, but today it infuriated me. To make matters worse, every time a car approached, I had to dive into hedges and ditches to avoid being seen. Not fun at all.

As I passed Drabbington Avenue, the sound of an engine reached my ears. There was no place to take cover. I had to act cool. Like I wasn't skipping school. Like I was supposed to be out there. Just acting cool.

The vehicle approached from behind, its exhaust like breath down the back of my neck. It rumbled past.

Phew. Close call.

Then it stopped.

I kept my head down. My foot started an anxious tap dance.

The vehicle reversed. And parked itself right in front of me. I wished for true invisibility.

I was so busted.

"Where to, darlin'?"

"Reggie?" I looked up. The 83 bus and its friendly driver greeted me with an open door and a wide smile.

"This isn't a school bus, but it looks like you need a ride." Tufts of sandy hair glinted beneath his cap, golden as the watch.

"I can walk."

"So can I, darlin'. You want an award or something?" He winked.

"No," I said, trying not to sound as cranky as I felt.

"Good, because I don't have one. All I can offer is a ride. Right on back to school. Where I'm pretty sure you're supposed to be."

I stuck my hands in my pockets. "I don't have any money."

"This one's on the house." He pressed a button and a little paper ticket emerged from the box on his dash. He handed it to me.

"Really?"

"As long as you don't stand there dillydallyin' a minute more. You know I like to keep my schedule running lickety-split."

At least I wouldn't have to dive into any more

hedges. "Thanks. I really appreciate it." I stuffed the ticket in my pocket and landed in the nearest seat. The bus was empty. "Where is everyone?"

"I'm just coming off my break. Saw you walking by yourself during school hours and figured I'd take a detour. You live on Drabbington?"

I looked down the sunny, inviting cul de sac. "No. Sometimes I wish I did."

"Not important where you live, as long as you're with your loved ones." He shifted the bus into gear and eased away from the curb.

"Reggie, I wasn't skipping school, just so you know. I had some . . . important family business to take care of."

He glanced in the mirror and gave me a little nod. He turned the wheel. "Next stop, Miss Muriel. She'll be waiting for us by her garden."

A few minutes later, we stopped in front of a grove of flowering magnolias ringed with tulips in every shade imaginable. Muriel stepped aboard. Her white-blue hair was swept in a loose spiral around her head, like cotton candy. She handed Reggie a cream-colored magnolia blossom instead of coins. He placed it on his dash and gave her a ticket.

"Hi, Muriel," I said, wondering what delicious spice she might smell like this morning.

"Ah, hello there," she said, her voice as crackly sweet as peanut brittle. "I would've brought you a flower, too, if I'd known you'd be here. Reginald adores them, don't you?"

"You know I'd rather ride a tractor than this bus, Miss Muriel. But your pretty flowers help. They make me feel like I'm driving outside again, where my heart wants to be."

"Your heart will find its place and its peace someday, Reginald. Don't you worry." Then she looked at me. "Usually I'm the very first pickup. Where'd you come from, honey?"

Where to start? It was a list nine cities long . . .

"Found this one by the side of the road," Reggie called over his shoulder.

"A stray." She patted my knee with her hand. A map of veins ran this way and that under her skin, thin and almost transparent, like crepe paper.

"I'm not a stray." Although I did feel like one lately. "I'm just late for school. Reggie's giving me a ride. That's all."

"Where's your mama and papa?" Muriel asked tenderly.

"My dad's at work. My mom is visiting my sister. Then she might go looking for a job."

"A job? Hear that, Reginald? Her mama's looking

for work. I'm trying to get rid of work. Life has a way of balancing itself out, doesn't it?"

"Sure does, Miss Muriel. Sure does."

"Tell me, what kind of job is your mama looking for?"

"She used to make pastries for restaurants and cafés. She was the best." Why was I speaking in the past tense? "I'm sure she still is. She's just out of practice."

"Mmhmm."

"She used to smell like you," I said. "Like spices. Cinnamon, and . . ." I inhaled deeply. "Cardamom? Maybe nutmeg too? Plus a note of magnolia, but that must be from your garden, not your kitchen."

The corners of her eyes crinkled. "You've got a good nose, honey."

"I do?"

"Miss Muriel knows noses!" Reggie said, opening the door at the next stop. Several passengers boarded, too engrossed in their midmorning routines to notice a kid who should already be at school sitting in the front row.

"That's my shop up ahead." Muriel pointed out the window at the bakery. "Been working there for over forty years. Think I'm due for a holiday."

"The bakery?" That sounded one hundred times better than the hardware store.

"Indeed." She reached into her purse and produced a small card. "Our apple pies made us famous, but when that orchard went kaput, we had to diversify."

"Diversify? Like with stocks?" I asked, trying to sound smart.

Muriel's laugh chimed like bells. "No, with sticky buns. And marble breads. And cakes and such. We had to adapt. It was difficult for a while. In the end, it made us stronger." She shook her head, sending white-blue wisps across her face. "I do miss making those pies, though. There must've been something mighty special in the water running through that orchard. Or maybe it was the soil. Who knows? Either way, I'd give my left foot for another one of those Melwick apples. Mmhmm."

"Nothin' like 'em!" Reggie agreed, smacking his lips.

"Did you say Melwick apples?" I sputtered.

Before she could answer, the bus stopped and the door opened. Muriel stood up. "Give this to your mama. Tell her to come see me when she's ready." She pressed the card into my hand.

"I will. Thank you!" I slipped it into the zipped pouch in my backpack, for safekeeping. I thought about the chance seedling and the watch I needed to bury beneath the ground. *We're running out of time to figure this out*, my parents had said yesterday. If everything worked like I imagined, the jewelry crop would solve our money problems and neither Mom nor Dad would need a job. But a backup plan couldn't hurt. Especially one that might involve sticky buns.

CHAPTER 23

I slid into my chair in the back row as if it were home base, right as the third period bell rang.

"Welcome back," Kira whispered from the next desk over. "How'd the secret mission go?"

I stealthily flashed the gold watch under the desk so she could see, then stashed it away.

"Nice!" Kira's attempt at a conspiratorial wink was horrendous. Anything but inconspicuous.

"Kira, the emergency eyewash station is located at the back of the room, if you need to use it," Ms. Perdilla said, looking concerned.

I tried to suppress a giggle. Which came out like a snort. Fantastic.

"And Isabel, if you need to see the nurse for any reason, please go right ahead. You don't need to ask."

"The nurse? Why?"

Ms. Perdilla walked over to my desk and said

quietly, "I wasn't sure you'd make it in at all today. You are a trooper."

I gave Kira a *what-the-heck* stare, but she just grinned and attempted that insane wink again.

Ms. Perdilla made her way to the front of the room and began taking attendance. I actually tried to pay attention for once, matching each name to each face and committing them to memory. When she got to my name, I responded with the standard, "Here!"

Several rows in front of me, Casey made a disgusting sound. Like he was puking all over his desk. Then Noah followed suit. And Leo. The class erupted with laughter.

I slowly turned in my chair. Kira nodded her head with satisfaction. "Good, huh?"

"What. Did. You. Do?" I muttered as quietly as possible.

"What's wrong? I made up an excuse. Just like you asked. I announced it in home room."

I grimaced. "Announced what exactly?"

"Food poisoning. Clever, right?" Her eyebrows waggled.

"Ugh." I slumped into my chair, feeling like I might actually throw up.

"That's enough. Settle down," Ms. Perdilla ordered. It was as if my make-believe malady was suddenly contagious. Kids were gripping their stomachs and practically rolling in the aisles with revolting sound effects.

"Class! Quiet down!"

I covered my head with my arms and tried to disappear.

"You're not mad, are you?" Kira whispered to my elbow.

I groaned, a little too loudly. Which ignited another puke fest from the middle row.

"Watch out! She's gonna blow!" someone yelled.

Ms. Perdilla flew down the aisle, waving detention slips, trying to regain control.

"I just wanted to help," Kira said.

I tilted my head and peered at her with one mortified eyeball. "I know. You only did what I asked. It's my own fault."

"Don't be so hard on yourself. You're like the most famous girl in school today."

School was actually one place I wanted to remain invisible. And now I was the exact opposite. "You mean *infamous*."

"Tomayto, tomahto!"

"Um, it's a big difference. More like tomato, armadillo."

"You ate an armadillo?" Casey snickered. "No wonder you got sick!"

The classroom exploded again. As a last, desperate resort, Ms. Perdilla lifted a foghorn from her desk drawer and blew it loudly. We all rocketed out of our seats, ears ringing. Someone whimpered.

"Imagine if our tree had sprouted some of those," Kira said under her breath. I tried my hardest not to laugh.

"May I please have your attention!" Ms. Perdilla said, which wasn't a question, but a command. The room went silent. "Thank you. Since we seem to be too distracted this morning to give our lesson plan the focus it truly deserves, we will spend the rest of the period working on our research projects. Don't forget—your topic statements are due next week."

There was a collective moan.

"This is supposed to be fun, ladies and gentlemen! You can choose to study anything. The world is your oyster!"

"Oysters?" Amelia looked up from doodling in her notebook. "Gross. They're like boogers in a shell."

Sensing another eruption, Ms. Perdilla raised the foghorn into the air as warning. "Thank you for that lovely insight. Now let's all try to settle down."

"Can we work in teams?" Leo asked.

Ms. Perdilla nodded. "Collaboration is an important

part of the scientific process. So, yes, if you would like to select a partner, you may."

"Sweet!" said Leo and Noah in unison, exchanging fist bumps.

Old me would have dreaded the idea of a group project. Not anymore. I turned to Kira. "Science buddies?" I mouthed.

Her giddy squeal was so loud that Ms. Perdilla almost had to blow the horn again.

***

We rearranged the desks so that we could work with our partners. Kira and I tapped our pencils. The pages in our notebooks stared blankly up at us.

"Any ideas?" I asked.

"I already used up my daily dose of creativity," Kira said.

"On what, food poisoning?"

"Hey! Lying doesn't exactly come easily to me."

I wished I could say the same for myself. Lately lies and excuses were flowing past my lips like water through a sieve. Too easily. Too quickly. Just thinking about softball practice invited a swarm of butterflies into my stomach.

"How are you ladies doing?" Ms. Perdilla said.

"What if I told you we were writing our report in invisible ink?"

She eyed the white sheets of paper and raised a single eyebrow. "I would call your bluff, Miss Fitzwilken." She placed a book on the desk. It looked positively ancient and smelled like the library basement. "Here. In case you need a little extra inspiration." A tree stretched across its dusty cover, embossed in gold. "You can choose a different topic if you'd like. I know we talked about amphibians, Isabel. But this caught my eye. Might be interesting, given the history of your family's property."

I looked down at the book. Twisting roots and limbs spelled out its title: *Restore Your Orchard: Bringing Fruit Trees Back to Life.*

"Thanks," I said. "We'll think about it."

"We will?" Kira asked, surprised by my willingness to discuss anything tree-related in public.

"Sure, why not?" The chance seedling had acted so odd that morning, with its gray bark and angry spikes. Maybe this book could explain what was going on. Maybe it could even help me speed up the next harvest.

"Fantastic," Ms. Perdilla said.

The lunch bell rang and I tucked the book into my bag. "Thanks again," I said, feeling inspired.

CHAPTER 24

Later that afternoon, the diamond beckoned.

An invitation. A challenge. An opportunity.

I seized it and ran.

From base to base. First, second, third. And back to home again. I had changed into my practice clothes quicker than my teammates so I could be the first one on the field. The grass had been mowed with a lattice pattern that reminded me of the crisscrossed crust of an apple pie.

Coach Naron jogged toward me. "Nice to see you, Fitzwilken. Heard through the grapevine you might not make it today. Feeling under the weather?"

"I'm fine. Ready to work. Ready to hustle!" I said a little too enthusiastically. I shuffled my cleats in the grass, trying to tone it down a notch.

"Glad to have you with us today. Here come the other ladies."

The locker-room door opened and girls flooded the field.

"Coach Naron?" I asked.

"Yup?" She opened her playbook, covered with barely legible diagrams and notes.

"Have you picked the starting lineup for the opener yet?"

"Why? You hungry?"

It took me a few seconds to decipher her sports speak. "Starving," I said, punching my fist into my glove.

"Good! Then let me see what you can serve up on the plate today." She blew an ear-splitting whistle. "Ladies! Drills start in five! Grab a ball."

Everyone paired off and spread out across the field. I looked for Kira but didn't see her.

"Think fast!" someone shouted, hurling a ball at my head. I snapped my arm up to catch it just in time.

"Jeez, watch it!" I yelled. The girl turned her head and I noticed a mile-long ponytail running down her back. It was Kira

"Good catch," Coach Naron said. "Ladies! The ready position is fundamental. You have to be prepared for any situation that may arise. Like Fitz and Ritts just demonstrated."

Coach gave us nicknames! I instantly forgave Kira for nearly knocking my head off.

I threw the ball back to her. She caught it and hollered, "Go long!"

I jogged backward, barely fast enough to snatch the ball from the sky. I returned a sizzling curveball, hoping Coach was still watching. We continued until our muscles were warm and loose.

"Huddle up!" Coach Naron called out. We gathered together as she described a series of drills. "As you know, the opening game against the Minnows is coming up. We need to start the season strong. Let me see what you've got. Break!"

We rushed into our positions and began executing the drills. I made a few mistakes, but so did everyone else. We were still getting into a groove as a team. Learning each other's strengths and weaknesses. Every time I was paired with Kira, we both did great. A silent trust carried the ball back and forth between us. Our midnight practice in the clearing paid off.

When we shifted into scrimmage mode, Coach pointed to me and then at the pitcher's mound. "Let's see what you're cooking, Fitz."

I yanked up my socks and adjusted the laces on my snazzy cleats. I wiggled my fingers. Time to initiate my lie-to-truth plan. No pressure.

Abigail Winthrop stepped up to the plate. I surprised myself by knowing her name. I also knew that she was twice my size and a slugger. "Yum, yum. I smell a home run," she taunted, gripping the bat.

I tried to remember Dad's advice. *Watch your catcher. Listen to her. She can see things you can't.*

Kira adjusted her catcher's mask, kicked the dust, and crouched down. She opened her mitt. I studied her signals. I twisted my shoulders, wheeled my arm around, and fired the ball.

Thwap!

"Strike!" Coach announced.

My heart leapt up. Two more to go.

Kira gestured. I scraped my cleats along the mound. I shifted my weight and threw the ball. It hurtled through the air.

Thwap!

"Strike two!"

The girls on the bench were hollering encouragements to Abigail. No one cheered for me, probably because I'd never cheered for them or even bothered to learn their names. But Kira nodded reassuringly and I felt the swarm of butterflies in my stomach settle.

She signaled. Just like we'd practiced in the orchard.

I looked at the batter. I shook my head. No way.

She signaled again.

I raised my arm. I lowered it. I raised it again. In that moment of hesitation, a million tiny doubts snuck in, scattering my focus. I released the ball. As soon as it left my hand, I knew it was bad.

Ping!

Abigail made contact with the ball. It flew behind the dugout.

"Foul!"

I rolled my shoulders back. Shook my head. I threw again. Off target.

"Ball one!"

I took a deep breath.

"Wait for yours!" the girls on the bench called. I tried to block out their voices, and Coach Naron's eyes studying my every move. I looked at Kira. *Don't be stubborn*, I told myself. We're partners, just like Dad said. I dipped my chin to tell her I was ready.

She signaled.

This time I didn't let a drop of doubt seep in. I lobbed the ball home.

Thwap!

"Steee-rike! Outta here!"

Two more batters followed. I struck them both out. I almost fell over on the mound, toppled by happiness. Kira lifted her mask and met my eyes. She grinned, giving me a thumbs-up.

"Nice teamwork, ladies. Let's switch this up a bit. Get some fresh blood out on the field. Dearborn! Hafiz!

You're up. Santos on deck. Let's hustle! Hup hup!"

Kira and I jogged to the dugout. Over the next several innings, we got better and better. By the end of the practice, the rest of our team was rooting loudly for us. And I cheered back, calling my teammates by name. Whatever Coach Naron decided about the starting lineup, at least I had tried my best. And according to my parents, that's all any of us could do.

***

"You should've seen us!" Kira crowed after practice. "We were a dynamic duo! Fitz and Ritts!"

"So proud of you, Pookie!" her mother gushed, steering the minivan onto Melwick Lane. There was no doubt in my mind that Mrs. Ritter would be at our opening game, and every game after that, even if Kira never made a single catch. I hoped I could say the same for my own parents.

"You two must be so pleased."

"Tickled pink," I said, looking up from the book Ms. Perdilla had given us. It was spread across my lap, the pages filled with illustrations of rosy apple blossoms. The flowers were pretty, but they were nothing compared to what the seedling could grow.

"We ruled the diamond!" Kira said, squeezing the

life from another innocent juice box. "Right, *diamond* buddy?!" Her catching skills were great, but her winking skills still needed major improvement.

"Posolutely." I reached into my backpack and wrapped my fingers around the watch, checking to make sure it was still there. The golden links were cool. The oval face, smooth. I wondered how many precious gems might bloom after I planted it. I envisioned oodles of diamonds, rubies, and sapphires. I tried to imagine the ticking sound hundreds of bejeweled watches would make once ripe and ready. It might even rival the bells.

I let go of the watch and closed the book. I sipped cold juice from my bendy straw. Everything in my life was still technically a mess, but at the same time, I felt like some puzzle pieces were settling into place. Softball practice had gone well. I had that business card from Muriel. Dad and Mom had even been noticing me a little more than usual.

Junie's surgery would go well. It had to. And the tree's jewelry harvest would more than cover all the bills. We might even have enough money left over to buy some fancy paper dolls, take gymnastics lessons, fix up our house, and give the neglected orchard the attention it deserved.

CHAPTER 25

"Do you want to come over?" I asked Kira as we pulled up to my house. "You could help me with our planting project."

"I do, but . . ." She stole a glance at the clock on the dashboard. "My dad's supposed to call me this afternoon."

"No problem. I totally understand."

She tugged her ponytail. "I'm excited, but also a little nervous," she whispered.

"You'll be fine." I gave her a quick hug.

She seemed surprised but grateful. She squeezed me back. "Thanks."

I gathered my stuff and opened the door. Fresh air flooded inside. I caught a faint whiff of honeysuckle.

Kira sneezed. The scent must have tickled her nose too. Her eyes watered.

"Are you okay?" I asked.

"Yeah, it's probably pollen. My allergies always act up this time of year. Good luck planting that seed." She waved, then sniffled and sneezed again. "Bye-bye, butterfly!"

"See you soon, raccoon!"

***

I raced through the orchard. The apple trees hadn't blossomed in over a decade, but dozens of bumblebees zipped through the air, buzzing hopefully. The scent of honeysuckle danced in the breeze. I couldn't tell if the smell was coming from actual honeysuckle flowers, which had just started to bloom in a thick hedge beside Dad's workshop, or if the seedling was releasing another blast of happy memory perfume. I didn't particularly care; I was just glad to breathe it in.

I entered the clearing and stepped over the foundation stones. I hesitated. The tree had given me a pretty clear message to back off earlier that morning. But now the buds and thorns were gone. The bark looked brighter and more inviting. I retrieved the watch from my bag. The wind pushed the rope swing back and forth, as if nodding. *Go ahead. Do it.*

I knelt at the base of the tree and dug a small hole, just as I'd done three times before. A slight jolt of electricity hummed through my hand when it grazed the trunk. The branches creaked as they bent toward the ground, sweeping and curving around me like willow fronds. I had no idea the tree was so flexible. The blue-streaked leaves fluttered and murmured as if they were admiring the watch. Even in the shade, the gold shined.

I placed the watch in the warm brown dirt. I waited until I saw the roots slithering through the earth, toward the precious seed. I filled the hole back up and pressed both my hands to the ground, trying to communicate the importance of this crop to the tree in our unspoken way.

The branches trembled for a second, then stretched back up into their regular positons, forming the tree's rounded crown.

"Did you understand me?" I said, rising to my feet. "After her surgery and her treatments, Junie will get better. She'll come home. When she does, I'll finally introduce you two."

There wasn't a cloud in the sky, yet the bark darkened, as if a shadow had fallen across the entire tree.

"You'll love her," I said, confused by the tree's reaction. "Everyone loves her." The branches inched upward, farther away from me, like they'd done earlier that morning. "What?" I burst out. "Junie will get better! She has to! As long as you help. I can't do this without you! We're running out of time."

The tree didn't respond. How rude! Here I was sharing seriously important information and it just stood there like it didn't believe me. Or like it knew something I didn't.

"Fine," I said, exasperated. "I'll let you rest. I'm crabby when I'm tired too."

It took most plants weeks and sometimes months to grow fruit. The tree had sprouted an entire bell crop in a matter of days, not to mention cookies and shoes before that. I needed to cut it some slack. It probably wasn't giving me attitude. It was just tired. Nothing to worry about.

Yet for some reason, that song from the radio stuck in my head, repeating over and over. *You can't always get what you want . . .*

✳✳✳

A car pulled into the driveway just as I crossed the front lawn.

"Dad!" Seeing him twice in one day was a rare occurrence lately. I caught him around the waist, squeezing like a boa constrictor. "Where's Mom?" I asked. Her car wasn't there. I hoped they hadn't sold it already.

"She's still at the hospital. She'll be home any min-ute. What do you say we have a quick catch before she gets back? My arm is pretty stiff from all that office work. I need to stretch it out. And I bet my star pitcher could use some practice."

"Yes!" I squeezed him again.

***

When we returned from playing catch, an incredible smell wafted through the house.

"Nel?" Dad said, peering into the kitchen, his nose twitching. "What's all this?"

"It's called dinner," she laughed, waving a spoon. "Eggplant parmesan, to be precise. Your favorite."

Dad stared. I could tell he was as stunned as I was.

"Don't just stand there gawking, you two!" she said, her voice warm and lilting. "Come help me set the table."

I jumped to action, grabbing napkins and forks and plates.

"What's the occasion?" Dad asked, wrapping an arm around Mom's waist and kissing her cheek.

"A promising call from the insurance company." She glanced toward the pile of bills on the counter. Maybe I wouldn't need the tree's help so desperately after all.

"That *is* worth celebrating." Dad kissed her again. It usually grossed me out to see them act mushy, but considering the circumstances, I'd let a few smooches slide.

I set three places at the table. A familiar ache wracked my insides. "How's Junie?" I asked, eying her empty chair. I missed her so much.

"She had a good day," Mom said. "She was a little tired, but she was happy. She kept talking about our visit yesterday. And the latest bloodwork showed that her counts are up. Dr. Ebbens thinks she'll be strong enough to have the surgery in a few days." Mom's eyes were bright. "I feel like this is a turning point."

Dad moved across the kitchen and took my hand. He spun me around. Then he pulled Mom away from the stove and gave her a twirl too. Swept up in the moment, we skipped and whirled around the room.

When the kitchen timer dinged, we stopped dancing and gathered around the table to enjoy the delicious home-cooked meal.

"Who's spending the night with Junie?" I asked between bites.

"I will," Dad said.

"Can I go too? I haven't seen her since . . ."

"Yesterday," Mom said with a slight smile.

I squinted at my purple wristwatch and did a

speedy calculation. "Technically twenty-two hours and seventeen minutes. But it feels like longer." I looked at Junie's empty chair again. "A lot longer. Sister withdrawal is a real thing, you know. Like an actual medical condition."

Mom glanced at Dad. She tilted her head to the side.

"It's okay with me," Dad said. "But we have to leave early in the morning. I can drop you at school on my way to work. And I'm warning you, that couch isn't very comfortable."

"I don't mind." I'd sleep on a cactus mattress for my sister.

"Don't stay up all night playing card games." Mom narrowed her eyes. "Junie needs to rest and build up her strength."

"Aye aye, captain!" I shoved a forkful of eggplant into my mouth, then saluted.

Mom was about to dole out second helpings when the phone rang.

"I'll get it!" I said, dropping my fork with a clang. "It might be Kira."

"The kid down the road?" Dad asked.

Mom nodded. "Helen Ritter's daughter."

"Remember? The girl I was hanging out with on Saturday? Actually, we hang out a lot now. She's my friend." The words came out so easily. It felt nice.

"A new friend? Really? That's wonderful," Dad said.

I stuck my tongue out at him. "Don't be so surprised." Although I understood why he was. Until recently, the don't-need-friends policy had been in full effect. "Hello?" I said, holding the receiver to my ear.

I recognized Dr. Ebbens' voice right away. "Good evening, Isabel. Are your parents available?" His voice was polite but rigid.

"Who is it, baby?" Mom asked, standing up. I'm sure she noticed my face, shot with color. She could tell something wasn't right.

"Dr. Ebbens," I said shakily.

Everything else was a blur. A second later, Mom was by my side, pulling the phone from my hands. Her voice was strained. Her words, choppy.

"But . . . this afternoon . . . she was . . . I know. Yes . . . We'll be right there."

Dad ran up the stairs, then back down. His car keys jangled. I felt like I might faint. I put my hands on my knees to steady myself. Mom dialed another number frantically.

"Helen? Yes. Yes. No . . . We'll see. Thank you so much."

I was still trying to catch my breath. Trying to make sense of everything that was happening.

Mom's hand was on my elbow. "Let's go," she said. "Now."

"What? Where?"

"The Ritters' house."

"I thought you said I could go to the hospital . . ."

"Isa! Now! In the car!" Her eyes were wild. Her voice scared me. Dad was already outside. The car's engine roared to life.

Mom shoved my backpack into my arms, then hustled me out the door in a total stupor. The dishes were still on the table. The pot of tomato sauce was uncovered, growing cold on the counter. I didn't even have time to pack a toothbrush or a pair of pajamas. The car lurched away from our house. Some of the lights were still on as we pulled away.

"What's happening?"

"Junie spiked a fever."

Dad zoomed down Melwick Lane like a race-car driver. For a healthy kid like me, a fever wasn't fun, but it wasn't the end of the world either. But for a cancer patient like Junie, a fever could quite literally mean just that.

"How did that happen?" I stuttered.

"An infection. A virus. Who knows? She could've been exposed to something from one of the other patients or from the staff. She's not in an isolation unit.

And even then, it's impossible to control everything." Mom was trying to be calm, but I knew she was panicking inside. So was I.

"All I know is that we need to get there now." Dad sped up. I checked to make sure my seatbelt was fastened.

"Why can't I go with you? If Junie's in trouble, I need to be there with her!"

"Not now, Isabel. Don't make this harder for us." Dad gripped the steering wheel and pulled with a screech into Kira's driveway.

"We'll call you as soon as we know what's going on, okay?" Mom turned to look at me. Then she got out of the car and hurried up the front steps.

"I don't want to stay here. I want to go with you," I stammered, but no one heard me. I stepped out of the car, completely numb.

Mrs. Ritter met us at the door, her eyes kind and concerned. She touched my cheek. She and Mom spoke in the doorway, their voices hushed. Kira took my hand and led me inside, closing the door behind us. I felt like someone had put my brain and heart into a blender. It was not a good feeling.

"Is everything okay?" Kira asked. Then she sneezed. She pulled a tissue from her pocket. She wiped her nose.

Something clicked inside me. The worry that had been simmering came to a boil. I exploded. "You! You got her sick!"

Kira backed away from me. "What are you talking about, Isa?" She sneezed again.

"I never should have invited you to come with me to the hospital." The words flew like poison arrows out of my mouth. "You've been sneezing all afternoon. I can't believe I didn't notice it sooner! How could I have been so stupid?"

Kira's eyes were wide. Her head shook from side to side.

"What is it? A cold? The flu? Do you have any idea what that could do to Junie?" I shouted at her. "How could you have been so reckless?"

"Isa, no. I told you, I have allergies. That's all. The pollen always does this to me. I was fine at softball practice. But it's worse around the orchard for some reason."

My eyes were mean slits. "It's all your fault!" I wanted to turn and run, but I had nowhere to go.

"I'm not sick. I didn't infect Junie, I swear. You saw me clean my hands that day. It must be something else. Please don't be mad."

Just then, Mrs. Ritter opened the front door and stepped inside the foyer. The car horn honked as my parents drove away. She looked at Kira and me standing in the hallway. The tension between us was thick and heavy.

"Everything all right, girls?" she asked, her face full of questions.

I swallowed and nodded. I was afraid more nastiness might escape my mouth if I opened it again. Kira sniffled and dabbed her nose with the tissue.

"Isa, I'll make up the guest room. Unless you'd like to stay upstairs in Kira's room? I'm sure she wouldn't mind having a slumber party."

"I wouldn't," Kira croaked, her voice fragile.

I fought back tears of my own. "The guest room is fine." My words were cold and hard. I followed Mrs. Ritter, refusing to make eye contact with Kira. I could hear her sniffle and sneeze, as she trailed several steps behind.

The guest room was on the main floor. It had paintings on the wall, shelves lined with books, and a big sleigh bed. Ruffled curtains adorned a wide window overlooking the northern slope of the orchard.

"Did you eat supper already?" Mrs. Ritter asked, smoothing a quilt over the bed and arranging some fluffy pillows.

"Yes." The fewer words I said, the better. Every time Kira tried to get close to me, I stepped away.

"Is there anything else I can get you, Isa?" Mrs. Ritter asked.

"No, thank you. I just want to go to sleep," I mumbled.

"Already?"

I nodded, gritting my teeth. I knew Mrs. Ritter was trying to be nice, but I needed to be alone. "I'm drained." If happiness can fill a person up, anger can do the exact opposite. I was mad at Kira and her germs. I was angry at myself for letting her into my life. I was even more furious at my parents for leaving me behind. It was so unfair, I could scream.

"The bathroom is down the hall, and there are leftovers in the fridge if you're hungry. Please, make yourself at home." Mrs. Ritter put a hand on Kira's shoulder. "Let's give Isa some privacy." They left the room and closed the door.

I sank into the bed, still wearing my clothes. I probably should've asked to borrow a pair of pajamas. But it didn't really matter, because as comfortable as that bed felt, I had no intention of actually staying there.

I rolled onto my stomach, leaned over the edge of the bed, and pulled the book Ms. Perdilla had given me from my backpack. I tried to pass the time reading through the yellowed pages, but I couldn't focus on the words or pictures. There was only one tree on my mind. I got up to turn off the lights, then I sat in a rocking chair by the window. I pulled the curtains aside and watched the stars gather in the sky. I could make out the scraggly silhouettes of our apple trees in the distance, dark as ink.

Eventually I heard footsteps in the hallway. They paused in front of my door, then continued walking up the stairs. The sliver of light that spilled between the door and the floor disappeared. I waited.

Finally, when I was pretty sure Kira and her mom were fast asleep, I opened the window and slipped outside into the cool night.

***

The moon cast a silvery glow over the orchard. I walked alone toward the clearing. I wasn't scared. I felt safe with the apple trees, like when Junie and I had pretended they were sentries guarding our make-believe castle.

I stepped over the old foundation stones, nearing the seedling. Usually the leaves rustled, or the branches shook when I approached, in a sort of greeting. This time the tree was still. It looked as tired as I felt. I didn't think trees actually slept at night, but then again, this wasn't an ordinary tree.

The bark was rough and cold like concrete. I pressed my palm against it, letting my warmth soak into the dreaming tree.

Suddenly the branches pulsed with light. I jumped back. "I didn't mean to wake you, I just . . ." It took me a minute to gather my words. The trunk grew brighter, from flat gray to vibrant green and turquoise. "And I thought you were impressive during the day. Look at you now!"

The gleaming leaves turned from blue to pinkish orange. "Are you blushing?" I teased. "You wear your heart on your leaves. We have a lot in common, I think." I breathed deeply. "My sister . . ." I said, feeling like I needed to explain why I'd come. I leaned my forehead against the trunk. Worries and sadness welled up, spilled out. My sobs sent a tremor through the orchard. The apple trees shuddered. Maybe they felt my pain.

I didn't need to say anything more. The seedling understood. A strong branch lowered and I climbed up, holding it tightly. It lifted me off the ground. More limbs curved loosely around me, weaving themselves into a sort of nest. It was as big and deep as a bathtub. I lay down. The huge leaves flattened across my back, covering me like a blanket. I said a silent thank you, then rested my head and fell into a deep sleep, comforted by the tree's embrace.

Hours later, the tree rustled, waking me gently. I rubbed my eyes. The sky was pink with dawn. I sat up and felt the branches stretch and move. The birds in the orchard began to sing their morning songs. I felt like one of them, waking up in a cozy nest amid the treetops. Nothing I'd dreamt could've rivaled that moment. The branches shifted, and I hopped down to the ground safely. I wanted to stay in the orchard, but I knew I needed to get back. The tree could carry me away from the world and my worries, but only for so long.

As I turned to leave, I looked back over my shoulder. My heart sank a little because there were no buds growing. Not yet, at least.

CHAPTER 26

Before Kira and her mom woke up, I snuck back into the house through the window, grateful that the guest room was on the first floor. I found a new toothbrush and a change of clean clothes on the bathroom counter, along with a sticky note on the mirror with a smiley face. I appreciated the toothbrush and note, but I didn't put on the outfit. I was still mad at Kira. I didn't want her germy clothes anywhere near me. I took a shower, soaking in the warm water, hoping it might wash away all the crummy feelings souring me like a pickle.

When I entered the kitchen, Mrs. Ritter was making breakfast. There was a glass of orange juice waiting for me on the table. "How did you sleep, dear?"

"Pretty well." Remarkably, it was the truth.

"I'm glad to hear that."

I sipped the juice. "Did my parents call?" I was desperate for news of Junie.

Mrs. Ritter stopped stirring a pot of oatmeal. "Nothing yet," she said. "You know what they say: no news is good news."

Even though every cell in my body wanted it to be true, I didn't believe her. Kira came downstairs a few minutes later, looking groggy. Her normally silky hair was matted and wild, as if she'd been tossing and turning all night. We ate our breakfasts in silence. Every time she sneezed, I fought the urge to send her a mean look.

"Why don't you take some of this, Pookie?" Mrs. Ritter set a bottle of nasal spray on the table for Kira. "Allergy season is rough on her," she said to me. "And apparently pollen counts are off the charts this year."

Kira took the medicine. A few minutes later, she stopped sniffling. Maybe she didn't have a cold after all. My heart kept insisting that it wasn't fair to blame her for everything. My stubborn brain wasn't so quick to give up its grudge.

After breakfast, Kira and I walked to the end of the driveway and waited for the bus.

"I didn't do anything wrong, Isa." Kira's voice was cautious.

I kicked a rock. If she made Junie sick, I didn't think I could ever forgive her.

"I know you're going through a lot. I just wish you'd talk to me. I know you left the house last night.

I know you went to the tree."

My eyes flicked up, wondering if she was threatening to tattle on me.

"I won't say anything to my mom. Or anyone. I'll keep your secret, you know I will. I promised you." Now she kicked a rock. "Sometimes I think you like that tree more than your own friends."

She didn't understand: the tree *was* my friend.

When the bus arrived, I found a seat in the back. I radiated enough nastiness that Kira didn't dare sit next to me. I knew I was being unfair. But I couldn't help myself.

***

The morning was torture. I felt guilty for taking Dad's watch, and guilty for treating Kira so cruelly. Most of all, I worried about Junie.

In the middle of science class, Principal Tam knocked on the door. "Sorry to interrupt," she said. "Is Isabel Fitzwilken here?"

Ms. Perdilla stopped writing on the board. "Yes. She's right over there."

I froze.

"Could you come with me, please?" Principal Tam asked, smoothing her blouse.

Everyone stared at me. Under his breath, Casey said, "Ooooh, you're totally busted."

My classmates probably all thought I was in trouble for being late to school the other day. But Principal Tam's voice was too gentle, her eyes too soft. If she'd come to punish me for tardiness, she wouldn't have looked or sounded like that. Ms. Perdilla gave me an encouraging nod, like she was trying to tell me everything would be okay. I had a sinking feeling it wouldn't.

I rose from my seat and walked with slow, stiff steps toward the door. I refused to look over at Kira, but I could feel her eyes on me.

Principal Tam closed the classroom door behind us and led me down the hallway.

"I'm sorry I was late to school yesterday," I said in the quietest voice imaginable, hoping that was the reason I'd been summoned.

"Isabel, your mother called," she said. I stopped and stared at the floor, my vision blurry with tears. Principal Tam reached out and gave my hand a little squeeze. "She's on hold. You can speak with her in my office."

I tugged my hand away and ran as fast as my legs could take me.

The secretary hardly blinked when I tore through the office door. All she said was, "She's on line one!"

I lifted the phone to my ear and pushed the flashing

red button. A second later, Principal Tam stuck her head inside the office. She was winded from chasing me down the hall.

"Do you want me to stay with you?" she asked. I shook my head, blinking back tears. "Of course. If you need anything, I'll be right outside." She shut the door with a soft click.

"Isa?" my mother said over the phone. "Is that you, baby?" The phone connection was poor. It kept crackling. "Are you there?"

I made a tiny hiccupping noise, fending off waves of crushing fear.

"Baby, I'm so sorry to pull you out of class like this. It's your sister . . ."

Principal Tam's office began to shrink. The walls closed in around me. There wasn't enough air. I was light-headed. I clutched the telephone with both hands, because I needed to hold on to something.

"It was a long night, baby," Mom said. Tears spilled down my cheeks. They splashed all over Principal Tam's big oak desk. The phone line crackled again. "Dad and I wanted to call you right away, to let you know." I bit my lip so hard I tasted blood.

My mother's voice rose up above the static. "Junie's doing better. The doctors were able to get the fever under control. It was an infection in her port. As soon as Edith noticed her temperature rising, they started antibiotics. I can't even imagine what might've happened if she hadn't been in such good hands."

My mother's words threw the windows of Principal Tam's office wide open. Air rushed in. The room expanded. The walls retreated. My lungs filled. If Junie was okay, I was okay. My family was okay.

"Can you come get me?" I said, breathing so loudly into the phone that I sounded like Darth Vader. "Please? I want to be with you."

"Dad's leaving soon. He'll pick you up around lunchtime. Think you can make it that long?"

"Uh huh." If Junie could make it through surgeries and blood tests and scans and chemotherapy and infections, I could certainly survive another hour or so at school. "Mom, I'm glad you called me. I'm so . . ."

"I know, baby. Me too." I could hear other voices in the background. "I've got to go. Dr. Ebbens is here. Dad will be there soon, all right?"

I wiped my nose with my sleeve. I didn't even care if it got smeared with snot. "Okay."

The line went quiet and I thought she'd hung up. Then I heard Mom's voice, clear as a bell. "I know I haven't said it enough lately, Isa, but I love you so much." Her words made me cry all over again. At least this time, they were happy tears.

CHAPTER 27

Junie was tangled in tubes. She was hard to hug, but easy to love.

"I was so worried about you," I said, holding her hand. "How do you feel?"

She blinked up at me. "Overwilmed."

"Aren't we all," Mom said, rubbing her temples.

"What's that?" Dad asked, putting down his cell phone. He'd been talking to someone from the insurance company about authorizations and payment plans and other confusing stuff.

"Junie invented a new word. Overwilmed." I explained, "Because we're overwhelmed. And totally over stupid Wilms. Get it?"

"Good one, Junebug. Me too. Most definitely. I find caffeine helps." He smiled at Junie. "For grownups, that is."

"Speaking of which . . ." Mom yawned. "I wonder

if the nurses could hook us up with a coffee IV?"

"Doubtful. But let's go check the cafeteria," Dad said. "We'll be back in a few minutes."

I pulled a chair close to Junie's bed.

"How's the tree?" she asked, her voice weak but eager.

I told her about sleeping in the nest made from branches.

"When I get the sleepy medicine before my surgery, I'm going to pretend I'm falling asleep in a giant nest like that. It sounds perfecterrific." She hugged her stuffed rabbit and rested her bald head on a pillow. "How's Rapunzel?" she asked.

Her question hit me like a punch to the stomach. I told Junie how I'd been a major grouch and wrongly accused Kira. "I feel awful," I said. "I don't know what to do." I slumped down into the chair.

"Just say you're sorry, Isa." She poked me in the ribs. "Easy peasy, allergy sneezy."

I sat up and gave her a peck on the cheek. "What would I do without you?"

It was an impossible question. I didn't dare think about the answer.

***

When we returned to Bridgebury that evening, I asked Dad to drop me at Kira's house for a few minutes, making up a story about our science project. I could've easily called her on the phone, but I felt like I needed to apologize in person. Dad said he'd wait in the car until I was done, because he didn't want me wandering home through the orchard in the dark. I wondered what he'd say if he knew I'd done just that last night.

I tapped the brass doorknocker.

"Isabel! Please come in." Mrs. Ritter greeted me pleasantly. Which I hadn't expected. I was prepared to take a well-deserved scolding for treating her daughter so terribly. "How's Junie?"

"She's better," I said. The words were a relief, like aloe on a bad sunburn.

"I'm so pleased to hear that." She led me down the hall. "Can I get you something to eat?"

"No, thanks. I just need to talk to Kira."

"She'll appreciate your visit. She's been feeling a little down. That pollen is driving her crazy. And I think she's a bit self-conscious too." Her voice dropped to a whisper. "I'm trying to be supportive. She's beautiful no matter what." I had no clue what Mrs. Ritter was talking about. "We'll all get used to it soon enough. I know seeing you will cheer her up."

I wasn't so sure about that.

"Go ahead, dear." She gestured toward the stairs. "She's in her room."

The smell of pot roast drifted through the house as I climbed the stairs. The carpets were soft, the lights bright. How could I be filled with so much dread in such a cozy, inviting place?

The second door on the left was open. I peered inside Kira's room. A boy in a baseball hat was sitting at the desk, scribbling away on a piece of paper. He turned when he heard my footsteps.

He wasn't a boy at all.

He was Kira. Her long hair must've been tucked under the hat.

I stepped into the room, trying to work up the nerve to apologize for being such a rotten friend. "What are you doing? Homework?" I said sheepishly, as if that was some great icebreaker.

"No. I'm writing a letter to my dad."

"How was your phone call the other day?"

She put down the pencil and pushed her chair back. "He never called. So I'm back to writing old-fashioned letters."

"Oh. That stinks." I wished I could think of something better to say. "You send him something every week, right?"

"So you *were* listening." Her tone had a slight edge.

"Of course I was."

"I do it so he won't forget about me."

If only I had some golden nugget of advice to give to her. Something brilliant and comforting. But the truth was, I was still struggling with many of the same feelings about my own family. "Does he send you anything back?"

"Other than the occasional postcard? Not really." She let out a long, disappointed sigh. "Like you said, it stinks."

I walked over to her desk.

"And you?" Kira said, swiveling around in her chair to face me. "When you move, will you forget about me too?"

My mouth hung open. "Move?"

"That's why you came, right? To say good-bye?" she said crisply.

"First of all, I despise good-byes. Second of all, I don't know what the heck you're talking about. I'm not moving anywhere."

She stared at me. "Oh." Her eyes dropped. "I thought I overheard my mom talking to someone on the phone about selling the Melwick place. I must've misunderstood."

I really, really hoped it was a misunderstanding, and nothing more. Moving was the absolute last thing us Fitzwilkens should be doing. We had enough on our plates already. "I didn't come to say good-bye. I came to say . . ." I took a deep breath. "I came to say I'm sorry. Kira, I feel crumbuckets. I shouldn't have yelled at you." Her eyebrows lifted up. "I was just really scared. I still am, actually. But it wasn't fair of me to take it out on you. I know you didn't make Junie sick."

Kira fidgeted with her baseball hat. "Thanks for saying that. I understand, sort of." She looked at me. "I care about you, Isa. And your sister, even though I only met her once."

"I care about you too."

"When Junie got that fever yesterday, I was afraid maybe I *had* accidentally done something terrible. And I wanted to fix it, or at least make it better somehow." She pulled the hat off her head and set it on her desk. I waited for her long chestnut locks to tumble down over her shoulders. They didn't.

"Whoa!" I said, shocked. Her hair was clipped to a blunt bob.

"That bad, huh?" She blushed and reached for the hat.

"No! Don't cover it up," I said. "It looks really nice. Just different."

She shrugged, tugging self-consciously at a few short pieces by her ears. "You think so?"

"I do. I mean it."

"I'm still getting used to it. Like I said, I wanted—"

"Wait," I interrupted, "is that why you cut your hair? For Junie?"

"Um, not entirely. I really did it out of necessity. If I was going to continue to be your lab buddy, that long ponytail had to go. Major fire hazard." I was surprised to hear the sound of my own laughter, and hers too. "Besides," she said, "I've been growing it because my dad liked it that way. After he flaked out on our call again, I thought, why am I holding onto this annoyingly long hair for someone else? So I chopped it off." She ran her fingers through it, a little more confidently than before.

I remembered a chapter on pruning from that book Ms. Perdilla gave me. "According to the orchard book, you have to let go of old things for new things to grow."

"I believe that," Kira said, a slight twinkle in her eye. "You know, I cut it myself. Which might not have been the best idea, but I was thinking about your sister and . . ."

"Kira, please tell me you didn't plant your hair under the tree hoping to grow Junie a wig or something?"

"No! Although that's an interesting idea. I did find a place where I can donate it. They make wigs for sick kids. I'm going to send it to them the next time I go to the post office."

"Oh. That's really nice of you. You didn't have to do that."

"I wanted to," she said. "And you know what? I feel better now. I really do." She shook her head from side to side, like an actress in a shampoo commercial.

"You might need a new nickname though. Rapunzel doesn't quite fit anymore." I reached out and gave a playful tug to her short hair. "This style suits you. It's perfecterrific."

"Prettiful?" she asked.

"Posolutely."

CHAPTER 28

Over the next two weeks, I waited for my sister to get better. I waited for the tree to bloom. I waited for Coach Naron to announce the starting lineup. Minutes and hours blurred, as if someone ran globs of finger paint across Junie's handmade calendar, smearing the wobbly lines between days until time became one grayish-brown smudge.

Whenever Junie and I were alone together in the hospital, I whispered stories about the orchard to her. They had a healing quality, lifting her spirits, bringing color to her pale cheeks. She improved more and more, until finally the doctors declared her strong enough for surgery. It was a weird thing to celebrate, but we were all relieved to say good-bye to that jerk Henry.

***

The day before her operation, I came home after softball practice to find both of my parents pacing the floor.

"Please don't be upset. I know we'll find it," Mom said, digging around in a hamper of laundry.

"I looked everywhere. It's gone, Nel."

"It can't be." She yanked cabinet drawers open, flinging old receipts, rubber bands, nails, and pens to the floor. And she claimed *I* was the one who turned the house upside down looking for lost treasures? Jeez. "We should file a police report," she said.

"A police report?" I asked, startled. "What happened?"

"The front door was open when I came home a couple of weeks ago. I assumed your father forgot to lock it on his way out. But now things are missing."

"Things? What things?" My stomach twisted in a queasy somersault.

"Well, just one thing. Your father's gold watch. He wanted to wear it to his big meeting this morning, but he couldn't find it." Mom shook her head. "You'd think a small town like Bridgebury would be safe, but I'm afraid we've been robbed."

"Robbed?" I gulped.

"We don't know that for sure, Nel. Let's not jump to conclusions."

"How else do you explain it?" She slammed a drawer shut. "I can't imagine what dreadful person would do this. Steal from us! Everyone knows we're struggling."

I opened my mouth to confess. Sure, they'd be mad at first, but once they cashed in my tree's latest crop and paid off those pesky bills, they'd forgive me. They'd be so happy, so grateful for my cleverness. I wouldn't be invisible, not in the slightest.

Dad exhaled. "It's just a watch."

"Exactly. We can get you another. A better one," I said, gathering the courage to begin my confession.

Mom looked up from the bookcase she was dismantling. "That watch was an heirloom, Isabel. It belonged to your grandfather. It's irreplaceable." A heap of cookbooks fell to the floor. Pages of cakes and casseroles smashed into the linoleum.

"That's beside the point," Dad said.

"Beside the point? How can you say that, Nathan?"

"Because I don't need it anymore."

Had the tree finally bloomed? Had Dad already plucked a glittering replacement from its branches? If so, why was his face swallowed in shadow instead of shining with happiness?

"You're not making any sense. I'm calling to report a theft." Mom marched across the room.

I had to stop this before it was too late. "Wait! Don't call the police."

She tore past me and lunged for the phone.

"Nel! Stop. Isa's right. Calm down." He lifted the receiver from my mom's hands and placed it back on the cradle. "Listen to me. Please." His eyes bore into hers, forcing them to focus. "I don't need the watch anymore."

"What are you talking about?" she snapped.

"Because," I said, stepping closer, lifting my chin. I was ready to tell them everything.

Dad interrupted me. "Because I've got all the time in the world now," he said glumly.

"What?" Mom and I asked in unison.

Dad went to the hallway, then returned holding a cardboard box. He dropped it onto the kitchen table. I leaned in to see if it contained the gleaming jewelry harvest. Nope. Only a jumble of papers, folders, and framed photographs.

Mom backed away. "What is that?" she asked, horrified. I didn't think a cardboard box could be so upsetting, but apparently this one was.

"What does it look like?" Dad's shoulders rolled forward, like the weight of everything resting on them was just too much to handle.

"A box?" I offered.

They both turned and stared blankly at me, as if they had forgotten I existed. A moment passed, then they returned their attention to the box.

Mom shook her head. "It can't be."

Something was clearly wrong with her brain, because it was definitely just a box. Square. Brown. Cardboard.

"I was laid off," Dad said.

"You mean transferred?" I stammered.

"No. It's worse than that, I'm afraid."

Worse? How was that even possible?

"The company is being reorganized." He pinched the space between his eyes. "That's what the meeting was about today. They cut half of our department." He shook his head and eyed the cardboard box miserably. "Said they were giving us time to re-evaluate our careers and seek out new opportunities. What a load of baloney."

Nothing moved or broke or crashed, but everything was suddenly destroyed.

"We don't need time," Mom cried out. "We need a paycheck. Plus, we rely on those health care benefits." She staggered backward, nearly tripping over the pile of cookbooks. "What are we supposed to do now?"

I could almost hear the call of bedsheets, luring her back upstairs. Away from us again. Dad must have, too, because he crossed the room in three quick strides and placed his hands on her shoulders. He guided her into a chair. Mascara ran down her face in black streaks.

"Anything . . . anything . . . is . . ." I tried pushing the words out, but they clung to the cliff of my lips and refused to budge. Mom blinked her raccooned eyes, looking defeated.

I could feel a giant mass growing in my gut, toxic as one of Junie's tumors. Guilt and doubt and worry and a whole bunch of other uglies ganging up together.

Mom turned and buried her face in Dad's shirt, smudging the crisp whiteness. He looked down at her and then back up at me. He shook his head, like he wanted to be everywhere at once. "We'll figure something out."

***

The screen door slammed behind me. The burrs and brambles in the meadow scratched my ankles worse than Mrs. Tolson's chickens. My muscles were exhausted from softball practice, but I made them sprint faster. I charged toward the clearing. Wishing. Hoping.

But also dreading.

I stopped and stared. I rubbed my eyes. No. Please no.

The branches were still barren. Not a single bloom or bud or brooch.

Worse than that, the seedling was sick. The leaves were cloudy and wrinkled. None of them rustled or sparkled. The trunk looked gaunt and gray. The limbs sagged. All the things I thought were coming together were now untethered. Adrift.

Falling.

Apart.

I replayed the conversation with my parents over and over in my head. *We don't need time. We need a paycheck*, Mom had said. I realized with horror that I'd made a terrible mistake planting the watch. The tree had misunderstood. There would be no gold or diamonds or rubies. Instead of expensive timepieces, my father, now jobless, had an abundance of time.

And my mother, who'd finally begun to come back to life, was teetering on the brink of someplace dark and distant again.

I was such a fool! I should've listened more carefully to the tales about our property. I should've realized that magic, like Junie's medicine, could have awful side effects.

I dropped to my knees and clawed through the dirt, ripping up clumps of grass. I reached my hands down, down. The earth was cold and damp. Root tendrils shriveled and shrank away from my fingers. The tree flinched. It wanted nothing to do with me. Fine. Maybe it was better this way. Anger welled up inside. I'd find the watch and leave. Then I'd never come back to this cursed orchard.

I dug another hole, then another. Each was empty. The tree's wilted crown drooped. I kicked wet dirt back into the holes. The ground was pocked and scarred. My heart felt the same.

Be careful what you wish for. I could hear Junie's voice in my head.

If only I'd heeded the advice of a very wise six-year-old.

CHAPTER 29

During the drive to the hospital early the next morning, my parents and I barely spoke, silenced by an unbearable heaviness. No one mentioned jobs or money or stolen watches. It was like we all pushed a giant pause button, even though the problems were still there.

We took the elevator up to the sixth floor, then checked in at the front desk. We'd gone through this routine many times before, but today it felt foreign and uncomfortable. We walked past the cheery activity room and the colorful murals. Edith waved when she saw me. I waved back, trying to look brave. In reality, I felt as flattened as the paper doll I held in my hand.

"Can I have a few minutes alone with Junie?" I asked my parents, while we stopped for a round of disinfecting squirts. "We have some sister stuff to discuss." Without grown-ups around, Junie and I were able to relax and talk freely, unfolding like flowers.

They nodded, looking weary. "We'll be down the hall if you need us."

I walked toward Room 612—just like our ages, easy to remember. Six for Junie, twelve for me. Beyond it was Room 613, which was the last room at the end of the hall. This struck me as a cruel joke. In October, I would turn thirteen. Would Junie turn seven in August? Or would we be stuck at six and thirteen, like the next room number plaque seemed to suggest? I tried to fling the thought as far away as I could, but it tangled around me, itchy and suffocating.

"Junie," I whispered, standing over her sleeping body. She was surrounded with stuffed animals. I placed the paper doll in her palm. "Junie," I said again.

She twitched. Her eyes opened slowly. She looked at me, then over at the doll. "NED!"

"No, it's me, Isa." I was frightened by the possibility that she might not recognize me.

"I know that!" She rolled her eyes, which was a huge relief. She held up the paper doll. "She's Ned."

"The doll's name is Ned?" It was an odd choice. She looked like a Briar Rose, or a Snow White, or something more princessy than . . . Ned.

"Soon I'll be NED too." She clutched the doll to her heart.

"Junie, what are you talking about?"

"NED! NED is the coolest, bestest thing to be."

Suddenly I remembered. NED stood for No Evidence of Disease, also known as remission, or cancer free.

She hugged the paper doll again. "Thanks for keeping her safe."

I wasn't sure that losing something in the back seat of the station wagon counted as safekeeping. "Let's just say I hid her so well, even I had a hard time finding her."

"Maybe she found you?"

I shrugged. Trouble was the only thing finding me lately.

"It's not my birthday yet," Junie said.

I felt my throat constrict. "I know. Think of the paper doll as a good-luck charm. For the surgery. And for everything that comes afterward." If we could ever find a way to afford it. I still had Muriel's card from the bakery, but I wasn't sure it would help enough.

Junie took a few deep breaths. "You . . . Isa . . . good . . . sister."

"You *are* a good sister," I corrected. As if this was an appropriate time for grammar.

"No, you are Isa. And Isa *is a* good sister."

"So is you," I replied, leaning closer.

"How do you feel?" she asked, lifting her hand to my face.

"Me?"

"You don't look right." She poked my cheek, lifted my eyelid, pinched my nose. "You look . . . hmmm . . . you look . . ." The wordwilken was lost for words. That was a first.

I didn't want to worry her about Dad's job, but I was as see-through as Muriel's crepe-paper-skin to Junie. So I told her about the watch and the tree's unwanted harvest.

She stayed quiet for a while, then said, "Time isn't such a bad thing. Around here, everyone talks about time. Everybody wants more time."

I knew she was probably right. It was just hard to appreciate at the moment.

"How do *you* feel?" I asked. "That's the more important question."

"Missing."

"What are you missing? Other than French-Fry-Fridays, of course."

"I miss me."

"You're right here." I tapped her knee with the paper doll, then made it do a silly dance across the bed, trying to lure out a laugh. "I see you. Ten fingers." I lifted up the blanket and tickled her feet. "Ten toes. Arms, legs, nose. All accounted for."

"Except Henry, that sneaky, meany blast-o-rama.

308

He'll be gone soon. Good riddance." She frowned. "What if they take out something else? Something important, Isa?"

"The doctors and nurses are very good at their jobs. Even if they do wear pajamas." I smiled at her. "They'll only remove the bad stuff."

She didn't seem convinced. I thought about Kira's hair, how cutting it helped her let go of some sadness about her dad. Then I remembered the book Ms. Perdilla had given me. I pulled it out of my backpack and flipped to a page with a diagram of a tree dashed with lines.

"Look. To keep an orchard healthy, you have to prune it. That means cutting branches."

"Doesn't that hurt?" She traced the lines in the picture with her fingertip. Then she touched her stomach. By the end of the day, more stitches would be dashed across her pale skin.

"Not if you do it right. I know it doesn't make much sense, but it works. Apparently." I turned the page, revealing a photograph of ripe, red fruit. "See? You have to remove old things to let new things grow. Like delicious apples."

She tugged the strings on her purple cap.

"Try to think of your surgery like that. A little Junie pruning. Once it's done, you'll grow big and strong."

"And delicious?" Finally, a giggle.

"Let me check." I bent over and gave her cheek a little nibble. "Mmm, I think it'll work like a charm." She giggled some more. "Oh yes, nice and sweet. What should we make with you? Junie pie? Junie strudel?" I nibbled her again. "I'm sure Mom has some great recipes for Junie pudding."

Her eyes bulged open. She sat up.

"What's wrong? I was only joking. We're not really going to cook you."

"I know that!" She reached for the book. "Maybe that's why your tree isn't working anymore. Why it's acting so strange."

"Strange? That's the best word you can come up with?! Try combining world-class jerk with about fifty curse words!" My muscles tensed. I remembered what Dad had said about our property. "It's more of a liability than an asset."

"Huh?"

"It means it's causing more harm than good. Come to think of it, I might chop the whole thing down. Have a bonfire! Roast some s'mores."

Junie gasped. "Don't say that! You can't get rid of it, just because it's a little broken. Would you chop me down and use me for firewood if I were a tree?"

"Stop. That's not the same at all."

"It is so." She shook a finger at me. "You said I need Junie pruning. Maybe the tree does too." She wheezed and reached for a cup of water on her bedside table. She took a sip. "Have you even watered it once?"

"No," I said sheepishly.

"Not even on Thirstday?"

"Nope. But it's been raining a lot lately."

Her forehead wrinkled. "It probably needs a nice cold drink and some attention. From you." She gulped the rest of her water. "That tree's been working hard lately, growing you all kinds of treasures. Poor thing could use some TLC." She sank back into her bed.

I thumbed through the book's pages. The words and diagrams all seemed to agree.

"Junie, I know you said you were a princess before. But I think you might also be a genius."

"Technically, I'm a Junius." Then she made a funny face, crossing her eyes, puffing up her cheeks, and wiggling side to side.

I laughed. "You are. A deliciously goofy Junius." I wrapped my arms around her in a squg. I breathed her in.

"Isa . . ."

"Yes?"

She wriggled free. "Would you be scared if you were me?"

"Of being devoured by a cannibalistic sister?" I bared my teeth. "Most definitely."

"No," she giggled, swatting me away. "I'm serious. Would you?"

I had told enough lies lately. Junie deserved the truth. "Yes, probably. But it's normal to be scared. You're going to be okay." I wanted to be strong for Junie, so I forbid myself from crying, which felt like holding a very determined Great Dane on a leash when all it wanted to do was run. "Everyone is going to take good care of you. The doctors, the nurses, the counselors. Mom, Dad. Me."

"The tree?"

"Maybe even the tree. If it gets better and starts behaving."

"I think it will. As long as you take care of it. Promise?"

I hooked my pinky with hers.

She looked at me with those big green eyes. "Isa, what if I'm not okay?"

An unsettling realization: anything is possible. Good and bad. I thought about the stats Dr. Ebbens gave us after Junie was diagnosed. Ninety percent of kids recover from Wilms. But ten percent don't. My brain crunched the numbers over and over again, trying to come up with a better calculation. The fact was, anything other than zero was too high.

I didn't know what to say. I tried to look confident, but I was terrified. I held Junie's hand and squeezed it gently. Three times. I. Love. You.

"I can't cry in front of Mom and Dad," she said, squeezing my hand back.

"Of course you can."

Even though she was only six years old, if you looked deep into her eyes, you'd think you were looking at a much older person. "No, Isa, it hurts worse. I don't want them to know."

"Know what, Junie?"

She swallowed. "It's a secret, Isa."

"You can tell me anything." I held up my pinky to seal the promise. And then Junie cried, sniffling sobs that swelled and rolled, so deep and shuddering that they got almost quiet. She told me how frightened she really was. How badly she hurt some days, even when her brave little face tried to hide it. Unlike the wishing pin or the countless other items I'd misplaced in my life, this was something I knew I'd never lose. Junie's secret was something I would carry forever.

I held her in my arms and we cried together, neither of us embarrassed by the snot that ran in gooey rivers from our noses. By the time a nurse knocked on the door, we had cried all those feelings right out. And we were almost to the place of smiling again.

"Hello, girls," the nurse said. "Everything all right in here?"

We nodded. Our eyes were probably red rimmed, our faces blotchy. But we both felt better. I was grateful the nurse left us in peace and didn't start poking and prodding Junie.

"Today is Chooseday," Junie reminded me once we were alone again.

"It is." I wiped her cheek with a tissue, sopping up all the leftover tears and snot, because loving someone means cleaning up their boogers and not minding one bit.

"So far today, I haven't been allowed to choose a single thing. Everyone is making decisions for me. I didn't even get to pick which flavor Jell-O I wanted to eat!"

"I thought you hated Jell-O. Isn't it a food unfittian? Not quite liquid, not quite solid?"

"You're missing the point, Isa."

"Okay, you want to make a choice. I get it. Maybe I can help." I wasn't feeling very capable of making anything but mistakes lately. But for Junie, I would always try my best.

She picked up the paper doll and waved it.

"What do you want me to do with her?"

"For goodness' sake, make the poor girl some clothes! Something prettiful. And a whole assortment of hairdos. Long, short. Curly, straight. Red, brown, black, blonde. Maybe a few wild ones too. Like a purple mohawk. Just for fun."

"Easy peasy. Consider it done. Anything else?"

She bit her lip. "Magic treesy. Yes, pleasey."

"What do you mean?"

"Plant one more thing."

"I don't think that's a good idea, Junie. I told you what happened with the watch."

"It has to be more special than that."

I shrugged. "I searched the whole house and the car. I don't have anything."

"I do." From beneath her pillow, she pulled a metal butterfly with crooked red wings. The wishing pin!

"Where did you find that?" I gasped, shocked to see it.

"You put it in my hospital bag, for safekeeping. Remember?" She pointed across the room at an old yellow duffle bag hanging from a hook.

"I did?" Suddenly I remembered stashing the pin in the bag's zippered pouch. "I mean . . . I did!" I clutched the pin. "Listen, Junie, if I plant this, you probably won't get it back. The seeds seem to disappear in the soil. Believe me, I tried to dig up the watch. Nothing but earthworms and grubs and a whole lot of regret under there now."

"That's okay. I don't want it back. Just don't forget . . ."

"What?" I asked.

"To make a wish. A wishing pin without a wish is just a hunk of junk."

I studied the red rhinestones. "What should I wish for? Money?"

"Oh, Isa," she huffed, from exhaustion or flusteration, or maybe both. "Even I know *that* doesn't grow on trees." She pulled off her knit cap and scratched her head, bare as the paper doll's. A machine next to her bed made some ticking sounds. "Whatever you wish for, make sure it comes from there." She pointed to the machine. A jagged mountain range of colored lines ran across its screen. Before she could explain further, a team of pajama-scrub clad doctors and nurses entered the room with my parents.

CHAPTER 30

After we helped Junie get ready for her operation and gave her oodles of kisses and squgs, my parents and I waited. The hospital waiting area had a television, magazines, even a snack bar. I had brought a deck of cards from home, but none of us was in the mood to play a game. It was hard to think about anything other than Junie. When Gregory's misfit orchestra blared down the hall, sounding more off tune than ever, I covered my ears. I wondered when the shipment of bells would arrive. I hoped it would be soon. This place was in desperate need of some music and magic.

"Come with me," someone whispered over my shoulder. I turned. Edith smiled and gestured to a set of double doors. Mom and Dad looked up from their magazines and nodded, giving me the okay to go.

I followed Edith down a long corridor and out a door into a garden full of herbs, lush ferns, and colorful flowers. There were even a few small trees. Magnolias, I thought, remembering the blossom Muriel had given Reggie as bus fare.

We walked along a smooth path, wide enough for at least two wheelchairs. We sat on a wooden bench and listened to a fountain bubbling. It wasn't the same as being out in the orchard, but it was comforting to be surrounded by green, growing things. Plus, the air smelled alive, like rosemary and honey, instead of bleach and cotton balls.

"This therapeutic garden is one of my favorite places," Edith said, leaning back. "We had one at my old hospital, too. A few hours in a place like this can work wonders."

"For you, or your patients?" I asked.

"For everyone," she said. "By the way, you forgot this." She reached into a folder that she had carried outside. She handed me the paper doll.

"Thank you," I said, holding it close.

"Your sister's in good hands. She's brave, and she needs you to be too." Her eyes flicked in the direction of my parents, visible across the garden, through the waiting room window. "So do they."

I lifted the paper doll and made her dance with all the bravado that I wished I felt.

"Good girl." Edith patted my knee. "I've got to get back to work."

"Wait," I said, still trying to figure something out. "That machine in Junie's room. What is it?"

"Which one? There are lots."

I tried to remember what it looked like. "It has colored lines going up and down."

"That's probably the electrocardiographic monitor."

"What's inside it?" I asked, still puzzled.

"Inside? Wires and chips and electronic bits and pieces, I imagine."

"No, I mean what does it do?"

Edith rose from the bench and straightened her scrubs. "It tracks cardiac activity, among other things."

"Translation, please?"

She placed a hand over the upper left part of her chest and gave a little *tap-tap*. "That machine helps us see what the heart is doing."

Now I understood. A sort of calm washed over me. Junie wanted me to make a wish from the heart.

***

Mom plopped down next to me on the bench in the garden, clutching a cup of coffee like it was the elixir of life. Her hands shook just the slightest bit. "Did I tell you? Junie said the oddest thing before I left her."

"What?" I asked, eager for news of my sister.

"Right when she was about to get her sleepy medicine, she told me she wanted something."

"Let me guess, an ice cream sundae? Or french fries? Wait, did she ask to change her name to Ned?"

Mom rubbed her forehead, like my answers were scrambling her brain. "No. She asked for a tree."

"A tree? Why would she want a tree?" I asked, even though I had a pretty good idea.

"Beats me." Mom took a sip of coffee. "I said, 'Baby, do you want a tree to climb? Because we've got an orchard full of them at home.' Junie said nope. Dad asked, 'Do you want a tree to give you fruit?' She said no. 'Do you need the wood to build a dollhouse?' Junie said no, no, no." Mom's eyes sort of glazed over. She was sitting next to me, but I felt her drift farther away.

"So? Did she ever tell you why she wanted a tree?"

Mom snapped out of whatever thought she was lost in. "She was getting drowsy at that point. Right before she fell asleep, she said she wanted a tree for dreaming." She tipped the coffee cup to her lips and drained it. "Must've been the medicine talking. Because for the life of me, I cannot figure out what a tree for dreaming could mean."

If she had turned to me, looked at me, I might've told her exactly what a tree for dreaming was. Maybe I would even take her to see the seedling once I'd nursed it back to health, just as I promised Junie I would. But all she did was stare into her empty coffee cup. The moment passed. I didn't say a word.

***

Later that day, we learned that Junie's surgery had gone very well. Henry was officially gone and Junie was on the road to recovery. I got to see her briefly, but the medicines made her loopy and tired.

Dad stayed at the hospital. Mom drove me home. As soon as we got in the front door, she disappeared upstairs. I gathered a few supplies, and then I disappeared too.

CHAPTER 31

The book lay open in the grass. I read the words and carefully studied the intricate diagrams. I'd gathered a wheelbarrow full of tools from the shed. I was ready to work.

I looked up at the seedling. Its withered leaves hung limply.

"I'm sorry for the way I acted the last time I saw you. I want you to know that I'm not really mad." My voice was tender and sincere. "Not at you. I'm mostly mad at me. For the record, I do wish Dad could keep his job. And maybe you could return Grandpa Isaac's watch, but I understand if you can't. At least I think I do. I'm trying."

I read a line of text printed on the page:

To reap the benefits of a successful harvest, an arbor-ist must develop a reciprocal relationship with his or

*her trees. Give your orchard as much as you expect
to receive.*

"I think this means you need a little TLC."
I touched the trunk with my palm. It brightened just
a little. "Junie was right. I've been selfish and greedy.
Harvesting away without giving anything back."
Hadn't the stories about Melwick Orchard warned
me that something like this could happen? "I want to
help you," I said. The bark grew warm to the touch.
I could almost sense a faint rhythm, like a heartbeat,
from somewhere deep inside its core.

*To revive a dormant or under-producing tree, follow
these steps:*
1. *Aerate soil.*
2. *Water roots.*
3. *Prune branches.*
4. *Nourish and protect.*

"Okay, we'll start at the beginning. Aeration.
I can't strap one of those hospital breathing machines
to you, but I think this will do the trick." I reached
into the rusty wheelbarrow and removed a rake. I con-
sulted the book again. A small note at the bottom of
the page said:

*Aeration can be a laborious process. Allowing chick-
ens to feed around the base of your trees can expedite
this work. Their claws and beaks do an excellent job
loosening topsoil, saving you time and energy.*

I shivered. "Don't worry. I would never let Mrs.
Tolson's flock near you. I'll do this job myself." I gripped
the rake and began scratching the hard-packed earth,
pulling up little clods of dirt and clumps of weeds and
grass. I leveled out the pockmarks my frantic digging
had caused when I'd tried to recover the watch.

When I finished aerating the soil, the ground
was smooth and loose. I wiped sweat from my brow
and leaned against the tree. Its warm bark cooled to a
refreshing temperature. A breeze wound through the
boughs. The apple trees along the edge of the clearing
stirred, their own branches perking up.

"You must be thirsty," I said. "Time for step two."
I hauled two sloshing buckets from the wheelbarrow.
I poured the fresh water in a spiral pattern around
the tree, watching as the earth soaked up every drop.
When I was done, the tree's leaves seemed plumper.

"Okay, step three. Time to cut." My stomach
turned. My foot tapped. I wasn't feeling particularly
confident about this part. I lifted a pair of loppers from
the wheelbarrow. I propped up a metal ladder and

inspected the tree's structure, visually marking a cut plan. "I don't want to hurt you. But I think we need to do this." I knelt down and studied the book once more, just to be sure.

Ample pruning is necessary for sunlight to reach a tree's inner leaves. Removing limbs also helps focus a tree's energy on fruit production. Do not be afraid to prune aggressively. Your orchard will thank you.

I eyed the branches and took a deep breath. "Here it goes. I'll be quick. Lickety-split. Like pulling off a Band-Aid."

I opened the loppers and clamped down. I cringed as I felt the sharp metal bite through the branch. Instead of making a snapping or cracking sound like regular wood, this branch sang out. Not a cry or a screech, but a single, clear note: *Do!*

I clipped another branch. *Re!* And another. *Mi!* Each limb sang, then fell noiselessly to the ground, as if even the thickest limb weighed no more than a feather. Moments after they struck the damp earth, they dissolved, just like the shoefruits and bells had before. Everywhere a branch landed, the soil flushed green as blades of fresh grass sprouted up.

Faaaa! Sol!

I continued to prune.

Laaaa! Ti! Do!

Soon a lush carpet of grass covered the ground and the canopy was open and bright. Streams of sunshine poured over the translucent leaves, dappling the ground with rainbows.

The book said the prune wounds may need some extra attention to prevent infection or decay. Miraculously, the tree appeared to be providing its own bandages. At the site of each cut, a milky substance oozed out. It was shimmery and sticky to the touch. Using the softest part of my fingertips, I smoothed the sap across the surface of a large cut. When I finished, a scab of silver bark hardened. I worked my way from cut to cut, tenderly dressing each wound like a pajama-clad nurse in Junie's hospital.

The final step called for nourishment and protection. I didn't have any fancy fertilizers, and I was pretty sure trees didn't eat jam sandwiches, so I tried a different approach. I wrapped my arms around the massive trunk, in as much of a squg as I could manage. I whispered encouraging words. The kinds of things my own heart ached to hear.

I reached up and held a branch in my hand. I squeezed.

One. Two. Three. I. Love. You.

I let go. The leaves fluttered gratefully.

The book's advice seemed to be working. The entire tree looked healthier. Surprisingly, a single acorn-shaped bud began to sprout on one of the lower branches. It started off green, then slowly darkened to a deep indigo blue. I hadn't planted anything since the watch, and I'd given up on the idea of the jewelry harvest. But maybe there was still hope. The bud pulsed and faded, glowing pale yellow, bright orange, and eventually iridescent blue again. I reached upward, but the tree lifted its branches, pulling the new bud out of my reach. Telling me to be patient.

"Message received," I said.

Junie's wishing pin was still nestled in my pocket. I rubbed my thumb across the pin's crooked wings. I pressed my other hand to my chest, trying to figure out the wish inside.

CHAPTER 32

The next morning, I slipped out of the house at dawn. The tree had continued to improve overnight. The bark was returning to that watercolor mix of marbled greens and grays. The blue veins in the leaves shined. The single bud was still small and tight, not yet ripe. I checked each prune wound. I poured a bucket of water at the base of the trunk and gave all the branches I could reach gentle squeezes in sets of three. Eventually, my watch beeped. I needed to get back home.

Dad was waiting by the station wagon, ready to return to the hospital. He and Mom had switched off last night, making sure Junie was never alone.

"Where have you been?" he asked. Nerves and lack of sleep made him grumpier than usual.

"Just getting some fresh air."

"The bus should be here soon."

"I know. I'm pretty good at keeping track of time, remember?"

He looked at his wrist, but of course his watch wasn't there.

"Could I skip school today and come with you?" I asked. "Just this once?"

"You'll see Junie this evening," he assured me. "In the meantime, it's best if you—"

"Maintain my routine, right?" I kicked the ground, scuffing my sneakers and sending a miniature avalanche of gravel skittering down the driveway.

"Exactly." Dad stared at me. "Besides, don't you have softball practice? I bet Junie would want her star-pitcher sister to stay in peak form." He reached out and gave my left arm a gentle bump. "Big game on Friday, right?"

I lifted my chin. He hadn't forgotten. I felt happy, but also uneasy. I had a good shot at making the starting lineup, but it wasn't guaranteed yet. I really didn't want to let him down.

***

The rest of the day I felt numb one minute, then overwhelmed—or overwilmed—the next. It was like a roller coaster ride, but not a fun one. I was so tired of the constant ups and downs. I just wanted to get off and walk on flat, solid ground for a while.

"How's your project coming?" Ms. Perdilla asked Kira and me after class.

Even though the question had been directed to both of us, Kira seemed to understand that I needed a little time alone with our teacher. She nodded and said she'd save me a seat at lunch while I hung back to talk to Ms. Perdilla.

"We might need an extension," I replied, not wanting to describe all the reasons I was feeling one hundred percent crumbuckets.

"Of course. Don't worry. We'll arrange something. You've been occupied with other issues lately. How is Junie?"

"Better, but still in unfittian mode."

"I see. That must be difficult." I was relieved when Ms. Perdilla changed the subject. "How's that orchard book working out?" she asked.

"Pretty handy, actually," I said, which was a total understatement. The book had literally helped me bring the seedling back to life.

"I'm so pleased to hear that." I was about to leave when Ms. Perdilla said, "You know, Isabel, you've inspired me."

"I've inspired *you*?" I wheeled around. "How?"

"In many ways." She smiled. "Each and every student inspires me. Ralph Waldo Emerson once said, 'The creation of a thousand forests is in one acorn.' I think of you and your classmates like that."

"Like acorns?" I scratched my head. The idea felt almost too immense to fit inside.

She laughed softly. "An acorn represents tremendous potential. It is quite literally a seed of possibility. So are you." Her words were warm as sunshine. "Speaking of seeds," she continued, "did you know that a two-thousand-year-old seed from a date palm was recently discovered during an archeological dig in Israel?"

"I didn't know that. But it sounds cool."

"I agree. What's even cooler is that some scientists decided to plant it. To their shock and delight, it sprouted! That single seed revived a species otherwise believed to be extinct. Isn't that astonishing?"

I nodded. The prisms hanging from the classroom windows cast flecks of colored light across the tiled floor, just like my tree's crystal leaves. "Where did you learn about that date palm?" I asked.

"After I found the orchard book for you, I went back to the library." She gestured to a stack of books and magazines on her desk. "Trees are fascinating. We depend on them for the very air we breathe. Not to mention food and shelter and warmth." She flipped through the crinkly pages of a book with a faded brown cover. "Even this paper was made from wood pulp."

She picked up a glossy science magazine. "Some of the oldest living organisms on earth are trees." She seemed to crave information the way my parents craved caffeine. Cracking open those word-filled pages gave her a jolt. "There's a single bristlecone pine tree in California that's over five-thousand years old. And scientists believe a group of quaking aspen trees in Utah could be close to eighty-thousand years old."

"Whoa." Even my time-counting brain could barely compute a number that high.

Ms. Perdilla grinned. "Whoa, indeed!" She held up another book. "This one explains how trees experience pain, help each other, and converse."

"Are you telling me there's a scientific explanation for a talking tree?" I could barely get the words out.

"Oh, yes! Trees don't speak with words, obviously. But they certainly communicate with each other."

"How?"

"By intertwining their roots, releasing chemicals from their leaves, and growing fungal networks underground." Ms. Perdilla showed me a photograph of massive acacia trees in Africa. "See these? If a giraffe starts eating the leaves of an acacia, the tree will emit a warning scent. In response, neighboring trees will produce a substance that makes their leaves taste unpleasant, forcing the hungry giraffe to find food elsewhere."

"So you're saying some trees protect each other?"

"Precisely." She added, "Did you know that other trees have incredible healing properties?"

I knew my tree calmed me. It distracted and entertained me. It reminded me to smile and laugh and dream and hope. It lifted me up, sometimes quite literally right off the ground.

"There's even a compound found in the ancient yew tree that's used to make cancer medicine," Ms. Perdilla said delicately.

The word *cancer* sort of took the wind out of my sails. But curiosity filled me back up again. "Do you have to cut the tree down to make the medicine?" I asked.

"Initially researchers stripped the trees of their bark, which, sadly, did end up killing them. Later they discovered they could make the drug using the tree's needles instead, which caused less harm."

I fidgeted, thinking. "I wonder if there are any yews on my property."

Ms. Perdilla grimaced. "Hmm, I hope not."

"Why? You just explained how wonderful they are."

"When used properly, yes, but they are also extremely poisonous. The leaves and berries are lethal if eaten."

"Yikes! And . . . yuck."

Ms. Perdilla straightened up. "The yew is an example of a life-saving plant, but one that must be handled with care. Does that make sense?"

"Mmhmm." I gave a knowing sigh. Without reading any of the books on her table, I had learned that very important lesson all on my own.

The lunch bell rang. "Can I take a few of these with me?" I asked, pointing at the stack of books. An idea was blossoming.

"Certainly!" She smiled broadly, as if I'd just made her day. When, in fact, she'd actually made mine.

CHAPTER 33

The sky was bright and cheery during softball practice. Coach Naron dodged my question about the starting lineup, but that was probably because she still needed to work out the other field positions and batting order. I was feeling confident. I'd been hustling, and I'd thrown strike after strike during our scrimmage.

Earlier that afternoon, legions of dandelions had begun releasing their fluffy seeds into the air. I knew there was probably a scientific explanation for what was going on, but the little white puffs looked surreal, floating across the playing fields like springtime snowflakes.

Yellow pollen dusted the sidewalks, making Kira sneeze nonstop. "Something weird is happening in Bridgebury," she snuffled. "My allergies have never been this bad before." She pulled a package of tissues from her pocket and dabbed her nose. "It's a little out of control. And I've never seen so many bugs."

It was true. An unusual number of bees and butterflies buzzed and flitted through the air. Even the birds in the orchard seemed to be chirping louder than normal lately, like they could sense change coming. I wondered what the apple trees and chance seedling might be saying to each other in that silent language of trees Ms. Perdilla had described.

As I walked to the parking lot with Kira, the books in my backpack felt as heavy as bricks, but my heart felt lighter than it had in days.

***

Mom was wearing her bathrobe when I came home, but at least she was downstairs. I was relieved to find her cleaning. When Junie was around, we kept the house as spic-and-span as possible. But in the last few days, it had become a total mess. Now, hampers of unfolded laundry sat on the couch. Vases and frames had been taken off the mantel, probably for a much-needed dusting. I hoped this was a sign that my sister would be returning home soon. If that was the case, I'd even volunteer to scrub the toilets.

"So? Would you like to tell us what you've been up to, young lady?" Mom said, pursing her lips.

"Uh, school and softball. Maintaining the old

routine. That's my job. Remember?"

"That's not what she means." Dad stepped into the living room. He was wearing a suit and tie, which meant he had probably been interviewing for a new job. I sensed trouble in his tone. I began tallying up the secrets and truth-stretchings of the past few weeks. Where to begin?

Mom lifted a crumpled piece of paper from the laundry pile. "What is this?" she asked.

I took it from her and smoothed it across my palm. It had been through the wash and the ink was smudged, but still legible.

A bus ticket. If only I had stuffed it into one of my holey pockets!

"Garbage?" I offered, trying to play dumb.

"I might have believed you, Isabel, if I hadn't found this one too." She held up another crumpled bus ticket. Heck. Sometimes the smallest things get you in the biggest trouble.

"Would you like to explain what this is all about?"

"No," I said truthfully.

"Where have you been going?" Dad asked.

I wasn't sure how to respond.

Mom's face was pinched. "We already have one child to worry about. The last thing we need is another."

Translation: Go back to being invisible.

Her words dredged up all the hurt and anger that had been building inside me for months. I felt like I'd been injected with a dose of Junie's feisty juice. "Right," I sneered, refusing to be quiet anymore. "Better to forget I'm here at all! Just like the trees in our orchard, huh?" If I couldn't escape, I might as well fight. "Where did I go? I'll tell you. I went to the hospital to see Junie. I took the bus by myself because neither of you would take me. Is that really so bad? I went because I love her. And I wanted her to know that." I was done being invisible. I planted my hands on my hips. "Because when you love someone, you show up! When someone needs you, you show up!"

The floorboards didn't creak, the curtains were still. Only a pot of soup on the stove in the kitchen dared make a sound, burbling away obliviously.

"Is this about your softball game? Because I promised you we'd be there, and we will," Dad said.

"We're doing our best." Mom looked out the window, unable to meet my eyes. "Don't punish us, Isabel."

"Punish *you*? What about *me*?"

"We just wish you'd been truthful with us."

"Truthful? Have you and Dad been truthful? Junie might be getting better, but I can see the bills on the counter and the looks on your faces. You pretend like everything's okay."

"Isabel." Mom came to my side. "We didn't say anything because we didn't want you to worry."

"Too late for that."

Dad paced back and forth, then came to a stop. "While we're being forthright, your mother and I have something to tell you." He loosened the tie around his neck. "We found a way to pay for Junie's hospital bills."

I inhaled a sharp breath. "You did?" I glanced cautiously around the room. I noticed several cardboard boxes stacked around the living room.

Mom wasn't cleaning. She was packing. Which meant we were moving.

"No." Two little letters. Small but big. "No!" I cried so loudly the windowpanes shook. The room spun. From molasses slow to warp speed.

"We have to sell the house. Without the health insurance from Dad's company, we have no other choice." Mom shook her head. "It's a tricky sort of property, but Helen Ritter helped us arrange a special sale through the bank. We're closing in a few days."

"A few days? Are you kidding me?" Her words were like an ax swinging through a forest, splintering me. I was a felled tree, helpless and in pain. "There has to be another way." Every inch of my body stung, inside and out. If only my last seed had worked!

Dad spoke quietly: "We wouldn't do this unless

we'd exhausted every other option. We're going to rent a small apartment in Carolton, the next town over. It's less expensive than anything we could find here, and we can't go too far from the hospital. We need to continue Junie's care at Delorna until she recovers. After that, Uncle Lewis said we could stay with him while we figure things out."

"Uncle Lewis lives in Cincinnati. That's hundreds of miles from here." My heart squeezed into something tight and hard. "I can't start over again." My voice was raw. "There are only a few months left in the school year. I have projects. And friends! Actual real friends."

"We're not moving to Cincinnati just yet. Carolton isn't far. Besides, it's just a temporary solution, until we get on our feet."

"Temporary is exactly the problem!" I shouted. "What about softball? You said . . ."

"Isa, about that." Dad cleared his throat. "I spoke to Coach Naron."

"Okay, okay!" I burst. I couldn't handle any more lies. They were like tiny grenades, ticking and fizzing, then exploding, one by one. I wanted to toss the rest away before they destroyed me from the inside out. "I might not be the starting pitcher. There! I said it. But I tried. Really hard. I did. Even if I just sit on the bench, I need to be there. You promised you would too!" I growled angrily. "I shouldn't have to lie for you to notice me."

"Lie?" Dad said.

"That night by the millpond. I told you I was starting, but Coach Naron hadn't even chosen the lineup. I knew it was wrong. It just came out, and then you seemed so happy and proud. I wanted to make it true. I thought I could."

"Isabel—"

I threw my hands in the air. "I know. I messed up. Ground me if you want. But please, let me play in that game!"

"You can play. I explained our situation to Coach Naron. She said you were doing a great job. Really hustling."

I lifted my eyes. "She said I was doing a great job?"

"She did." He gave me a crooked smile. "Which is why she'll be so sad to lose such a strong player." He moved closer. "Listen, I never, ever want you to feel like you need to lie to get my attention. Or Mom's."

I interrupted him. "Wait, I don't get it. Why is Coach going to lose me?"

"Sweetheart, because we're moving."

"But you said I could play . . ."

"You can. And you will. Except you'll be playing for the other team. Carolton Minnows, remember?"

He reached out to muss my hair. "More like piranhas, especially with you on the mound."

"What? No way!" I pushed his hand away. "I can't play for the opposing team. I won't!"

He looked tired. "Fine. Then you won't play at all, Isa. It's your choice."

But it wasn't. It wasn't Chooseday at all.

"Dad!"

"Enough. I'm not debating this with you right now."

"Mom!" I turned, looking for an ally. Her face was in her hands. I was on my own. I sprinted for the door, but Dad blocked my path.

"Don't you run away!" he bellowed, his patience dissolving faster than a fallen shoefruit.

"I'm not running away. That's the last thing I want! Didn't you hear anything I said? All I want is to stay here." I stamped the floor with my foot. "You're always making us leave. Making us say good-bye and pulling us up like weeds as soon as we start growing roots someplace."

"I know you're upset."

I rolled my eyes. "That's the understatement of the century." I tried to nudge my way through the door. "I need some fresh air. Please." I felt dizzy and light-headed.

He sighed and stepped aside. "Fine. But stay on our

property. Don't wander too far. It's dangerous."

"Dangerous?" I whipped around. "Why? Because of Mrs. Tolson's chickens?"

"Did you forget we were victims of a robbery?" Mom's face emerged from her hands. "There's a thief on the loose in Bridgebury. Your grandfather's watch still hasn't shown up."

I moaned. "The watch wasn't stolen," I said. "It was borrowed."

"Borrowed?"

No point keeping secrets. We were selling the land and all that came with it. My tree would be discovered soon enough. I couldn't protect it, or myself, any longer.

"Who took the watch, baby? You can tell us," Mom said.

My lower lip quivered. My toes tapped. "I did." As soon as I admitted it, I felt better.

"You?" Dad stepped backward. "Why?"

The rest was surprisingly easy. That's the funny thing about the truth: once it starts trickling out, you can't stop it. Before you know it, it busts right through the wall of lies you constructed, the way water breaks down a dam. "I took it and planted it under a special tree. I hoped jewelry would sprout and we would make a lot of money. Then Junie could get her medicine and everything would be fixed."

I watched for signs of anger or forgiveness or . . . something. My parents wore paper-doll-flat expressions.

"It's true!" I said. "I'll show you right now. I'll take you to the tree. As long as you promise not to hurt it. I can't explain how it works, but Ms. Perdilla says . . ." I studied their faces. Still blank. When I realized they didn't believe me, flusterations bubbled up. "Are you listening to me?" I reached for my dad's hand and tugged him toward the front door. "Come with me. I'll show you!"

"What are you talking about?" he rumbled, pulling back.

My cheeks blazed. "First I planted a shoe. Two shoes, actually. When the tree was just a sapling. It sounds crazy, but there was this squirrel and he actually encouraged me to do it, and then . . ."

"That's enough!" Mom shouted. "Sneaking around. Stealing. Telling outlandish lies! Nathan, her behavior has gotten out of control."

"Don't look at *me*, Nel."

My parents turned on each other, yelling about me, not at me. I went from the center of their attention to invisible again.

They didn't even notice me leave.

CHAPTER 34

The orchard accepted me with gnarled, outstretched arms. The leaves hushed the sounds of fighting. The wind carried the angry voices from my ears, even though they echoed in my head. I touched the rough bark of the apple trees with my palms. I liked the crooked angles of their branches. They weren't as graceful as willows, or as statuesque as oaks, but they were beautiful and wise in their own way. Even if they were stubborn and awfully scraggly.

I tried to picture them blossoming again. The rolling hills, a sea of pale pink waves. Each tiny flower holding the promise of a harvest come autumn. Bushels and bushels of those mythical apples that seemed to linger in people's memories long after they'd taken the last bite. Muriel's pies with crisscrossed crusts. Fresh cider. Tarts. Sauces. Strudels. People lined up all the way to Drabbington Avenue to have a taste.

The leaves and wind whispered to each other, like they, too, were imagining and remembering. I wished I had the time and strength to take care of them all, the way I had cared for the chance seedling. Aerating the soil, watering, pruning, nurturing. I'd planned to study the books Ms. Perdilla had given me and crack the Melwick mystery once and for all.

Now I wouldn't even get the chance to try.

I walked and walked, dazed and broken, letting the long grasses tickle my open palms. I ducked beneath a leafy branch and blinked.

Scoops of sherbet-colored clouds crowded the sky. Puffs of dandelion seed were suspended in the air. I stepped into the clearing. The air was cool and fresh. I lifted a hand to my forehead, shading my eyes. A small smile tugged at my reluctant cheeks.

The tree looked healthy, fuller and brighter than ever.

"Hey!"

I jumped at the sound.

Kira waved from across the clearing, where she was sitting on the swing. She got up and jogged over to me. "What happened? You look like a wreck."

I sighed and sat down beneath the seedling, resting my back against the strong trunk.

"Is Junie okay?" She sat next to me.

"She's fine. It's something else." The words were sticky. It was difficult to get them out. To admit they were real. "We're moving." I hung my head and felt tears roll down my cheeks. They dripped into the grass, seeped through the ground. "Your mom found a buyer. It's happening soon. My parents need the money."

Kira's face blanched. "No, Isa. We can't give up so easily."

"What are we supposed to do?"

"I'll talk to my mom about delaying the sale. Maybe you can still fix things."

"How?" I sniffled.

She reached into her pocket and fished out a fresh tissue. She handed it to me. "Follow Junie's advice."

"A wish from the heart? Easier said than done," I said. "I'm pretty sure my heart is permanently busted." I thought about the yew tree, which Ms. Perdilla said had the power to both heal and kill. "What if I accidentally make things worse?"

Kira looked at me with her kind brown eyes. "During the cookie harvest when I was freaking out, you told me you trusted this tree. Do you still feel that way?"

I closed my eyes. I nodded. "Yes."

"Then plant the pin. Take a chance. Make your wish."

Above me, the tree bowed and swayed. Was it nodding? Its bark rippled and twisted behind my back, nudging me lightly.

"Okay, okay." I admired its powers of persuasion. "Any ideas?"

Kira shook her head. "You know the extent of my creative genius. I maxed out on food poisoning, remember? Besides, it has to come from your heart. No one else's."

Unfortunately, I felt flat out of inspiration. I stood up and shoved my hands into my jean pockets. Something jabbed my finger. "Ouch!" I yelped. A small bead of blood appeared on my thumb.

"Oh my gosh! Are you hurt?"

I pulled the wishing pin from my pocket.

"I can't believe that apple brooch pricked you! Here!" Kira handed me another tissue.

"It's nothing serious," I said, blotting the blood. "Wait, did you say apple?"

"Uh, yeah. Why?"

I held the brooch up to the light. "It's a butterfly, not an apple."

Kira took the pin from me and frowned. "Nope. I've seen about a hundred butterflies this afternoon, and none of them look like this." She rotated the pin. "Yup. I'm pretty sure this is an apple." She polished the rhinestones with the edge of her sleeve. They shined. Bright ruby red. "See? An apple. Cut right down the middle."

"Naw, those are wings." I peered over her shoulder. "They're just bent a little." I tilted my head. "It's missing one antenna, but . . ."

"That's the apple's stem, not an antenna, silly." She handed it back to me.

I turned the pin over and inspected it closer. I remembered my father's pitching pep talk about trusting your teammate. *She can see things you can't*, he'd said. He was right. And so was Kira. I had seen it wrong, all along. My mind whirred. A well of fresh hope sprang up inside of me.

I flung my arms around Kira, letting that squg say all the things that words could not. Because best friends, like trees and sisters, speak all kinds of languages. And many of them don't require words.

CHAPTER 35

A peace offering filled my nostrils the next morning. Cinnamon and nutmeg. My nose sent a signal to my stomach, which sent a message to my eyes. Open. Wake up.

Mom stood over me, a plate of warm, fragrant sticky buns in her hands. Her eyes were puffy and tired. But not wild. And not blank. She sat down and ran her fingers through my frizzy hair. She placed the plate on the bedside table and a kiss squarely on my forehead.

"You were right, Isabel. We should have been more open with you. We wanted to protect you, that's all. I'm sorry if that hurt you." She reached over and opened the window behind my bed, letting sunshine and fresh air spill inside. She took a deep breath. "This hasn't been easy for any of us. There's no instruction manual for this kind of thing." She handed me a sticky bun.

I couldn't resist. I sat up, accepting the bun. And her apology. A grudge was a pointless thing to hold on to. Kira had taught me that.

"Do you know why I like baking so much?" she asked.

I took a bite of the sticky bun. "Because you get to eat what you make? And it tastes so darn delicious?"

She laughed and kissed me again. "That certainly helps. But it's more than that. I like the recipes. They're predictable and reliable. They tell me how much sugar, how much flour, how much butter to use. I know that if I follow the rules, the result will be good." She licked cinnamon glaze from her fingertip. "Life isn't like that. I wish it was." She sounded like herself, her real self. The mother I remembered from before. She pressed her hand to my heart, as if she was trying to mend what was broken inside.

"I've missed you, Mom."

"I know. I've missed me too. Mostly I've missed you, Isabel. You and Junie and Dad. Us."

Us. Two letters, small but so big.

"I didn't mean to make you and Dad fight."

"Of course you didn't." She dusted powdered sugar from my chin. "You actually helped us."

"I did?"

"Sometimes people need to argue. It's healthy. You

forced us to talk about a lot of things we've been avoiding lately."

"So you're not mad?"

"No. But promise us there will be no more lying. Or sneaking. Or stealing."

"Borrowing," I corrected.

She raised an eyebrow. I decided not to push it.

"We've all made mistakes these past few months. How long has it been?"

"I sort of stopped counting, but . . ." I glanced at the clock on my bedside table. I quickly did the math. "Six months, one week, three days, eleven hours, twenty-four minutes."

"That's a long time to be cooking without a recipe."

I nodded, sinking my teeth into the last bite of sweet dough.

"We've got a plan now," she said. "And we're in this together."

Dad stepped into my room, probably lured inside by the scent. "Special-occasion sticky buns, huh?"

"I thought the spices might make the house smell more appealing when the bank appraiser comes today," Mom said, although in my heart, I knew she had made them just for me.

"Powerful potpourri, indeed." He wrapped an arm around Mom's shoulders.

She smiled. "I'll let you two chat. I need to clean up the kitchen."

I pulled the blankets around me and pouted. How could the bank put a price tag on our house and orchard? There was so much more to a home than walls and ceilings and acres of land.

"Isa?"

I peered out from my blanket cocoon.

"You've got a bus to catch, and I have an interview over in Carolton. But I think there's just enough time for a quick morning catch. What do you say?" It was his own version of a peace offering. "It'll help us clear our heads. Things are going to happen pretty quickly with this move."

"Ugh. I don't want to move. I need more time," I croaked. Plus, the tree needed more time. I glanced at my clock. I'd only planted the wishing pin twelve hours and fifty-four minutes ago.

"I'm sorry, sweetheart. I really am. Tick-tock," he said glumly, tapping the spot on his wrist where his own watch should have been. He left the room. The stairs whined as he descended.

I lay there for another minute, gathering my courage. I stared up at the cracks in my plaster ceiling. Today the pattern looked just like roots. I had an idea.

I sprang out of bed and threw on some clothes,

then skidded across the hall and down the stairs. I laced up my sneakers, grabbed my softball glove and dashed through the mudroom. The screen door clapped as I exited.

"Dad! Dad?" Maybe if I showed him how magnificent the seedling was, I could change his mind about selling the house.

I ran across the backyard. Past the shed. Up the hill.

My father was frozen. Still as stone.

"Dad?" I ran to him and tugged his shirt. "What's wrong?"

He didn't say a word. He looked down. I followed his gaze.

His open palm cradled a single blossom with five petals.

"A flower? Dad, what's going on?"

He lifted his arm and pointed. Just beyond the fence, the horizon was pink, erupting with apple blossoms. Every single tree was covered with hundreds of them.

Neither of us said a word. Dad lowered his arm and took my hand.

We walked toward the trees in a daze. The entire hillside was blushing with color, brimming with perfume. A blizzard of pink petals filled the air and half-drunken bees buzzed with pure joy.

"The trees . . . they're awake. Alive. Thriving. All of them." He inhaled the sweet fragrance, even better than sticky buns fresh from the oven. "I never thought it was possible. It's . . ."

"A miracle?"

"A wish come true," he stammered.

Yes, it was.

We walked deeper into the orchard, hand in hand. Exchanging squeezes in sets of three. I wondered how he would react to a giant tree with swirling bark and crystal leaves. My explanation yesterday hadn't exactly gone over well, but sometimes seeing is believing.

We ducked beneath the last row of apple branches, crowded with flowers. I held his hand extra tight. We stepped into the clearing. I looked left. I looked right.

The seedling was gone.

I ran to the spot where it had stood, horrified I might find a stump, severed and bleeding silvery sap. The only trace of the tree was a circular patch of grass, shorter and more vibrantly green than the rest of the meadow. My whole body ached. I hadn't even been able to say good-bye. I fell to my knees and pressed my hands to the ground.

I felt a faint electric pulse. Once, twice, three times. Then it faded away. As quickly as it had appeared, the chance seedling disappeared. I choked back a sob.

The apple trees swayed in the breeze, as if to say, *There, there. Don't be sad.* I looked around at their flowering branches. My beloved seedling was gone, but the orchard was full of new life. I touched the ground once more. My heart squeezed, not so much from pain but from gratitude.

"Thank you," I whispered.

"What are you doing?" Dad asked.

"Looking for magic," I answered, knowing it would sound crazy.

"Sweetheart, there's magic all around." The apple trees rustled in agreement.

We walked across the clearing toward the swing that he had built months ago. I sat down and he started to push me. I soared, Junie-to-the-moonie high. I had a pretty nice view from up there. Not quite a bird's-eye view. More like a squirrel's-eye view.

"Isabel, if all these blossoms yield fruit . . ." Dad started to calculate the numbers in his head. "We'll have a record harvest."

"The Melwick apples are pretty famous. I bet folks would come by the busload just to taste one."

"You're right. Imagine that!" A boyish, hiccupping chuckle. "We could make a fortune." Dad slowed the swing to a stop. He came around to face me, kneeling down so our eyes matched up perfectly.

"As long as we don't get too greedy," I warned. "An orchard like this needs a lot of attention."

"You're right," he said solemnly. "If we take care of these trees, they might just take care of us."

I didn't say it, but I already knew that.

"Does this mean we can stay?" I asked.

He studied the orchard. Bewildering. Beautiful. And now bountiful. "It does." He laughed. He scooped me up and twirled me around. "Let's go tell your mother the good news!"

On our way back home, I filled my softball glove with apple blossoms.

"Nel! Call the bank! Cancel the meeting," Dad hollered from the front porch. "We're not selling the house! Come outside. You won't believe it!"

Dad swept Mom off her feet as soon as she opened the door, catching her in an embrace full of contagious, bubbly hope. He was talking a mile a minute, almost as fast as Kira. Mom shook her head in disbelief. I tossed the flowers into the air, like confetti. They both wrapped their arms around me. A family knot, tied up tight. Together. Only one thread was still missing: Junie.

CHAPTER 36

Four months, six days, five hours, and nineteen minutes after Dad and I discovered the apple trees blossoming, another miracle happened: Junie turned seven years old.

On the day of her birthday party, Mom was busy in the kitchen, humming as she whipped up cupcakes by the dozen. The recipe was a hit at Muriel's bakery, where Mom had taken a job as head pastry chef, thanks to a little help from me.

Dad came in from the orchard with a bouquet of wildflowers. His crooked ties and stiff suits were long gone. Now he could wear his flannel shirts and grass-stained jeans every day. A few leaves and twigs were stuck in his hair. Mom plucked them out, grooming him lovingly like a gorilla at the zoo. He leaned in and tried to steal a smooch and a swipe of frosting from the bowl on the counter. Mom swatted him with her spatula, then smiled, planting a kiss square on his lips.

I filled the old tin can with water and placed the wildflowers inside. It had been empty for a while, but not because we didn't have lunch money to put inside. Once our land bloomed with the promise of profits, the bank was suddenly more than happy to give us a loan. Most of the money went toward Junie's medical bills, but we still had some left over. And judging by the bushels of apples ripening on the trees each day, we wouldn't have any problems paying it back in the fall.

Now the tin can made a perfect vase to display the orchard's finest flowers, of which there were many. In fact, as part of our science project, Kira and I had decided to catalog some of the more unusual plants on the Melwick land. We didn't mention the chance seedling in our report, but we did discover seventeen different varieties of wildflowers, some of which were extremely rare.

"Where would you like these, darlin'?" Reggie asked, picking up a tray of crustless sandwiches. The bones had already been delivered to the ducks by Kira and me that morning, on our way to a pickup ballgame with the kids on Drabbington Avenue. The weekend games were a great way to keep our skills sharp over the summer, and make some new friends in the process. Even though our school softball team hadn't advanced to the playoffs, I still considered the season a success. Mom and Dad made it to most of my games, even the opener, where they cheered extra loud as I stepped up to the mound and threw the very first pitch (a window-breaker, of course).

"Sandwiches go on the buffet. Thanks, Reg," Mom said.

When Dad realized he needed help tending the orchard, Reggie had been the first to apply, and I gladly gave him a glowing reference.

"Did you girls get the balloons?" Mom asked.

"Yes!" Kira and I called in unison. She pulled her shoulder-length hair into a ponytail, then tied brightly colored streamers to seven giant helium balloons. I spread a roll of parchment paper borrowed from the bakery across the floor and began painting a birthday banner. I attached the paper doll named NED, who now sported a funky purple mohawk and a matching purple tutu.

Ms. Perdilla and Coach Naron set the dining room table with plates and napkins printed with happy green frogs. Junie had had a change of heart about unfittians, and seemed particularly sympathetic lately to all things in-between. Edith turned some knobs on the radio, filling the room with music. Dr. Ebbens danced to the beat. Muriel sprinkled powdered sugar, white as her hair, over a tray of special-occasion sticky buns. Even our neighbor, Mrs. Tolson, joined us, carrying a platter of deviled eggs.

"Did you find a pin?" Dad asked me.

"Not yet." The original wishing pin was long gone, but as soon as I finished painting my banner, I'd turn the entire house upside down to find something sharp enough to do the balloon-popping honors.

"We don't need one," someone said.

I recognized that voice in an instant. "Junie!" I dropped my paintbrush. I raced to the door and caught her in a squg.

Mom peered out from the kitchen. "Surprise!"

Everyone cheered.

"Come meet my aunt and uncle," I said to Kira. Uncle Lewis and Aunt Sheila had come to town for a weeklong visit and had agreed to take Junie to her gymnastics lesson that morning so we could get the party ready. I hugged them and introduced Kira like she was part of our family.

"The birthday girl has arrived!" Dad said, picking Junie up. She was still pint-size and bony, but her cheeks were slowly returning to their former state of pinchable pudginess. Her hair had started to grow back spikey and wild, which made her look like a blonde hedgehog. She was awful cute. I loved her something fierce.

No matter how hard I'd wished, my tree couldn't cure Junie. Thankfully, medicine could. Daily doses of love and an occasional story about magic helped too. Day by day, Junie got stronger. She came home in June, which seemed fitting. There was a lot of flusterating waiting along the way, and we knew that she would need continual checkups to make sure blast-o-ramas like Willie, Pablo, and Henry never came back. But according to the doctors and nurses, Junie could finally be called NED.

The doorbell rang. Gregory and James entered and waved. Gregory was still undergoing chemo, but he was well enough to come home between treatments. "The full orchestra couldn't make it today, but I think these will do for a birthday serenade." He jingled a handful of shiny bells. "They make the most amazing sound. Ever since someone donated them, our orchestra has gotten so much better. We're a total hit."

I winked at Kira and she winked back.

"Now that the guest of honor is here, I think we should get started. Everyone help yourself to food. Junie, look! Muriel and I made your favorite cupcakes. Have as many as you like."

Before Junie could stuff her face with treats, Dad helped me carry a large present over to her. We set it down carefully. "Open it!" I said, clapping with excitement.

Her eyes were wide as she peeled back the wrapping paper. Dad and I had finally finished building the dollhouse, and it looked pretty darn good if you asked me.

Junie agreed. "A home of my very own. Thank you! Thank you!" she sang.

"Oh! One more thing. Isa, did you find that pin?" Mom asked.

"I told you, we don't need it," Junie said. "I used to pop balloons to make wishes," she explained to Gregory. "But not anymore."

"Why?" he asked.

She turned to look at me. "Because I got my wish."

We all had.

For the first time in a really, really long time, everything felt perfecterrific.

* * *

After the party, Junie, Kira, and I went outside to explore. The three of us wove through the trees, braiding the orchard with ribbons of laughter. Apples grew on every bough. Soon they would ripen and turn red, and we'd have a bumper crop. My mouth watered imagining taking a bite of my very first Melwick apple.

We played in the clearing, showing Junie for the millionth time where the chance seedling had stood. It was hard to believe that it had ever been real.

I watched my little sister's healthy grin as Kira pushed her on the swing. I knew Ms. Perdilla had been right: there were many unexplainable things in this world, like mysteries and miracles. Anything was possible, after all.

When we felt tired, we rested in the grass together, not minding the crickets and ants trekking across our bare shins or the sun beating down on our cheeks and noses. We were just happy to be.

***

As the sun waned in the sky, we heard the tinkling music of a bell echoing over the rolling hills. Mom had found the large copper bell in my backpack one day and often rang it like a dinner bell to call us in from the fields because its song could travel much farther than her voice.

"Let's go!" Junie leapt up. The prospect of another round of birthday cupcakes had her running as fast as her skinny legs could carry her.

"You coming?" Kira asked.

"Go ahead. I'll be there in a minute."

The wildflowers whispered. The crickets chirped. The grasses rippled. I crossed the clearing. I knelt and touched the ground, remembering the seedling. Missing it deeply. My fingers grazed something hard and round in the grass. A small unripe apple, perhaps. Probably knocked off its branch by a deer or a strong gust of wind. I picked it up.

It wasn't an apple at all. It was an acorn. Smack dab in the middle of the clearing. My heart sped up. I turned the acorn over in my palm. A cloud passed overhead. When the sun broke through again, I could've sworn that tiny acorn shimmered with just the faintest hint of blue. My fingers tingled as I slipped it into my pocket. For safekeeping.

The apple trees swished. A twig snapped. "Just another minute," I said, hearing the sound and thinking Kira was still there, waiting for me on the edge of the orchard.

I looked up. Kira was gone.

All I could see was a bushy tail disappearing through the trees.

ACKNOWLEDGMENTS

Like a magical tree, this story grew in unexpected and wonderful ways. I extend heartfelt thanks:

To my parents, after whom the Melwick Orchard is lovingly named, for teaching me that anything is possible. I'm so grateful that you made books such an important part of my childhood, and that you continue to squeeze my hand in sets of three. To Robert, for being my favorite fiend and showing me how much love siblings can share. To the cousin club, for giving the best squgs. To my family and friends, near and far, for all of your encouragement and support—*grazie mille!*

To my agent, Christa Heschke, and the team at McIntosh & Otis, for spotting this manuscript in the slush pile, nurturing it, and making sure it found the right publishing home. To Laura Diehl, for creating cover art that perfectly captures the mood and whimsy of this story. To everyone at Carolrhoda Books and Lerner Publishing Group, particularly my incredible editor, Alix Reid, for your enthusiasm, patience, and reminding me to have fun during the revision process. This book is one hundred percent more awesomesauce thanks to your guidance. To Amy Fitzgerald, Kayla Hechsel, Libby Stille, and Lindsay Matvick, for helping to usher this book into the world.

To all of the marvelous teachers and librarians who pushed me to see and think and create in new ways. To my friends and colleagues at Cornell University, the University of Calgary, and Studio G Architects for cheering me on as I shifted course from a career designing buildings to writing books.

To Christy Griffith, Krissy Dietrich Gallagher, Francesca Agostini, and their families, for bravely sharing their stories, along with Dana-Farber, Boston Children's Hospital, St. Jude, and Johns Hopkins for providing answers to my medical questions. In some instances, I took artistic liberties to aid the story's plot; any inaccuracies are my own.

To the orchards of New England, where I gladly tasted apples (and far too many cider donuts) in the name of research. Peter Wohlleben's book, *The Hidden Life of Trees*, was a fascinating resource, as was Michael Phillips's *The Apple Grower*.

To the Society of Children's Book Writers and Illustrators for teaching me the ins and outs of publishing, and for welcoming me into such a vibrant and supportive community of writers, readers, and book-loving superheroes. To the Big Sur Writing Workshop, where the first chapter of this book was born, and the Writers' Loft where I continue to learn.

To the Lucky 13s: Austin Gilkeson, Jessica Rubinkowski, Julie C. Dao, Heather Kaczynski, Mara Fitzgerald, Kevin van Whye, and Jordan Villegas, for keeping me sane during the submission roller coaster, with extra special gratitude to Kati Gardner for such thorough and thoughtful notes. High fives to my fellow Electric Eighteens—I am thrilled and honored to join you on this debut author journey.

To Sally Hinkley, Sarah S. Brannen, Craig Bouchard, Susan Link, and all the Mixed Bag critique group members for your feedback on the earliest draft, and to Jenny Bagdigian, Stephen Anderson, Carol Gordon Ekster, Joy Wieder, Brian Schmidt, and Margaret Bridges, for your ongoing help with each new project.

To Rainbow Children Home in Pokhara, Nepal, for changing the direction of my life.

To my sweet Joys—you live up to your names each day. I began writing a story of sisterhood before I ever knew I'd have little girls of my own. Watching you grow is sheer magic. I love you a bushel and a peck!

Last, but certainly not least, to Stefano, most perfecterrific husband and father, for your steadfast love and support, your sense of adventure, and your delicious cooking. Thank you for never letting me give up on this dream, even when I doubted myself. *Ti amo. Per sempre tuo.*

ABOUT THE AUTHOR

Rebecca Caprara grew up in a small New England town surrounded by apple orchards. She graduated from Cornell University and practiced architecture for several years, before shifting her focus from bricks to books. An avid globetrotter, she has traveled to over fifty countries, and has lived in Italy, Singapore, and Canada. She is now growing roots in Massachusetts with her family.